Witch Hunt

By Casey Moores

INTER CAELUM ET INFERNUM

13

Three Ravens Publishing
Chickamauga, GA USA

WITCH HUNT By Casey Moores
Published by Three Ravens Publishing
threeravenspublishing@gmail.com
P.O. Box 851 Chickamauga, Ga 30707
https://www.threeravenspublishing.com
Copyright © 2021 by Three Ravens Publishing

Credits:
Witch Hunts was written by Casey Moores
Cover art by J.F. Posthumus

Witch Hunt by: Casey Moores, Three Ravens Publishing, 1st edition, 2021

Trade Paperback ISBN: 978-1-951768-40-9

Unit Thirteen Hymn

From the swamps of Roanoke Island
To the shores of Saint Augustine;
We fight the unseen evil
On the land, and on the sea;
First to fight for faith and prudence;
And to keep our honor clean;
We are proud to claim the title
Of Unit Thirteen Marines.
Our flag's unfurled to every breeze
From dusk to rise of sun;
We have fought in every wretched place
With Bowie knife, axe, and gun;
In the muck of cursed southern lands
And in moonlit battle scenes,
You will find us always on the job
The Unit Thirteen Marines.
Here's health to you and to the Corps
Which we are proud to serve;
In many a strife we've fought for life
And never lost our nerve.
If the Union Navy or Army;
Ever look on Hell's minions,
They will find the gates are guarded
By Unit Thirteen Marines.

Casey Moores

Chapter 1: Holding the Governor

"By God, Marines!" Major Reynolds shouted above the din of the crashing waves. "I know you feel whipped, but we're not played out yet! The only thing holding this damn ship afloat is the strength and grit of United States Marines, and, by God, I swear that's all we need! Now come on, keep to it!"

Our ship, the *Governor*, was sinking.

Reynolds was the battalion commander for the expedition. As I'd served under him at Bull Run, there was no other officer I'd rather had to lead us through such a desperate situation. The other marines and I struggled in the belly of the beast, ropes lashed about its ribs in a desperate fight to hold the bloated creature together.

"You heard the Major! Hold to!" I shouted for my men of Company C. By rights, our young, new lieutenant led the company. Our original commander, Captain Lewis, had been struck down in an incredible accident when a barrel, of all things, flew off a train. The lieutenant merely sat to the side fighting his illness and stared at us. For the duration of the crisis, true leadership of the company fell to me. When Major Reynolds came by to check on us, he made a show of speaking to the lieutenant, but locked eyes with me as a clear sign as to whom he truly spoke. Turning my head so the men wouldn't see I was the one to respond, I informed him we would hold forever if need be. With a nod of approval, he headed off to other companies.

After he'd left, I attempted to speak with the lieutenant.

"Sir, perhaps a few words would encourage the men?" I lied.

"Damn the Big Bugs, Sergeant, damn them to hell," he replied. I failed to see what the admirals and generals had to do with our immediate situation.

"Sir?"

"We should've been spread all around the fleet, Sergeant," the lieutenant said. "But some fool general saw a couple damn Confederate guns, wanted to keep us close to the far shore, and instead here we are, all the eggs in one basket, loaded up on a miserable ship for sea going. It's a river boat, for God's sake, and this storm will be the end of us. Then this *Great Naval Expedition* will have no marines left. The Union will never take Port Royal without us, but no matter to us because we'll be dead. . . swallowed up by the ocean."

Though I agreed, it didn't seem like the time to dwell on it.

"All right sir, you rest here a bit and I'll see to the men," I said. I did my best to nod respectfully and turned to go.

"See there!" the lieutenant said. He pointed to a man who stumbled down the stairwell. It was the ship's civilian captain, and he did not stumble due to the storm. "Captain's gotten himself properly wallpapered. Whole damn crew's of no account, but it wouldn't make any difference anyway."

"Yes, sir, but Master Weidman's taken the reins and he'll keep us afloat until help can come. Private Smith knows how to work the pump, and we'll hold the hog braces together as long as we can, sir. Major Reynolds will see us through this, sir, we just need to keep the faith."

"By all means, Sergeant," the lieutenant said. He gave a feeble wave toward the men and turned his head aside. I returned to the men.

A tremendous crack and bang, followed by a long hiss, heralded the collapse of the smokestack and the bursting of the steam pipe. Men leapt aside and we suffered a few injuries, but we'd lost all power to the pumps. The bucket brigades became the sole source of bailing out the ship, and Company C was directed to join them.

Major Reynolds had the horse sense to fire off the distress rockets, but to no avail. Later, something on the engine blew. The smarter marines had no sooner jury-rigged the thing back to operation, when we lost the rudder chain. The rudder head itself broke next, and we were completely subject to the inclinations of the sinister sea. I've no knowledge of God's will, but the storm seemed personally opposed to our journey.

Exhaustion took on new meaning as the several hundred marines aboard the ship worked into their thirty-sixth hour. The storm had begun to threaten the civilian steamboat *Governor,* chartered by the US Navy, at ten o'clock the previous morning, and on the night of 2 November, 1861, nearly three hundred United States Marines still labored to hold the poor ship together.

Over the course of the next day, several smaller ships came by in hopes of a rescue. One attempted to secure a hawser, a thick rope, with which to steady us and perhaps transfer men, but those efforts failed. Another ship assured us they would stay with us to the end. This roused a cheer from some men, though I failed to see how that would help.

Major Reynolds came by with the news that the *USS Sabine* would soon be there to take us aboard. This, finally, lightened my spirits and gave renewed strength to myself and the men of Company C.

The frigate, as promised, arrived as the sun was setting yet again. It laid anchor next to us, and successfully secured two hawsers to hold us together. The turbulent seas continued to pound the ship, which necessitated an excruciatingly slow method of transfer. A single marine secured himself to a spar with a chain and was passed between the boats by a rope pulley. A mere thirty of our three hundred were moved before the hawsers tore apart. Some of the Navy sailors aboard the frigate leapt across to re-secure them. Unfortunately, the greatest of our hawsers became snagged by the stem of the *Governor* and cut clean through. They tried to secure a chain, but the pitch of the seas became so fierce that even the chain snapped.

Someone called for us to heave on the last hawser. The boats drew together, and dozens of marines leapt across to the *Sabine* as they did so. One unfortunate boy, Private David Sampson, fell between the ships. Some might claim it impossible, but even above the noise of the shouts, waves, and crashing hulls, I heard the crunch of the poor marine's bones when the ships pressed together.

As the ships drifted apart, I spied the officer who directed the men on the frigate. His eyes focused on the water between us. Something caused a look of sheer horror to overcome his face and he shouted for the hawser to be released. With trepidation, I allowed my eyes to fall to the water.

I never considered myself a gullible man, a superstitious man, nor one easily shaken. That said, what I saw in that moment horrified me to my core. At first, when I recognized the immense, dark shape, I thought something had simply spilled into the water between the ships, like tar or some other viscous thing. Then, arms reached out of the water. They were not the arms of a man, or any other creature I had ever seen, but tendrils, like the roots of a tree, which sprung from the water. Lined up on one side of each arm were little circles. In school, I'd learned of the octopus and the squid, but never seen one in real life. What I saw seemed far more sinister than those plain sea creatures. Pure evil, spawned from hell, had risen into the gap between our ships.

As the two ships drifted apart, a few more marines made a desperate leap from the *Governor*. They had no reasonable chance of jumping the distance, but I imagine they all jumped with the confidence they could swim the distance and be safely helped out of the water by the crew of the *Sabine*. As I watched them run to make their leap, I shouted a frantic word of warning, but none heard me over the tremendous noise. Six men splashed into the water, and I thought it would be the end of them at once. The group included my hapless lieutenant, but I did not recognize any of the others. A small part of me was thankful none of the others were from C Company.

One by one, their heads bobbed back up, and they all stroked their way, undisturbed, through the turbulent sea toward the *Sabine*. I could not see the strange creature I thought I had seen. For the briefest moment, I found myself gaining hope that I'd imagined it, that the six men might make their destination.

I was wrong.

The tendrils returned to the surface, tentatively at first, but then, hungrily. One rolled up in a spiral and smoothly snaked itself around one poor private at the rear of the group. My hand went to the cross I wore on a necklace under my shirt, and I screamed at the top of my lungs, but no one on the other ship seemed to hear me. I searched the rails of the *Sabine* with the desperate hope that someone witnessed the same as I, but all seemed focused on keeping their own ship afloat. The crew aboard the other ship appeared wholly unaware of the six swimmers. The officer I'd seen on the *Sabine* had retreated from the railing, perhaps in shock or disbelief. Then, I surveyed the attention of my own shipmates to see if I watched this horror alone. All others were too occupied in struggling with the failing *Governor*.

Helpless, I stared as the tendrils engulfed the next swimmer, pulled them below, and returned to grab another. When the process started, I knew only that they disappeared into the darkness below. However, as the creature pulled the fourth marine below, concentric rings of teeth became visible just below the surface. The marine screamed in increasingly greater intensity as the rings of white pulsed upwards along his body. When they reached his midsection, something snapped inside, he spasmed, and then went limp. The screams alerted his two remaining fellows, who scrambled to swim faster. They shouted for help, but to no avail. The dark, sinister sea beast seemed to sense this, and grabbed the last two simultaneously. The lieutenant maintained a free arm which he used to pummel the tendril without effect. The tendrils completely constricted the arms of the other man, so he could only wriggle about. Both struggled in vain.

Something bumped against me. I found Major Reynolds next to me, offering a rifle.

"I've kept them dry," he shouted. "There's no hope for them, Sergeant, but we can give them a quick death. I'll not make you shoot your own officer, besides, prudence forbids it. You help see to that poor soul, and I'll relieve your lieutenant."

"Yes, sir." The words escaped my lips, as if from someone else. Dumbfounded, I nodded and retrieved the rifle from his hands. I brought it to my shoulder and braced as best I could against the railing. Soaked to the bone, I found no good reason to bother choking back the tears as I took careful aim. I didn't think I could do it, in fact, I almost decided I *should* not. Good Christian men and United States Marines did not shoot their fellow man, much less their fellow marines. While this struggle churned within me, those vicious rings of teeth returned, just below the surface. The beast's tendrils maneuvered my fellow marine toward them.

"Now, Sergeant," Major Reynolds said.

I aimed and fired. A part of my soul slipped away. The report of Major Reynold's rifle followed shortly after. The man who'd led us all at Bull Run straightened. Gently, he took the rifle from my hands and cradled both rifles in his left arm. Though the *Governor* still rocked violently, he maintained his balance well enough to hold out his hand to me.

"Fine job, Sergeant Phillips," he said, as I took his hand and clasped it as hard as I have ever clasped another man's hand. His gaze scanned the topside of our ship. "Tend to your company now. It's yours until I can find you another lieutenant. . . which may be a while."

His expression indicated that something flashed through his mind. A look of concern, or perhaps comprehension, came over his face, as if some distant, ancient memory floated to the forefront to make a connection he'd never before made.

"I'll make inquiries," he eventually said. "I think I know the right man. Anyway, go tend to your Company."

I stared mournfully into the water for a brief moment, and then turned to go as ordered. The major caught me by the arm and dragged me so close that I almost retched at the overpowering fish, whiskey, and tobacco on the major's breath.

"One last thing, Sergeant," the major said directly into my ear. "Not a word of this to anyone. No good will come of it. And don't worry about the ships, I don't think it'll pull us down. But. . . if this ship sinks before we get everyone off of it, well, you know what'll happen. Go to your men and keep this damn ship afloat 'til the other captains can figure out how to help us."

Casey Moores

Chapter 2: Escaping the Governor

The ordeal on the *Governor* only lasted a few more hours, and the beast did not show itself again. The seas calmed and our struggle to keep afloat eased somewhat. Light slowly crept over the horizon when a call rang out.

"Marines! All officers, report to the deck! You too, Sergeant Phillips!" I heard Major Reynolds announce. I stumbled wearily up the stairwell from inside, made my way past the bucket line, and found the officers assembled near the starboard railing. Their attention focused on something in the water. I felt the color drain from my face, and my stomach turned. Curiously, none seemed perturbed by what they saw. Trembling, I approached the rail and came within hearing range of the major's directions. A boat awaited in the water, with a few eager sailors staring up at us.

"—down there will haul each of us aboard," the major explained. "The captain of the *Sabine* claims they have no more suitable hawsers, and he cannot risk drawing us close, even if he did. Thus, the sailors down there recommend that each man tie themselves to a rope, throw the other end of the rope to them," he gestured two the boat, "and then jump into the water," his eyes contacted mine, and we shared a grim, apprehensive look, "where they will haul him onto the boat. When the boat's full, they'll take the load to the *Sabine,* unload, and return for more."

The officers nodded their heads and smiled. Reynolds and I stared into the water with dread, searching for any sign of the evil creature.

"Sir, is that all?" a pale-faced lieutenant asked.

"Yes, Lieutenant," Major Reynolds answered. "You get A Company moving, then B," again, he made eye contact with me, "then D Company. Orderly Sergeant, you keep the rest of C Company bailing until everyone else is off, and you take up the tail. Everyone understand?"

"Yes, Major!" we all responded. Doing my best to hide all signs of fear, I walked away from the rail and returned below deck to my bailing marines. I told myself that, if the creature were to surface and resume its assault, screams and shouts would alert me. For a few more incredibly long hours, I led the Marines of C Company in the futile attempt to rid the failing ship of seawater. In the back of my mind, I imagined the beast so vividly I could *feel* its tentacles pull me into those pulsing rings of teeth. Every crack against the hull drew my attention.

"Orderly Sergeant Phillips!" Major Reynolds bellowed. "That's it. C Company is off last!"

My stomach twisted and churned, and then tightened into a heavy lump, like a cannonball.

"C Company! Your work's done, on deck!" I repeated. "Time to be saved!"

Though my head knew the call meant that the entire battalion preceded us without incident, I could not help but imagine the creature guzzling me down, with snaps and crunches of my bones. Numbly, I marshaled my men to the deck and ordered them to do as directed. Even as I watched them go, one by one, I could not shake the feeling of a condemned man awaiting his turn for execution. On the bright side, my tremendous fear held my exhaustion at bay.

"That's it, Sergeant," the major relayed, grabbing my elbow and shaking me from my stupor. "You're the last. You and I know it is the height of cowardice for us to be the last two, but appearances tell the men, who know no better, that this is an act of bravery. If I could go before you, I would. But consider this, I can encourage you to make that plunge. Once you're gone, there will be no one here to do the same for me. Moreover, if I were to jump first, *you* would then be required to make the leap on your own."

As he spoke, he tied the rope around me. Words and knots complete, he tossed the loose rope end below, as had been done for countless other marines.

"Go now," he said grimly. "For the men, you must jump on your own. I cannot push you. Go!"

If there was one thing I had learned in training, in combat, and in all my time in the US Marines, it was how

Casey Moores

to leap. I mean that in the spiritual and the emotional sense, though I found myself required to do it in the physical sense. When your heart and your mind agree that the action you must take is the worst possible action *to* take, but duty demands it, *those* are the moments which make one a Marine. I felt for the cross against my chest and spoke a silent prayer. Although the foul, abysmal creature existed in my mind, tendrils wrapped tightly around me, teeth dug into every inch of my flesh. . . I leapt.

The icy cold water engulfed me. Though I held my mouth closed, water still intruded through my nostrils until I remembered to breathe out slowly. My lungs burned with the knowledge that air was nowhere to be found, and I wrestled with the instinct to open my mouth in search of it. Part of me considered whether it would, in fact, be better to let myself drown than to be devoured by the beast below.

I defended myself against the internal anguish with visions of home. I conjured up memories of my mother's clam chowder, a treat upon which we feasted once a week, when she could collect the proper ingredients. Memories of the gang of boys I'd grown up with at the

Philadelphia docks came to mind. I pictured Cassandra Paul, the daughter of one of my father's fellow fishermen. Her gorgeous brown curls always framed those almond shaped, amber eyes so perfectly. The little button nose and those lush, inviting lips made my heart melt every time. I'd only kissed her the once, the day I enlisted and went home to say goodbye. My family threw a small party for me, with the neighbors gathered about. They all wished me well and flooded me with random stories of their own experiences of war or tales they'd heard from this relative or that. Cassie had found a moment of privacy, pulled me away, wrapped her arms around my neck, drawn me tight, and given me the most tender kiss I'd ever received.

"You come home to me, Alex Phillips!" she'd demanded. "You promise me!"

I smiled, nodded, and promised. In retrospect, it was such a stupid thing to promise. In my icy tomb, with a sea creature from the depths of hell waiting to swallow me, I knew in my soul I could never keep the promise. My fate lay waiting in that dark water.

Whether it was my imagination or not, I cannot tell, but I swear I felt slight swirls of water churn around my legs. More than once, I know something brushed past them. All memory of Cassie Paul dispersed, replaced with visions of the deep itself grabbing hold of me. Inky black tendrils would soon snake up and around me. They would draw me into that wretched maw. A ring of teeth would press into my legs from all sides, rending flesh and breaking bone. Slowly, the rings would pulse up along me, grab higher on my person and reach for more vital areas. When the teeth dug into my stomach, my innards would spill out and float lazily in the water. Somewhere around the time it cracked my ribs, my soul would leak out into the dark. This too, the evil creature from the depths would devour. My eternal soul would exist forever in the belly of the beast, in the dark depths of the sea, with the souls of other marines as companions.

After countless hours trapped in a mental hell, perhaps all of a minute, something grasped at my shoulders. Something else scrambled to tear at my arms. *The tentacles of the beast*, I told myself, *soon it will all be over.* Then, my body smacked against a wooden wall and scraped over the top of it.

Water drained away from my face. With a cough and a sputter, I drew in the sweet, life-giving air. I opened my eyes to find a dozen of my marines crowded around me.

"Weren't so bad now, were it Sergeant?" Corporal Wilkes, my chatty New Yorker, said in his usual, cheerful voice.

"No, of course not," I coughed out. "A pleasant, refreshing dip. Thank you. Now, let's see to the major."

"Come on, Major, it's just you now!" the boat chief called. I noticed, at that moment, that the boat chief was one of the sailors who'd leapt aboard the *Governor* in the attempt to re-secure the hawsers. I watched his gaze as it swept over the water in the same manner mine did. Unable to ask what I wished to ask in front of the others, my attention returned to the major.

Our major nodded and tossed his rope to the boat crew, who collected it. Then, our major came to rigid attention, saluted the *Governor,* and turned back to face us. He locked eyes with me, smiled, nodded, and leapt into the water. I grabbed a hold of the rope myself and pulled as if his life depended on it, just in case it did. It was a few short seconds before we pulled him out and dragged him into the boat.

"Took you boys long enough," he grumbled as we hauled him up. Soaking wet, he righted himself and found a spot to collect his legs to sit better. He lifted his chin toward the *Sabine* and gave a wave to her captain. The sailors on its deck cheered in response, and the crew rowed us over to our savior. Major Reynolds and I shared the occasional awkward glance during the trip, but we spoke nary a word.

Casey Moores

Chapter 3: Idle Marines

"Non hai capito una sega!" Leo "Lion" Tomasini shouted at his opponent. He threw a stiff jab and missed. The tall brown-haired man squared off against Chowderhead Nick, a slightly shorter but more heavily built black-haired man. Nick was short for Niculescu, as I couldn't even begin to pronounce his first name. No one could. "You ain't no Roman, stop sayin' it ya damned fool!"

"Ro-muuuun, yes!" Nick shouted in reply, as he always did. With his fists up defensively, he proceeded to use the only other English words he seemed to know. "Mareeens, yes? This, no!"

The Italian marine feinted with his left arm and threw a hard hook punch with his right fist, which caught the black-haired man on the side of the face. Nick's head barely budged from the blow, and he responded with a hard, straight jab into Tomasini's face.

Several short days earlier, we'd arrived at the Port Royal Sound, where we discovered the attack succeeded immediately prior to our arrival. Calm winds, which had helped the attack itself, had also stranded us a painfully short distance from the action. A steady bombardment from our fleet encouraged the Confederates to abandon Forts Walker and Beauregard with little resistance. Hilton Head became a part of the

United States once again. The South Atlantic Blockading Squadron, under the command of Captain Samuel DuPont, had achieved greater success than anything the entire Union Army could claim. Though tuckered out, we were rightly exuberant. For a brief moment, I nearly forgot the events of that horror-filled night aboard the *Governor*.

Orders soon came which directed us to form up for a very somber funeral procession, in which seventeen boats from five of the larger ships delivered lost seamen to their final resting place. We'd missed the action and now watched the Navy honor its dead. Meanwhile, our brave comrades who were lost from the *Governor* received almost no mention, save for a few words from Major Reynolds while we were still aboard the *Sabine*.

As will happen when marines find themselves with an abundance of leisure time, scraps between the men became more common. Within no time, I found my hands full breaking up quarrels between longtime friends, separating agitated trouble-seekers from different companies, and dragging poor, wallpapered bastards back to their bivouacs. Nick found himself consistently favored as a Jonah upon which to vent frustrations. This was mostly due to his near total lack of English. Somehow, the only words he seemed to understand were drill orders. I surmised he learned this in training by imitating the other's actions until, at some point, he recognized the orders themselves.

"Come on guys, knock it off before the provost shows up!" the relatively diminutive Private Samuel Cash cried out, and marched up to interject himself. Deftly, Tomasini turned, put his left hand on Cash's chest and gave a hard shove backwards. Nick scored a body blow while Tomasini was distracted, and the Italian came back with a flurry of jabs and hooks. Cash stumbled backward until I caught him.

"Heh, they' ya go, they' ya go," Tomasini said with a laugh, enjoying himself. The rate of blows traded between the two accelerated. "Muh-reens, Muh-reens!" Tomasini mocked.

"Private Cash," I said calmly, as I helped to right him. "Can you explain what's going on?"

"Sorry, Sergeant, but Leo and Nick are goin' at it again," Cash told me. Tomasini's abuse of Nick had been a regular occurrence back at Hampton Roads. Early on, the other marines discovered that Nick would tell them his home country was "Romun", which everyone interpreted as "Roman". Tomasini, a second-generation Italian, took personal offense to this, as Nick was clearly not "Roman". Being in different companies, the matter disappeared during sea voyages, but resumed when we found ourselves camped near each other for long periods. "Boys got Nick all riled up again, asking where he's from, 'cause they knew Tomasini was nearby."

Another large man waded into the action, with his hands to the side as if to proclaim peace. The large, muscular blonde man was Corporal Emile Van Benthuysen, our only Swede.

All the regular army units were arranged either by ethnicity or by home state. Thus, most regiments in the Union Army were filled with people who either knew each other or shared a common ancestry. The Marines were not organized in this manner and carried men from all kinds of places.

"Privates! Stop!" the corporal announced in his curt accent. I assumed he hadn't seen me approach, as he was attempting to resolve the matter himself. Tomasini ducked into him and slammed him toward Nick. The fight immediately became a three-way affair. I cleared my throat to bark orders, but glanced to my left and the words caught in my throat.

Major Reynolds leaned casually against a thin tree, sipped from a tin cup, and watched quietly from a distance. Far from appearing angry or annoyed, the major seemed interested or, even, calculating. My attention returned when someone fired a pistol into the air. Shouts of encouragement and admonishment ceased, and the combatants froze in mid-blow.

Lieutenant Cartter, from one of the other companies, marched up with a group of provosts as support. Van Benthuysen and Nick attempted to protest, while

Tomasini smiled with his hands raised loosely in the air. Cartter raised a hand for silence.

"You three!" he shouted. "I'm putting you all on charges." He addressed the group he'd arrived with. "Lock them up, men."

"Lieutenant, sir, if I may—" I started.

"You may not, Sergeant," Lieutenant Cartter said sharply. "If you'd done your job, maybe this could have been prevented. But you did not. Maybe you can keep the *other* men under better control in the future. To the rest of you, this behavior is not tolerated among United States Marines. Now. . . disperse!"

The lieutenant snapped his fingers and waved his hand to direct the men away. I looked back to Major Reynolds, but he'd walked off.

If I believed Major Reynolds to be indifferent to the whole affair, I, and the other members of the Battalion, discovered the opposite. The next morning, a message arrived for me to muster the men of C Company. The message specifically directed all the members to resume wear of their stocks, the uncomfortable hard leather collars which all Marines were required to wear. Their use had slacked off a bit, as the officers loosened up after the success on the forts. The marines in my company grumbled when I announced stocks were, once again, mandatory.

As I mustered the men, I found the other companies mustering as well. Once formed up, Major Reynolds addressed the lot of us.

"Gentlemen, it has come to my attention that I have been remiss in my duties as your commander," he explained with a voice that was not a shout, but raised enough so that we could all ear him clearly. "I commend how you all performed aboard the *Governor.* Furthermore, I can honestly say that I was proud to learn of the marines who manned the guns and stormed the forts to make this entire endeavor a success. However, since those events, I have failed you. I have allowed this Battalion to become lazy and ornery in recent days. I will now work to remedy that situation. Company commanders! I have designated grounds for each of you to run the men through drills. You will continue to do so until I am satisfied that my neglect has been corrected. Proceed!"

It occurred to me that, not being a proper officer, I was not particularly qualified to direct drill. However, it did not seem the appropriate time to raise a protest on the matter. I recalled all the orders I'd been given, the few I'd regularly given in my current position, imitated the orders being shouted by the other company commanders, and did my level best. As ordered, I ran C Company through marching drill and various formations for the next couple hours. As I started to go hoarse from shouting orders, I paused to take a drink from my canteen. The men relaxed for a moment, and I allowed it.

"Orderly Sergeant Phillips!" A voice bellowed, and I chilled. Major Reynolds appeared from nowhere. "Sergeant, explain to me why these men are not moving."

That I was in the midst of wetting my whistle was obvious, so I chose not to retort with the excuse.

"Apologies, Major, sir, it will not happen again," I answered. He nodded.

"See that it doesn't," he ordered. At that moment, Private Cash collapsed in the middle of the ranks.

"See to your men, Sergeant," the major said. In a strange contradiction to his immediately prior implication, he said. "Give them a brief respite. Get that man to Company Q. Then resume."

"Yes, Major," I responded. I sent Private Cash to join the growing sick list and re-formed the company.

Ten hours passed before the order came to cease for the day. Exhausted, with necks chafed, bleeding, and stinging from sweat, C Company and all the other companies retired. Never before, save perhaps for the evening after Bull Run, had I experienced such a quiet camp. I tended to the boys as best as I could and passed out cloth strips to wrap around their necks. The following morning, I awoke to find orders to resume the thinly-veiled punitive torture.

In no time, Major Reynolds, our very own hero of Bull Run and the great leader who'd kept us afloat on the *Governor*, became the focus of all our ire. Our idleness was cured, but our bitterness grew fervently. We did find more and more time at the end of the day to relax before we fully retired. During these times, I discovered one of the boys from another company had written a full song about the sinking of the *Governor*. This became an immediate camp favorite.

After a few days of this, we found ourselves subject to somewhat arbitrary muster re-organization. The powers that be assigned the other companies to various outbound ships. They were destined for further operations. C Company found itself both depleted in numbers and stranded at Hilton Head. Finally, after another week, Major Reynolds halted our drill and drew me aside to address privately.

"Sergeant Phillips, I am having your company returned to Hampton Roads," he explained. "There you will meet with your new lieutenant."

My heart sank slightly at the news. I'd heard of other experienced Marine non-commissioned officers applying for, and receiving, full commissions as officers as the United States Marines increased numbers. I'd held out hope that Major Reynolds might support a bid on my part, but those hopes dashed away.

"Furthermore, C Company is being officially re-formed under other leadership at Hampton Roads as we speak," he continued, "and they should be underway to support the South Atlantic Blockading Squadron. I've sent a request to Colonel Harris to re-designate your company as M Company. You'll also be in charge of all of our hotheads and jailbirds as well, who will, in fact, be assigned to M Company as well."

"Yes, sir," I replied somewhat numbly. I opened my mouth to speak again, but confusion overcame me, and I could not think of which question to ask first.

"Doubtless this seems like quite a blow," he said grimly. "However, there *is* a reason for this." He glanced around suspiciously, and verified we were alone. "You and I both know quite well what we alone witnessed the last night of the affair aboard the *Governor*. All I can supply at this time is that such events are not as unique as you might think. That's all I'll say on the matter. That said, the new officer you'll receive at Hampton Roads will need a good deal of your support."

"Major Reynolds, sir, if I may ask, why—" The major hushed me as a corporal approached with a message. Disappointment welled inside me as the major left to meet with the new lieutenant in charge of my old company. It was my last opportunity to talk with Major Reynolds, as we departed the next day.

I stood on the deck of the *USS St Lawrence*, which had arrived some weeks after the forts were taken and immediately tasked with our return to Hampton Roads. From its deck I watched the shoreline. Major Reynolds gave a wave and I felt certain it was specifically meant for me.

The mystery of my strange situation, coupled with dark visions of the sea demon, ate at my mind and my soul for the entire trip. When I could muster the courage, I drew myself up the deck to search the sea behind us, to see if anything followed. I found schools of fish and a number of sharks, but nothing like the creature I'd seen.

Chapter 4: Pumpkin Rinds

The new lieutenant, when he arrived, proved to be the strangest person I've ever met.

Upon our return to Hampton Roads, a captain directed us to our barracks, conspicuously distant from the few other marines. As mentioned, all the hotheads, jailbirds, no accounts, and parlor soldiers, such as Tomasini and Niculescu, remained assigned to my new company. Colonel Harris himself signed an order removing the charges from all in my company, contingent on their agreement to serve in it. This caused a great deal of confusion as all understood themselves to already be legally bound to serve in the United States Marines. Private Tomasini, in fact, became quite vocal that he would make no agreement which led to his service with Chowderhead Nick, the "Pretender Italian" as he'd taken to calling him. Worse, he and some others acted empowered by the new arrangement. I advised the involved officers of his defiance and was met with shrugs of indifference. It seemed the *agreement* was assumed on the parts of all my marines. Consequently, if Colonel Harris thought such a reprieve would diminish my company's appetite for brawling, he was mistaken.

We arrived back in Hampton Roads a few days before Christmas, and my time was filled with either breaking up rows or drilling the men. In addition, I found myself responsible for the endless managerial minutiae required to keep a company in operation. I yearned for an officer to arrive so I would no longer be responsible for such things.

No other marines, from the provost or any other company, involved themselves in our affairs. The first time I went to request help in restraining my men from a scrap, Orderly Sergeant Fisk directed me to inquire with Lieutenant Cartter, who'd returned to Hampton Roads as well.

"See to your company, Sergeant," Lieutenant Cartter replied, with an annoyed demeanor. "If those boys of yours were manageable, we'd assign them to real companies."

When I, respectfully, asked exactly what he meant by the statement, he repeated the phrase, "See to your company, Sergeant."

No further guidance, or assistance, would be forthcoming.

I did, during this time, receive my new non-commissioned officer sword, which I'm told was identical to those the Army officers were issued. They'd recently replaced the Mameluke swords, which Marines had carried for almost forty years. When I was not breaking up fights, I did what I could to learn how to use it.

For Christmas itself, the officers received invitations to some fancy ball somewhere to dance with local debutantes. Marines from the other companies received invitations to dinners at various homes in the area. M Company received explicit instructions that we were, under no circumstances, to leave the barracks. This had the expected effect on the Company's morale.

On Christmas Day, Privates Tomasini, Archibald, and Doyle took it upon themselves to protest their treatment by assaulting some of the other marines, who'd returned in drunken revelry. In this manner, we discovered the guards were heavily on the side of any marines who were not assigned to M Company. In a strange inconsistency, M Company also discovered charges would not be brought against us. Shortly after, a Captain came to me and confirmed the only punishment members of M Company could receive was capital. I warned the Company against working to determine where that line lay.

One week into the New Year, I awoke to find a new member of our company. Short cropped brown hair stuck out from where he lay buried contentedly in a thick, standard issue blanket. A Mameluke sword, the kind the

Marines had just replaced, and a Colt Dragoon Revolver hung over one corner of the empty bed he'd chosen- our barracks had quite a few. Over another corner was the man's coat, a tattered, decades old Marine officer's coat with numerous patches sewn onto it. On its shoulders lay the gold officers braid we called "chicken guts", with a simple red background and nothing else. A second lieutenant had arrived to command us. I walked quietly to Corporal Horne, a gangly redheaded man from Albany, who'd awakened before me.

"When did he blow in?" I asked. He simply glared and shrugged.

"No one seems to know, Sergeant," he answered. "Snug as a bug, ain't he? Just found him there this morning. No one had the grit to wake him. We figured that'd be your job, when you were ready, Sergeant."

"It's about damn time," I said, and started at the sleeping figure. "Thank you, Corporal. Muster the men, try to get them into something that looks like a formation and try to keep another row from breaking out. I'll see to our new lieutenant, as you said. Have them ready to receive words, I imagine he'll want to address the boys."

"One more thing, Sergeant," the corporal continued. "He's got a great big chest over by the door, or at least, boys and me have assumed it's his. Ain't none of ours and weren't there yesterday eve. Locked up, not that we checked." He winked. I looked to where he motioned and found there was, indeed, a large, leather covered chest with brass corners and a big brass lock on the front. A variety of intricate, but not matching, carvings adorned the leather. One caught my eye, a large black blob with concentric circles in the center and an abundance of wavy arms extending from it.

"Sergeant?" Corporal Horne asked.

"You've got your orders, Corporal," I stated.

With a nod, the corporal barked some orders and the men, eager to disperse before the new officer awakened, flooded out.

I gave them a moment to clear out. Major Reynolds' words returned to mind.

The new officer you'll receive at Hampton Roads will need a good deal of your support.

Did the major mean they'd gotten another greenhorn lieutenant? Since they seemed to be the official prison detail of the Marines, how would such a man not be eaten alive by the boys? What other possibility was there?

"Sir," I said quietly, as I approached the bunk. His mere presence in the barracks was a cause for confusion. Officers did not sleep in the barracks with enlisted men, they had their own quarters. The man did not stir. I cleared my throat a little louder. I then noticed a terribly worn pair of boots, which sat at the base of his bunk, covered in slightly dried mud.

"Sir," I announced even louder. This time, he responded with an angry huff.

"Lieutenant, sir!" I shouted at long length. "Orderly Sergeant Phillips, sir! It is my honor to welcome you to M Company!"

A hand reached up to the top of the blanket and peeled it slowly downward. Worn, hollow eyes peered back at me. Those eyes told me he'd been through the mill. They were so dark, in fact, that they conjured images of the beast from the *Governor*.

"Sergeant Phillips, is it?" he growled. His voice was deep, gruff, and had a hint of a New Englander's accent. "You got a first name?"

New officers asking a sergeant's first name identified them as new to the military. Whether this man had seen the elephant or not, he'd clearly never served before. The two newly learned facts clarified my impression of why Major Reynolds had said what he'd said.

"Orderly Sergeant Alexander Phillips, sir," I replied. Sometimes, a new officer could be dissuaded from becoming too familiar with the enlisted men with persistent professionalism. The instinct came from good intentions, but seldom ended in a good manner.

"Alex, then?" he responded, though he made no move to venture further from his blanket. Our new lieutenant would not be easily dissuaded from foolish pursuits. The best course of action in this case was to remain formal, no matter how hard the officer tried to become familiar. "Chilly here, isn't it?"

"I presume you are our new company commander, Lieutenant. . ." I let the word hang, hoping beyond hope he would supply me with an answer.

"I'm guessing you found my chest," he said.

"Yes, sir, it's intact. I did not let the boys touch it," I answered. With another groan, he freed a hand well enough to point at his coat.

"Key," he muttered. As I fumbled in the coat to find a key, he continued. "The chest is full of Arkansas toothpicks. See the men train up on them."

He pulled the sheets over his face as I retrieved the key.

"Sir?" I said. "Arkansas. . .?"

"Toothpicks," he barked. "Bowie knives! Get them out of the chest, pass them around, and train up the men on them. I'll be out in a bit."

"Yes, sir," I replied uneasily. "Sir, may I ask one more—"

"You may not," he answered. "Let me sleep, Alex."

Train up the boys on the knives? Who the heck doesn't know how to use a darn knife?

Nonetheless, I enlisted Corporal Wilkes to help me distribute the Bowie knives I found piled loosely in the chest. The reaction from the Marines of M Company matched my expectation.

"Our new pumpkin rinds wants us to do what, Sergeant?" Wilkes asked, staring in wonderment at his knife. "And where is he, in a loose state? Is he a beat?"

"You will refer to the *lieutenant* with respect, Corporal," I admonished. He shrugged with an embarrassed look, and we continued out to the men. I formed them up, Corporal Wilkes distributed the large knives, and I addressed the company.

"Our new lieutenant has arrived," I explained. "He reported in very late last night and is recovering from his trip. While he rests up, his direction is for us to familiarize ourselves with these fine knives with which he has provided us. So, form up the men. Just have them stab at the bayonet bags for a while."

M Company half-heartedly stabbed at the hanging bags we'd set up for bayonet practice. After half an hour or so, we returned to some regular drill, and then I released them to the dog robber for lunch.

"What you got in the way of black gold around here?" I heard the lieutenant say in his rough New England drawl. I nearly released my bowels. I'd had no indication he'd even awoken until he appeared behind me and made the inquiry. As I jumped up to reply, I almost knocked over the worn, wood plank table at which I sat. My chair did fall over, and he casually righted it for me. The man wore the same worn trousers I imagine he'd arrived in, with a white shirt. Though he wore his dark blue, double breasted frock coat, he'd left it entirely unbuttoned. His coat was the "undress" version, without epaulets and with plain collar, cuffs, and shirt pockets.

"Sir!" I shouted, with a bit too much excitement. "Good morning, Lieutenant, sir!"

"Please, it's Addison," he replied. "And about the coffee. . ."

"Lieutenant Addison, sir," I stated. Flustered with his appearance, I took it on myself to button his coat. Thankfully, he let me.

"Not just Addison," he retorted, but then he sighed in frustration. "Lieutenant Greene if you must, I'm not too familiar with Marine ways. So. . . coffee?"

Not too familiar with Marine ways? How the hell did he get to be our lieutenant?

"Corporal Archibald, would you be so good as to get *Lieutenant Greene*," I loudly enunciated the name so all would hear it, "a cup of coffee. Not the essence, get him a real cup."

"Yes, Sergeant," Thomas Archibald replied, and scuttled off to do so.

"Vittles, Lieutenant?" I asked. "Private Conyers boiled up a sort of fish stew. It's not too bad, sir."

Lieutenant Greene nodded and took a seat.

"Sir, with the other officers in the barracks, the custom is to wear the full-dress uniform," I informed him. "And

I'll have Private Cash look into getting you the proper trousers."

"I already told them, I'm not spending my own darned money buying some useless uniform," he grumbled. Wilkes set a tin cup full of java sludge onto the table in front of him. "I joined up to help with the fighting, since you men are *wholly* unprepared for the job at hand. On that, how'd the knife training go?"

"Well, sir, I passed the pig stickers out, as you said," I replied. Conyers, a tall, brown-haired, bespectacled man, and fellow Philadelphian came up with a bowl of steaming fish stew. Greene happily dug straight in. "I had them work over the bayonet bags, I think the boys are—"

"You keep calling them 'boys'," Greene said, and slammed his spoon against the table. "I don't plan to take any *boys* into a fight. This Unit has men, or I don't want them, do you understand? I had this talk with Johnny, uh, that's Major Reynolds to you, I suppose, but—"

Johnny?

"Unit Thirteen only has *men* in it, do you understand? I don't care much for this Marine vernacular of yours."

"You mean the company, sir?" I asked in sudden confusion. Corporal Wilkes, who stood by in expectation of orders, shot me a questioning look.

"No, I mean the Unit," Lieutenant Greene replied. With dismay, he paused again and bored holes into me with his gaze. "This *is* Special Unit Thirteen, is it not? Am I in the wrong place? The clerk told me it was the right place, then tried to direct me to Officer's quarters, as if I wouldn't be living among my men. Honestly, am I in the right place, Alex? I came a long way, and I gave you all those knives."

"Sir, first off, it is proper for you to refer to me as *sergeant*, and, to answer your question, this is M Company," I explained. We stared at each other for a long moment, with puzzlement on his face and befuddlement on mine. At length, he cracked a smile and broke into a chuckle.

"'M' Company, is it?" He continued to laugh and resumed eating. With a full mouth, he sputtered, "Tell me, Alex, is there an 'L' Company, or a 'K' Company? 'J' even?"

"None that I know of, sir," I answered, curious as to where the discussion led. I'd had these exact same thoughts and resolved that no reasonable answer existed. My best guess, and that of the other boys, had been that we were *Misfit* Company, though I dared not vocalize the rumination.

"Tell me," he said, and tiny bits of stew flew from his mouth. "Do you know what letter of the alphabet 'M' is?"

While I started counting the letters in my head, he shoveled more stew into his mouth. After a few moments, he lost patience and supplied the answer.

"Thirteen, Alex, it is the thirteenth letter," he gawked at me with an excited smirk, looking for my reaction. I remained as confounded as ever. "Do you not understand the significance?"

The excitement drifted back into frustration as I failed to supply an answer.

"Does no one here know anything about Unit Thirteen?" he asked. Deep passion seemed to overtake him. Both fists slammed onto the table, and the bowl of fish stew bounced up and overturned. "The heroes of Molina Del Rey? The legendary stand against the Quinametzin? The entire Mexican War would have been lost without their sacrifice! My Father—!" Our lieutenant shot up, knocking his chair away, and brushed stew off his coat. Then, he returned to his admonishment, slightly calmed. "How do you not know what I'm talking about?"

"Lieutenant, sir, my apologies, I do not mean to offend, I. . ."

He threw a hand up, closed his eyes, and let out a long, deep sigh.

"It's not your fault, Alex," he said, and relaxed. "It's not you, it's not you. You can't be blamed if the damned journalists and the politicians. . . And then there's the fact this sort of thing hasn't existed for well more than a decade. . . Anyway, let's get our men together. See how they're coming with those knives."

Chapter 5: A Different Kind of Unit

"What in the hell is this?" he growled. Lieutenant Greene stomped up to the sacks which dangled from an overhead crossbar. "How do you expect to learn how to use a knife stabbing a sack of. . . what the hell *is* this? Sand? Sand has never done anything to me, I'll have you know!"

"Lieutenant Greene, sir, this is how we train," I explained. "And, sir, if I may say, the boy—, the *men*, sir, know how to use knives."

"Not anymore, Alex, you do not train like this anymore," he said. He cast his gaze around the formation, who awkwardly held the large knives in place of their M1855 Springfield rifle muskets. "And no, I'll bet a month's wage, *my new officer's wage*, that you do not. You!"

He pointed at Chowderhead Nick.

"You!" he repeated and waved his hand invitingly. "Come here and stab me."

"Sir, you can't—"

"Can't I?" Greene retorted, animated. "I'm the lieutenant, am I not? Even if I don't know a damn thing about being a Marine or fighting a damn war."

There it was. He had just admitted, before the entire Company, to a total lack of knowledge about our service.

Any credibility he might have had evaporated into the cold, humid air.

"But I can sure as hell teach you how to kill something with a knife," he straightened and settled a bit. In slow, dramatic fashion, he unbuttoned his coat while he spoke. "You all think you know how to use a knife, don't you? Well, let's find out. Come on, big man with the black hair, what's your name?"

"That's Private Niculescu, sir," I informed him. "He doesn't speak much English. He claims to be a Roman, we think."

"Roman?" Greene asked. The lieutenant squirmed out of his coat and tossed it to me casually. He regarded Chowderhead for a moment. "*Este Romîn?*"

Nick lost all bearing and his jaw dropped open. He turned to look at me with something between despair, relief, or confusion. It was hard to tell.

"Dah!" Nick answered. He'd used the word a lot in the past, we'd taken for it to mean "Yes". The rest of the conversation came across as pure gibberish. "*Vorbeshti romaneste?*"

"Dah," Greene replied. "*Înveti Engleza?*"

"Yes, I t-rrry," Nick said, with a half shrug. Lieutenant Greene nodded in satisfaction and turned to me.

"He's not Roman, he's Romanian," Lieutenant Greene explained. "Good hunters in Romania. Lot to learn from those people." He returned his attention to Nick. "*Bine. Atacă-mă.*"

Nick stepped forward, uncertain, and his gaze darted between the lieutenant and me.

"*Bine*, Niculescu," Greene repeated. "*Ajută-mă să-i învăţ. Atacă-mă.*"

Determination seemed to build up with our newly discovered Romanian. He clenched the knife tightly, looked around at the other men, and stepped toward the lieutenant. Greene put both hands up, hunched a little, and bent his knees slightly. Half a second too late, I understood what was about to happen. Nick launched himself at Greene, leading with the knife.

In a flash, Greene straightened up and kicked Nick's shin, which halted Nick's rush. Greene planted his foot on Nick's foot, grabbed the sleeve of the knife arm, jerked his body along, grabbed his collar with the other hand, and shoved Nick's face down into the dirt. As if plucked directly out of heaven, Lieutenant Greene's credibility returned with the resounding thud of Nick's head hitting the ground.

"Now, men, I don't want to see you doing something this stupid out in a fight, but I'm trying to prove a point," Greene explained. "If it's just you and someone else has a knife, run and go find your own knife, or a gun, with a bayonet if you can. Or try to slow them down long enough for one of these other men to shoot them for you. My point is, you men could learn quite a bit more about

Casey Moores

how to fight with a knife. If this man can't cut me, and you'll all get your chance, too, but if none of you can even cut me before I knock you down, you've all got a lot to learn. A man with a knife should always at least get himself some blood."

"Lieutenant, that man shouldn't have--"

"I told him to attack me, Alex," Greene said. He let go of Nick and stood up. "*Scuze, mulțumesc.*"

Nick rolled over and dragged himself back to his spot in the formation. Greene began low, but became more agitated the longer he spoke. "If you hadn't noticed, we're out here by ourselves, away from the other marines. The *real* Marines as all of them see it. But they're all wrong. *We* are the real Marines, the ones who deal with all the dark things they can't handle. This country's forgotten all about us, which is fine by me, because we don't need them. We're here. . . once again, in honor of the good Marines, like my father, who lost their lives doing a mighty important job, one I understand you've never heard of. We're the reason Marines still wear those stocks, did you know that? We are the newly reformed Special *Unit* Thirteen. M Company works just fine as well, and that's who you *say* we are. And I am proud to be in this company. 'M' Company. . . M for *Misfits*. . . M for *Murderers*. . . M for *Monsters*. Hell, M for *Marines*, because we are the true Marines of the entire United States of America."

The formation stared at him in silence. They seemed torn between pride and confusion. I can only imagine they wondered at the sanity of their new officer. I would have as well, and I even began to, until the dark, tentacled, evil creature intruded upon my mind. Memories of marines, of my previous lieutenant, of those vicious rows of teeth pulsing up those poor men, bones cracking, the screams. . .

"Alex, I'm speaking to you!" Lieutenant Greene shouted, and I snapped back to the barracks. "Get these men lined up, they'll each have a shot at me. Anyone draws blood, well, I got a present for you to carry into your next fight, help you kill whatever it is we're fighting."

Whatever it is we're fighting? My blood chilled as I considered the implication.

"Damnit, what's the order for 'line up and attack me', Alex?" Greene asked. I blinked twice and turned to the formation.

"You heard the lieutenant!" I shouted. "By file, men."

The line of marines attacked the lieutenant, as ordered, one at a time. Most simply rushed forward and took a wild swing. The first few went down the same way Nick had. Van Benthuysen made a wild bull rush for the lieutenant's legs, which took Greene to the ground. However, the big Swede got punched in the head several times and forgot about his knife in the process. Greene did give him some encouragement though, for making the best showing yet. The affair turned into a bit of a game, with Wilkes collecting bets.

A few more, to include Tomasini, went down easy. Little Samuel Cash surprised everyone by keeping his distance, dodging the kick, and making a whole lot of quick jabs. He successfully scored a scratch on Greene's forearm before taking a solid punch to the face. No one else drew any blood.

I went last.

I mirrored his posture, with my arms up as if boxing. I figured I would play it slow, feel him out, so that, at the very least, I would last longer than all the other men. We paced around each other a bit and I feigned a few jabs. Then I jabbed with my left hand, threw a stronger feint with the knife, skipped outside the kick, which I'd expected, and thrust the knife forward with all my weight. I felt the knife press into his shirt.

Then, my vision exploded with stars.

"Damn!" Greene shouted. As the bright points of light and blanket of darkness dissipated from my sight, I found myself laid out on the ground. My head rang like a bell. The lieutenant stood, admiring a small red stain on the lower left side of his white shirt.

"That's the stuff, Alex!"

"Sergeant Phillips!" I heard Lieutenant Cartter bellow. I found him stomping up with his pistol out, as if he planned to shoot me. "My apologies, Lieutenant, let me send for a nurse. I had not yet had the opportunity to inform you of the ornery nature of your—"

"I ordered him to do this, um, I'm sorry, who are you?" Lieutenant Greene said. As he did, Greene moved forward to hold out a hand and help me up. Cartter paused and glared back and forth between Greene and me.

"*First* Lieutenant William Cartter, and may I presume you to be *Second* Lieutenant Addison Greene?" Cartter announced. "Ordered, you say? I must have misheard you. As I was saying, I'm sorry no one was here on your arrival to explain that these boys—"

"I am perfectly aware of who these *men* are, William," Greene said, as I made it to my feet beside him.

"Call him Lieutenant Cartter," I advised in the smallest of whispers, facing away from Cartter. Then, I turned about.

"Lieutenant Cartter, I mean," Greene grumbled. "But as *I* was saying, I know who these *men* are, and I ordered them to come at me with a knife so that I could assess their abilities. Fine bunch, wouldn't you say? I will be honored to take these men into battle."

"Ordered them? You *did* say that, didn't you? Well, *Second* Lieutenant Greene, let me inform you that—"

"If you take issue with how I lead my men, *Lieutenant Cartter,*" disdain dripped from Greene's words, "I would ask that you please take it up with Major Johnny Reynolds, so that he may discuss the matter with—"

He grabbed my elbow and whispered, "Who's in charge of the Marines, just now?"

"Colonel Harris, sir."

"—Colonel Harris." Greene said aloud.

Cartter sputtered for a moment, and his gaze flowed around all of the assembled men.

"I do not need to take this up with them, *Second* Lieutenant Greene, I am taking it up with you, at this very instant," Cartter said. "In the United States Marine Corps—"

"Lieutenant Cartter!" a new voice announced. The entire Company turned to see a much older officer, with slicked over black hair that connected down to a full beard, but no moustache. I recognized the new arrival as Major Jacob Zeilin, with whom I had fought at Bull Run. He'd been shot in the left arm, and I'd helped escort him away in the retreat. "Thank you for helping to welcome our new lieutenant."

Cartter became dumbfounded once again and was completely lost for words.

"My stars, if it isn't Addison Greene. . . good to finally meet you as a full-grown man," Zeilin said. "You wouldn't remember, but I met you as a small child. I knew your father, you see. Incredible man. Saved my life. Hell, he saved the whole damn war down there in Mexico." The major turned to me. "And Sergeant Phillips, so good to see you again as well. Lieutenant

Cartter, you were there, you remember Sergeant Phillips from Bull Run, don't you?"

"Uh, Major, I--"

"Of course you do. I still can't thank you enough for carrying me off the field that day, Sergeant. Horrible day, but we Marines fought with honor, didn't we?"

"Yes, sir," I replied, and glanced at Lieutenant Cartter. A moment earlier he'd been the lord of the barracks, prepared to render God's judgment. He'd transformed into a mouse, surrounded by predators.

"Addison, I've taken personal interest in your requisitions, and I'll ensure you get everything you need," Major Zeilin continued. He leaned a little to regard Greene's stained shirt. "I'll see to it we get that replaced. And we'll get you some appropriate trousers as well. Do you need a full dress coat?"

"Yes, Major, I was told I'd have to purchase one, so I'll look into it," Greene answered.

"Nonsense. . . Lieutenant Cartter?"

"Yes, sir?"

"See to it Lieutenant Greene is provided with a full dress coat," Major Zeilin ordered.

"Yes, sir," Cartter replied softly.

Major Zeilin clapped a hand on Greene's shoulder. "You've quite the task ahead of you, and I'll be damned if you were to fail because of me. Myself, Major Reynolds, and dare I say, the Commandant are all behind your endeavor."

Casey Moores

"Thank you, Major," Greene replied. "And give Major Reynolds my thanks when you see him."

That was the last occasion on which I ever witnessed any marine officer make any complaints with regard to M Company. However, we still had no answer as to exactly what kind of unit we'd found ourselves in, only more questions.

Chapter 6: Unusual Ordnance

After our unorthodox introduction to our new lieutenant, we only spent a few more days at Hampton Roads before being assigned to the North Atlantic Blockading Squadron. In those few short days, I'd learned that Greene had never served as a soldier in any capacity and lacked any knowledge whatsoever on the ways of Marines.

Those last few days were spent training with the knives and familiarizing ourselves with shotguns, which he produced from that same trunk. The barrels had each been shortened by over a foot. The *men* greatly enjoyed practicing with the muzzle-loading shotguns. Some had used similar guns in their youth, "fowling guns" according to some, messenger guns according to those who'd witnessed them on mail carriers, and "plain old short-barreled muskets" according to most. Either way, all the men of M Company loved them, even those who questioned their usefulness in an actual battle. Lieutenant Greene attempted to mollify them with the word that Confederate troops used them quite a bit with great, murderous effect, but that made few feel any better.

I, personally, felt particularly honored to have received a breech-loading version the lieutenant received from Europe. It used hard paper cartridges with a pin that stuck out the top. Once I'd learned how to align the pin correctly, I found I could reload and fire it far more rapidly than the muzzle loaders.

Two of the corporals, Van Benthuysen and Wilkes, received short, quick firing rifles called carbines. Where Greene had procured cartridges for the variety of weapons I could only guess at. He assigned Private Cash as our quartermaster. It was a position I'd failed to assign as we'd previously had little supply and I, as the sole sergeant, had handled it myself. I explained to Lieutenant Greene that the quartermaster was a sergeant's position but, as usual, he dismissed my words and informed me he'd handle promotions later.

"Sergeant, are we gonna carry these instead of our rifles?" Corporal Van Benthuysen asked me, after a few hours of practice with the weapons.

"You'll carry them both," Lieutenant Greene announced, breaking his characteristic silence. He only seemed to intrude into conversations when the men questioned our new weapons. "With the shotguns on a leather cord so you can't lose them. And you'll carry two more pouches for its powder and ammunition."

Several murmurs of consternation followed, which he seemed not to hear.

Despite the joy of learning to use the shotgun, something still ate at me, and that was the lieutenant's lack of interest in learning how to lead us in drill. After we dismissed the men for lunch, he requested I join him, and I took the opportunity to encourage him.

"Proper set of hardheads and bruisers we got here, haven't we?" Greene asked. "And thank the heavens no one's decided to send us a priest or something equally useless."

"Lieutenant, may I suggest you lead the men in drill this afternoon, sir?" I asked, while Greene slurped away on a bowl of stew.

"That's where the men line up and fire all at once, right, Alexander?" he replied, and scooped another dripping spoonful into his mouth.

"Well, sir, that's the overall point, but there are quite a few commands to learn to form them up, march them forward, turn them--"

"How do I split them up and get them to spread out?" he asked, between spoonful's.

"That would be a skirmish drill, sir," I answered.

"That, then," he stated.

"Sorry, sir?" I asked.

"Skirmish drill, that's what we'll work on," he said.

"Well, sir, that's a progression, as it were," I explained. "Sir, first we need to work on platoon drill, so we can form the men up, move them about on a battlefield--"

"Don't expect we'll ever be fighting on a proper battlefield, Alex," Greene said, and turned his head to lock eyes with me. He smacked the spoon onto the table. "Do we understand each other, *Sergeant?*"

Since our first meeting, he'd reserved the term *sergeant* for moments when he expected me to shut up and follow.

"Yes, sir, I understand you, but. . . sir, if we were to come across a situation in which we needed to--"

"In such a situation, I imagine you would do an admirable job, translating my directions into the appropriate orders, would you not?" he asked, gaze held firm.

"Yes, sir," I replied, exasperated.

We began the afternoon with some skirmish drills. With perplexingly few inputs from the lieutenant, I formed the company into one large platoon. This was mostly due to the fact that, despite my repeated requests, we had yet to assign any other sergeants to the company. Greene informed me he'd make no decisions to that effect before "he'd tried our metal".

"First Platoon, as skirmishers, on the left file, take interval, march!" I shouted. As they moved as ordered, I explained to the lieutenant what he was witnessing. "You see, sir, the left four men, or *Comrades in Battle,* move forward. Meanwhile, all the others move forward and right as they go. The next Comrades in Battle over go twenty paces to the left of this first one, the next one over goes another twenty paces over, and so on. Now, I'm about to order 'Halt', at which time each group of four--"

"Comrades in Battle," Greene said.

"Yes, sir, you're getting it now, Comrades in Battle," I said with an encouraging smile. "Now, when I say 'Halt', the first man will stop and the other three will line up, each five paces to the right of the previous man, so that they're all spread out in a skirmish line, as you asked. Now. . . *Halt!*"

The line ceased moving forward and, as I'd described, the groups of four spread out into a thin line. I turned back to Lieutenant Greene, with plans to describe how I could re-assemble the men.

"Now, can we order them to act independently as Comrades in Battle?" Greene asked. As usual, I found myself lost for words. He noticed my stunned look. "I mean, which one of the men is in charge of each *Comrades in Battle*? Is it the man on the left, the one they, uh, move off from? Can I tell that man to take charge of his," he sighed in frustration, "*Comrades in Battle*? And is there something else we can call them? *Comrades in Battle* is a hellacious mouthful, especially if I'm shouting orders at them all the time."

"Well, sir, you see, you never shout orders at specific Comrades in Battle," I explained. "They all still move as a Platoon or a Company, which would be much easier to direct if we had more sergeants and maybe another lieutenant or two, but we still give one order to direct them all. But we can put them in this position in a variety of ways, let me show--"

Casey Moores

"Squad?" he asked, and I responded with my usual confusion. He rolled his eyes. "Can I call them a squad? Instead of Comrades in Battle?"

"Well, yes sir," I answered. "Two or three of those constitutes a squad, and they arrange themselves as such, but that's just to help them form up, unless we're on a ship, we almost never order them to do anything as a--"

"That's it then," he said. "I need to designate someone to command each squad. Then I can order them to go off and operate independently." He bobbed his head and smiled as if he'd just dreamed up some revolutionary battlefield tactic. "I can't be sending these men forward into the sorts of things we're going to be facing in a big long, obvious line. We gotta be able to move about, forward and back, with each squad acting in the best manner to deal with whatever it is we're going to be dealing with!"

The sorts of things we're going to be facing. . . I chilled every time he said something to that effect.

When we re-mustered in the early evening, he introduced us to something called the Ketchum Hand Grenade, a strange item which looked like a cross between a giant dart and an oblong iron ball. Greene informed us his *friend,* Billy Ketchum, had given him a few to test. No one openly commented on our introduction to a weapon which was loaded with explosives, meant to be thrown, and named "Ketchum". We attempted to try one, and only one, out in an empty field, a good distance from the barracks. Greene explained it was meant to explode when the plunger on the front tip rammed against the ground. To demonstrate, he tossed one out as hard as he could, in a high arc. It did not explode.

Over the next few seconds, the men and I heard Greene properly curse for the first time.

"Alex, who's our best sharpshooter?" he asked me, after he'd calmed a bit.

"Hard to say, sir, we haven't exactly had a competition or anything," I answered. "Though Conyers and Meier are pretty good."

"Well, we'll have one now," he said. "Gather together whoever thinks they're the best shot. Come up with some kind of target and some kind of rules and work out who our top four marksmen are. I'll be right back."

As he was known to do, he walked off and disappeared. Per his direction, I set up a few targets, collected the candidates, and led them up with their Model 1855 rifle muskets. After a few rounds of firing, Paul Meier placed first, Alan Conyers second, Michael Clarke third, and John Parker fourth.

By then, Lieutenant Greene had returned with a sort of rifle none of us had seen before. The rifle was unusual in that, when you looked down the barrel, it had a six-sided groove instead of a circle. The barrel stretched a little over three feet, making the entire weapon about four and half feet long.

"Sir, you didn't get that out of that chest of yours, now did you?" I asked. I jested that it was much too long, though I suppose he could have carried it in pieces. Either way, we'd already dug through the chest to see what other *presents* he might've been holding back. We hadn't seen this contraption in there.

"Of course not, Alex," he replied. "I wouldn't trust you scoundrels with a beauty like this. I know you picked that damn chest two days after I arrived. No, I left this at the armory, where I hoped it'd be safe. But, as with everything in that chest of mine, I'd always intended to give it to one of you. So, in order of your ranking, you four get to shoot that grenade from a few hundred yards away. The one who blows it up gets this one of a kind, worth-more-than-you-and-your-parents-and-your-grandparents-all-combined, Whitworth Rifle."

Lieutenant Greene then produced its strange, blocky ammunition, demonstrated how to load it, and fired it into the air. Then, he handed it to Private Meier.

Private Meier took the rifle, loaded it, and kneeled down right where we'd gathered. On his first try, Meier hit the iron ball dead center, but to no effect.

Private Alan Conyers walked left and right a good ways. Eventually, he found the position he wanted. He knelt, took aim, and hit the front of the iron ball. The explosion itself was not as exciting as we expected, as far away as we were, but explode it did, followed by whoops and hollers from the men. Conyers had accomplished the prescribed feat and became the company's first sharpshooter. After the cheering subsided, Lieutenant Greene ceremoniously put his hand on the unusual rifle, which Conyers still held.

"This rifle is now your entire life, Private," Greene announced, loud enough for all to hear. "There are not many like it. The day may come when your sharp eye and this terrifically expensive rifle may be the difference between the life and death of this entire Company. You've proven yourself our best shot, but from now on, with every shot you take, you must continue to prove yourself worthy of it. There's only so many cartridges for this rifle, though I got a kit to give you with molds to make more. In any event, by God, you'd better make every single shot count."

Conyers nodded, glowing with excitement and respect.

"I won't let you down, sir," Conyers replied. "You point me at the Johnny Rebs, I'll kill whichever ones you want me to."

Casey Moores

"I'm sure you will, Alan," Greene said. Private Conyers turned pale, and the rest of the marines hushed. It may have been the first time he directly addressed someone other than me and Niculescu, and his familiar manner had not lost its ability to shock them. On one hand, I was constantly perturbed by his infuriating use of the men's first names. On the other, I found myself greatly impressed that he'd already *learned* all their first names. He'd even tried using Niculescu's, but that had only caused confusion and he'd stopped.

Oblivious to the reaction, Greene retrieved a long, cylindrical object from his knapsack, turned, and offered it to Private Meier. "Have you ever used a telescope before?"

"No, sir," Meier responded, and accepted the telescope, looking it over with wonder.

"Well, Paul, you'll learn how to use it. This telescope comes with two standing orders. One is that you are to dedicate yourself to helping Alan spot things to shoot at. The other is that you'll learn to use the rifle as well, in case Alan here gets himself killed. Can I count on you?"

"Yes, sir," Meier glanced at Private Conyers, then to me, and uncomfortably around at all the other men of the company. I got the sense he was torn between pride at the orders and discomfort with the lieutenant's familiar manner.

"That is all, Private Meier." The company shuffled in surprise again, this time at his unexpected use of Meier's rank. He shocked us even more when he barked, "Attention, Company!"

As trained, each one of us snapped to attention, but we could not help but let our gaze wander around a bit. The confusion cleared a moment later at his next words.

"Lieutenant Cartter, sir!" he shouted. "Fine group of men I've got here, they're a bunch of Jim Dandies, are they not? How may we help you sir?"

The young Bull Run veteran stomped up around the assembled group and straight to Greene. He held out a letter, which Greene accepted.

"Orders, Lieutenant," Cartter explained. His gaze swept up and down the line, and he gave a slight smirk. "The North Atlantic Blockading Squadron, with M Company included, is directed to depart tomorrow. You'll find your assigned vessel and its dock in those instructions. Do not be late, Lieutenant, or it will reflect poorly on the United States Marine Corps and the commander of the Marine contingent for this expedition."

"Which is who, Lieutenant Cartter?" Greene asked. Somehow, I knew the answer before the reply came.

"Me, Lieutenant Greene," Cartter said with a grin. "For the duration of this expedition, you will answer to me."

Casey Moores

Chapter 7: Shipping Out

"**A**lex, I demand that you shoot me," Lieutenant Greene groaned. "That's an order from your lieutenant. Shoot me now, end my misery for the sake of all that is decent and—" He retched the meager contents of his stomach into a bucket.

He'd repeated that specific request a dozen times a day ever since we'd departed Hampton Roads. Sea travel was not to his liking.

"I would love to, sir, but then I would lose the guardian angel who protects me from Lieutenant Cartter," I replied. First Lieutenant William Cartter had been assigned as the leader of the small contingent of Marines attached to the expedition. Major General Ambrose Burnsides led the entire expedition of over ten thousand men, or so it was rumored, carried on a motley flotilla of gunboats, river steamers, ferry boats, tugboats, and all other sorts of ships.

"And worst of all," he said after he'd ceased heaving, "there's no damn coffee on this ship. Just brackish water and. . . ungghh. . . bust-head."

"No, sir, it's another chartered civilian ship," I replied. "They're generally short on the sorts of things soldiers and marines need to survive. That, and they keep the best stuff for themselves, despite our best attempts to requisition such."

"Bastards," he replied. He buried his face in the bucket and retched again.

I'll admit a slight amount of guilt in taking advantage of the lieutenant in his poor state, but I decided it was time to get answers.

"Lieutenant Greene, sir," I said, as I let myself into his cabin. He dry-heaved into the bucket and put a hand up for me to wait, which I did.

"Addison, please," he moaned. "What's on your mind?"

"Well, sir, the boys--"

"Men."

"Yes, sir, the men. . . " He heaved again, and I waited. "They're wondering what it is we're really doing. They know we're doing something, well, *irregular*, and uh, well. . . "

"Tell me about the *Governor*," he muttered. Panting heavily, he leaned back into his bunk, but focused his sickly gaze intently upon me. The beast appeared once again in my head. I feared what he was truly asking, but I'd also become adept at telling the "official" story of the event, so I began with that.

"Well, sir, it was never quite seaworthy, not particularly suited to sailing in storms at least, um, so. . . once the waves got particularly harsh, uh--"

"Not *on* the *Governor*, Alex, I mean. . ." He gagged for a moment, swallowed, and resumed. "Tell me what you saw *below it*."

I told him. It all sounded so strange, those words coming out of my own mouth, almost as if someone else spoke them. As I said it all aloud, I also doubted whether I'd even witnessed it. Those images burned into my mind, could I be certain they weren't some nightmare I'd had afterward? Reynolds *had* witnessed it as well, hadn't he? Or was that another trick of the mind? Throughout my description, he simply nodded and encouraged me to continue.

"Sounds like a kraken, but a very small one, at least," he said slowly. Some color returned to his face. "Might've been something else, Leviathan maybe, sounds *far* too small, but you can never quite tell. Pulled up by Kur Oto maybe, or one of his followers."

"Sir, you said Kur. . .?"

"Oto. I'll get to that," he said. He swung his legs over, sat up, and shook his head as if to shake off the nausea. "Sergeant, what you saw was part of something that's been going on much longer than anyone can remember. Essentially, would you say you saw a monster?"

"Well. . . yes, sir, I would." I had never admitted such to myself, but as he asked, it became an unavoidable conclusion.

"That's better than most would admit to," he said. He cleared his throat. "Most I've known would still be explaining it away or blocking it out altogether. Alex, I'm going to tell you that the demons of the Bible, the monsters of myths and legends," he stopped, reached toward the bucket, but then paused and took a few deep breaths. A moment later, he continued. "Almost all of them are real. Generally, very poorly described, but real."

"Pardon my asking, sir, but how do you know all this, seeing as no one else seems to?" I asked.

"How much do you know of the war down in Mexico, Alex?" Greene appeared fully recovered and became possessed with a great intensity.

"Well, I mean, I know we beat Santa Anna in his own country," I answered. "Last time Mexico will ever be a problem for us. But we were fighting for Texas, as I understand it, who, of course, have joined all the other secesh states in rebellion, ungrateful bastards."

"Do you know what the Marines did in that war?" he asked. I vaguely remembered something about it, but had to ponder a moment to find an answer.

"Well, they helped take Mexico City, right?" I asked. He nodded and I smiled.

"Chapultepec, yes," he said. His gaze wandered off to the ceiling and he laid back down, turning pale again. "They talk about that part. Reynolds was there. There's a pretty big part of it they don't talk about, though.

marines, a whole mess of them, fought at a place called Molino Del Rey."

"Never heard of it," I said.

"You wouldn't have," he replied, and closed his eyes. "There was a battle there, but there were no reports of marines being there. Newspapers, the ones I could find, only talk about how General Worth defeated a garrison there, a few days before Chapultepec. But there was another fight there.

"The Mexicans woke the Quinametzin, ancient giants, and got them all frenzied. I'm not sure how, seeing as the Quinametzin were no friends to the Mexicans, but nonetheless, the Mexicans set a trap using those giants, and damn near destroyed Worth's army, which would have left Santa Anna free to roll up the rest of our army. Except, there was a *special unit* of marines there to stop them."

"Special Unit Thirteen," I said in wonder. It all became clear in my head, like a vision. The regular army charged off across some field and attacked the Mexican Army. Meanwhile, a smaller group of marines lined up, firing rifles into massive, unnatural men, who hurled boulders and swung trees as clubs.

"Special *Unit* Thirteen," he said.

"What happened?" I asked.

"They stopped the giants," he replied, voice soft and distant. "But they died, to a man. Reynolds, and some others, found them afterwards, after they'd taken

Chapultepec, when someone sent him with a group to find out what happened. Found the marines and the giants all slaughtered. Parts and pieces of men and giant alike all strewn about. Cut, shot, ripped apart, blasted with cannon. . . some of ours even looked like they'd been chewed on. Says it looked like they'd all killed each other. My father. . . Johnny Reynolds found him on top of the biggest one of them. Says he was all limp and bruised, as if every bone in his body'd been broken. His saber was lodged firmly in the big demon's neck, with buckets of blood pooled about."

I caught my breath.

"Yes, marines, and regular army even, still talk of the storming of Chapultepec," Greene said, "and the great number of marines who bravely died there. But if they speak of Molino Del Rey, they do so in hushed tones and suspicious glances. To the greater public, the story of my father and his fellows simply does not exist."

"I'm sorry to hear that, sir," I stated. A quiet moment later, I said, "So, did Major Reynolds do this too?"

"No, he was, and still is, *just* a marine," Greene answered. "I imagine he would've been, and might've even asked to be, in the unit, but there *was* no unit between then and now."

"Why not?" I asked, finally dropping the formality. "Or, maybe I should ask, why now?"

"That is the better question, Alex," he said. Though still pale, all other signs of illness had departed. "After all, this Special Unit's been fighting evil on this continent since we beat out the British. Now, obviously, we haven't had to deal with Quinametzin or anything like them since my father and the Unit killed them all down in Mexico. And these things, well, they generally stay kinda small, or local, when there's no major fighting going on. Solitary black dog here, some large possessed mountain cat over there, but usually nothing big. Whenever there's a war or something, that's when they come out in droves. Not sure why that is, but it is. Only a war coulda woken up those Mexican giants, but those Mexicans were smart enough to know how to play them, enough to point them at us. I've heard over in old Europe, those wars they're always having wake up all manner of beasts, big old mean bridge trolls, little winged devils, and whatnot. All the demons of the Bible become real, physical manifestations when they think they can profit from death and chaos."

Insanity. He can't be serious. The Bible was a great list of metaphors, of guidelines and stories to teach us how to be better people, not real tales of real creatures. My parents told me that none of those stories they told me when I was a boy were true. Monsters aren't real. Well, except for the one I saw. . . Good lord, where have I found myself?

My stomach lurched and I grabbed his bucket. I'd grown up a fisherman's son and didn't remember a time when the sea had made me ill. Even so, I emptied more fish stew and partially digested bread than I remembered eating into that bucket.

"Hard to take in, I know," he said. "We never know how people are going to handle it until they do. Reynolds tried to find me the kinds of people who he thought would take it well, but I still don't know until they either have or haven't."

"So, are we heading south to find that creature I saw?" I asked. The idea filled me with excitement and terror all together. Excitement at the prospect of hunting the evil sea beast. Terror at the prospect of encountering it again. I vomited again into the bucket as I re-envisioned it.

"No, I mean, well. . . sort of," he said. "That's the sort of thing we may never see again. No telling if it just bubbled up because it happened across an opportunity to snack on sailors, or if it was conjured up by someone or some. . . *thing*. I've a theory there's an old evil, here since before anyone came from Europe, that's played in the affairs of men for eons. But. . . to answer your question, Major Reynolds made the case to reinstate this unit when you and he saw what you saw. Went straight to some fairly important people to make it happen. When they approved it, he requested I lead it."

"Why you?" I asked. "If this has not existed in, what, fifteen or so years, how do you know what you know?"

"Well. . ." he gave a sly smile.

Someone knocked at the door.

"Message for Lieutenant Greene, sir!" the new arrival announced.

"Come on in," Greene said, then burped.

A sandy-haired young Midshipman entered with a letter. He looked at me with pity as he stepped inside the cabin.

"Haven't gotten your sea legs yet?" he asked. Before I could reply, he smiled with compassion and continued. "It'll come in time. Don't you worry, one day soon it'll simply vanish, and you won't remember ever getting sick."

My stomach settled instantly, and I crafted a protest in my head.

"Thank you, Midshipman," Greene said, as he yanked the letter from the man's hand. The midshipman nodded smartly, gave a sloppy, cuffed-hand salute, and departed. Greene unfolded the message and read its contents.

"Well, we might soon see which of our men can handle it, and which can't," he said. His gaze swept up and down the page again. "*Maybe*. . . Could be we don't find anything at all. Looks like were chasing an old ghost story."

"And that is?" I asked.

"One of the first colonies here, a place called Roanoke, just up and disappeared over two hundred years ago," he said. "Ever hear of it?"

"Can't say I have," I replied.

"Well, there's all kinds of guesses into what might have happened," he explained. "But the truth is, no one really knows. My kind have spent those centuries trying to work it out, but, between you and me, I think they just starved, and wandered off looking for food, and then Indians got them. I don't believe anything crazy happened to them, but you never know. We could get lucky."

With no warning, he tossed the page to the side, dropped to his knees, retrieved the bucket once more, and heaved.

Chapter 8: Roanoke Island

"Tell me again what this is called?" Greene asked me, as we set up our tents.

"Bivouacking, sir." I said.

According to the ship's crew, we'd arrived in Croatoan Sound, inside the Hatteras Islands. Though we had more men than when we'd taken Port Royal, we'd also had a more ragtag fleet. The Rebel "Mosquito Fleet", as the crew called it, traded shots at us for several hours before sailing off, as if out of boredom. A minuscule shore battery fired at us from an islet as we sailed past, and the entire fleet blasted it in retaliation. After the Reb guns went silent, orders passed through the fleet, directing a landing on the island.

Greene had stormed up to the captain and explained M Company was meant to land as well, to which the captain replied that all marines were to remain aboard. After Greene showed him the message, the captain arranged for boats to take us ashore.

A small collection of Confederate soldiers formed up on the beach where we planned to land. However, they scattered like flies from a swatter when the gunboats sent a few shells their way.

After landing, we were directed to make camp, since the commander of the army forces decided it was too late in the day to mount a proper assault. Greene located the commander of the First Brigade and demanded a bivouac site in the forward and left corner of the encampment, right against the edge of the swamp.

Shortly after arrival, a collection of colored men emerged from the swamp, which we assumed to be escaped slaves. By their scared expressions, we couldn't discern whether they'd come out to get help, or if they'd been scared out of their hiding place by the Rebels. We'd directed them to a makeshift camp further south, per the orders of General Foster, the commander of the First Brigade.

It was the first time I'd seen their kind. I'd seen the occasional freed colored man in Philadelphia, and the few I'd met seemed sharp enough. These, however, were a different breed altogether- gaunt, starved, quiet, and with tattered clothes. They were nervous and skittish, as if they expected any of us to take a swing at them, or shoot them, at any moment. They herded around the few women and children in the group in a protective manner.

I wondered how long they'd lived in that swamp. Had it been days, weeks, months? Had any lived there for more than a year? If so, how? With great pity, I tried to imagine what it must have been like to live in the brambles, mud, and filth. The stench alone could have, eventually, driven me mad.

"Sure stinks to high heaven out here, doesn't it, Alex?" Greene asked. As he did, his gaze swept toward the swamp and he paused, as if he pondered some unknown question.

"Yes, sir," I answered. As I looked around, I found the other men of M Company had tied strips of cloth around their faces to help combat the awful smell. "Not the normal stench of docks or the sea. It smells more like a whole mess of skunks up and died right over there."

He frowned and continued to help pound stakes into the soft earth. Naturally, I attempted to explain that officers generally did not involve themselves with setting up camp, but I was as successful as all my other attempts to encourage him to be a proper officer.

"Why can't they just call it camping?" he mumbled. "Anyway, let's hurry up, then help with the others. I have a feeling we're here on a fool's errand, and I can't wait to get a proper night's sleep on solid ground—"

"Lieutenant Greene!" Lieutenant Cartter shouted. Greene sighed, grumbled, and then straightened up with a big smile.

"Lieutenant Cartter, sir!" he shouted back. "How may I be of service, sir?"

Cartter strolled up and gazed around disdainfully.

"A word in private, Lieutenant?" Cartter said. Greene nodded and set his sledgehammer down. The two walked off. I heard nothing of what Lieutenant Cartter said, but his demeanor suggested he gave Greene a significant dressing down. Greene repeatedly shouted "Yes, sir!"

and remained in a rough approximation of the position of attention.

When he returned, he smiled at me and retrieved the hammer. Cartter shook his head in disgust and wandered off through the camp.

"Sir, might I inquire as to the nature of that discussion?" I asked. He maintained the smile and resumed his work on the stakes.

"You may," he replied, and then became silent. I was just about to relent and ask more specifically when he spoke.

"The illustrious Marine commander of the North Atlantic Blockading Squadron has informed me that it is not an officer's place to take part in the construction of the Bee-voo-wack."

He chuckled and took a swing, driving a stake deeper into the earth.

"Furthermore, I am directed not to take my detachment on any unauthorized excursions," he stated, with a sarcastic tone. "Which contradicts my *other* standing orders from an authority higher than he." Greene had said plenty of similarly vague proclamations, but I knew I'd receive no clarification. "But it's perfectly fine by me. Really just proves he has no idea what this company's meant to do. Anyway, I'm serious. The sooner I can get to sleep, the better. That much time spent in the belly of an angry sea beast- uh, mmm, sorry Alex, I didn't mean. . . I mean, I was only being. . ."

"It's fine, Lieutenant, and I get your meaning," I said. I glanced to the side and, once again, tried to push my memories of the creature away. In so doing, I found Private Cash walking up with a concerned look on his face. Corporal Van Benthuysen strode faster up behind him and grabbed him by the arm. The two argued over something, and I walked up to investigate.

"—doesn't need to hear you been daydreaming, Private! Colored's put ideas in your head is all." Van Benthuysen said in hushed tones as I approached.

"What are you two going on about, Corporal?" I asked.

Van Benthuysen straightened up in attention, and Cash followed suit.

"Nothing worth bothering you over, Sergeant," Van Benthuysen said, and glared down at Cash. "*Private* Cash needs to return to his sentry duty, and I'll see to the bivouac, Sergeant."

"Private Cash, do you think it's worth bothering me over?" I asked. Cash glanced at the corporal, and then back to me with a nervous look.

"No, he does not, Sergeant, he—"

"I asked the Private, Corporal," I said, and gave Van Benthuysen a look that told him to shut up. "Go ahead, Private."

Cash shuffled his feet, and his gaze floated about nervously.

"Private Cash. Tell me what you saw."

"Well, Sergeant," his voice was as meek as he looked. "I was setting up our tent, just like we were ordered, and I started thinking about how close we were to this swamp, I mean we really are up on the edge of this swamp."

"Get to it, Private, so we can get back to work!" Van Benthuysen demanded.

"That is all, Corporal!" I replied. "Go on, Private, and take your time. Tell me what you need to tell me."

"Yes, Sam, go on, and leave nothing out." Lieutenant Greene appeared behind me. I'd had no indication of his approach. Corporal Van Benthuysen, who should have seen him coming, jumped as well. All three of us snapped up straight and saluted. He waved back dismissively.

"Yes, sir!" Cash nodded and gulped. "You see, sir, I was, uh, well, I was there by the swamp, see, and, well, I started thinking about how those coloreds had been living there. You might not have heard it, but the one's that came through said they'd seen some things. Didn't make any sense, like a white woman or something."

Van Benthuysen scoffed. Greene put up a hand in warning, and then nodded encouragingly to Cash.

"Well, sir," he continued, "got me to thinking that all manner of creatures probably lived out there, sir, you know, I've heard tell of gators and the like, and, well, I imagined wolves, but, I'm guessing there ain't any wolves in a swamp this far south, but, sir, you never know, you know."

"Okay, Sam, okay, now stay calm," Greene said softly. "Go on."

"Yes, sir." Cash swallowed again. "Well, as I said, sir, I looked out there, and," his eyes narrowed down to thin slits and he leaned forward a touch, "well, sir, I could swear I saw, I mean, it sounds kinda foolish now, sir. . ."

Greene held his gaze and remained quiet. Cash looked to Van Benthuysen again, then to me, and, eventually, realizing he was not getting out of it, resumed.

"I swear I saw a woman out there," Cash said. "Just like those coloreds said there were."

"There you have it, sir, just his imagination," Van Benthuysen said and chuckled, but still seemed agitated. Van Benthuysen grabbed Cash's elbow and turned as if to leave.

"Just a few weeks out and he's already dreaming about the girls back at Hampton Roads. Sorry to bother you, sir."

"Go on, Private," Greene repeated. Van Benthuysen froze. Cash spun back to face the lieutenant. "What did she look like?"

Cash's face scrunched up again, as if he focused on the picture in his mind.

"She was all dressed in white, sir," he said. "Which, seeing a woman in a swamp is one thing, but that really stood out, sir. Even if some woman was somehow lost in a swamp, why would she have gone into it all dressed in white? In a long, flowing white dress. It just didn't make any sense."

"I see," Greene said. "Then what?"

"She saw me, sir," Cash explained. "And I motioned to her, you know, figuring I could help her, but she just stood there and stared at me, standing straight as one of these poles," he glanced over to our tent, which was not quite properly upright. "Well, straight as one of *our* poles, sir. I mean no disrespect."

"Continue," Greene said. "Did you go to her, did she come to you? Did you see anything else out there? Anyone else? Or maybe some animals around her?"

"No, sir," Cash said. "The corporal here yelled at me because I'd stopped, and I looked at him, and then I looked back, and she was just gone."

"You see, sir," Van Benthuysen said. "This was just a marine daydreaming when he should've been working. Made up some story when his Corporal, that's me sir, barked at him. I'm sorry we bothered you, sir."

"Have the men hurry up and finish the *bee-voo-wack*, Sergeant," Greene said. "Go make sure our dog robber gets the men a good meal, and quick. Then, quick as you can, get them under arms and form them up. By *squad*, as we discussed. Bayonets, too, Sergeant. Wait here for me."

The other three of us eyed each other in confusion.
"Yes, sir," I said.

Greene nodded and stalked off before we could salute.

Shadows grew long and rain clouds formed overhead before we received any other direction. It came in the form of a baby-face young midshipman, who directed a team of men to drag a twelve-pound boat howitzer our way. A large wooden box, presumably rounds for the big gun, was lashed to the axle.

"Come on Daniels! Come on Meeker!" the boy shouted with great excitement. "You keep moving that along, I'll go scout the best position for it!"

The spirited teenager marched on up to our camp, stopped, and scanned around. He locked his gaze on me.

"Is this the Marine detachment?" he asked, with tremendous intensity.

"Yes, sir, it is," I replied. "Sergeant Phillips at your service, sir."

"Bully!" he said. His voice sounded like a boy, as I'd expected by the look of him. I anticipated his voice cracking at every other word, but it did not. "I'm Midshipman Benjamin Porter, United States Navy and commander of a six-gun howitzer battery in support of this assault. I have the requested gun coming up just now. Sergeant, have you seen your Lieutenant?"

Requested gun?

"No, sir, not for quite a while."

"Well, he expressed concern that the Johnny Rebs might attempt to tramp their way through the swamp and attempt a raid on this flank. These boys weren't doing anything, so I agreed to support him. Now, any ideas on where this might find the best use?"

Truth be told, I hadn't really considered the possibility. We'd completed the bivouac and the men were in the process of attending to the inner man. Joel Mossberg, our cook, had made a stew of crumbled up hardtack and salt pork. Just about the entire Company had kept an eye on the swamp in hopes of a glimpse of the mystery woman, but we'd seen neither hide nor hair of our lieutenant in about an hour.

The midshipman and his two subordinates, Acting Master Charlie Daniels and Flag Officer's Clerk Eddy Meeker, walked around our encampment. I preferred a spot on the corner of the camp, where I thought Rebs were most likely to come out. The other three found another spot further west, toward the beach, where the gun could sit on a very slight rise and have a little more open area in front of it. I spent the discussion lost in wonder at what our lieutenant was getting us into.

Satisfied, the midshipman directed his men to move the howitzer to the agreed upon location. Then, he cleared off all but Daniels and Meeker, and he left to command the rest of his detachment, somewhere else in the camp.

"That's your *commander*?" I asked the Acting Master, when the midshipman was gone.

"That he is," Daniels replied with a grin. His voice was deep and gruff. "Looks like a baby fresh fish, don't he? But I tell you that Mr. Porter's got a fire in his belly. Top rail as I've ever seen for one so young. Now. . . if you're good lieutenant thinks there's a fight coming, then where is he? I'd ask if he absquatulated, but I can't imagine where he'd go."

"No, he didn't absquatulate," I replied. "If he isn't here, he's doing something, but heaven knows what. He's an odd duck, and, well, he's a good man."

"Hmmm," Daniels grumbled. "I'll note you did not say 'good officer'. This whole thing sounds like a humbug to me. But, I've been wrong before. We'll be here and ready to blast whatever comes out. We'll load this up with a pleasant gift in case any grey backs come creeping out, until Mr. Porter or your lieutenant tell me to do otherwise. I'm thinking your pumpkin rinds wants you boys formed up as well?"

"The *men,* yes." I restrained a smile as I recognized I'd come around to Greene's way of thinking. Instinctively, I almost gave a shout to form the men up, but thought better of it and walked around to form them up, by squads, as quietly as I could. There was no point letting any Reb skulkers know we were readying ourselves for an attack, and no point alarming the whole camp if nothing happened. I directed each squad to load both their rifles and their shotguns, formed them up in rough lines a bit back from the swamp, and we waited for God knew what.

As we did, a light rain began.

Chapter 9: Into the Darkness

As light dwindled and the rain picked up, I found the naval howitzer pair had set up a couple torches. I roused myself, from a near stupor of boredom, to do the same.

A crack echoed from the swamp. A muffled shout followed it. I, and everyone else, snapped our attention to the murky wood. To a man, we searched about. My squad leaders, taking the initiative Greene had given them, instructed the men to ready their rifles.

For an uncomfortably long moment, we heard nothing but the dull sound of raindrops.

Then, another crack sounded, this one much closer.

"Ready the men!" Greene shouted. His voice was barely audible, but unmistakable.

"Unit Thirteen, ready!" I shouted. Everyone snapped to attention and readied their arms. Squad leaders set to dressing the lines.

The rate of cracks and snaps increased, all localized to one area. "Where's the gun?"

"Here, sir!" I shouted. "We're over here!"

"Keep shouting, I'm coming to you!" Greene replied. "Everyone ready?"

"Yes, sir!" I answered. "Right here, sir, keep coming this way!

Casey Moores

A tiny rumble developed in the swamp further back from the sound of Greene's approach. As I identified the figure of Greene stomping his way toward us, the rumble increased into a raging cacophony of destruction. It sounded as if a wide arc of Rebs were trampling through the swamp behind him.

I ran out to help drag him through the last few feet of bramble. His Colt Dragoon Revolver was tight in his right hand, and he fired blindly back into the swamp as I approached. At that moment, I wondered why none of the Rebs had tried shooting at him as they pursued.

"Ready!" Van Benthuysen shouted to his squad, closely followed by similar orders in other squads.

"For God sakes, shut the hell up!" Greene ordered. Then, he scrambled back to his feet, ran to the howitzer, and flapped his arms wildly. "Over here, you smelly apes! Over here!"

He grabbed a torch from Daniels and continued. The sound of cracking wood overcame the area. Through it, however, I heard a chorus of fiendish growls. Somewhere behind me, I heard someone call out "what the Hell's going on over there?"

"Be ready, sailor!" Greene said to Daniels, who nodded. "What you got in there?"

"Canister," Daniels replied, gaze intent upon the woods. "I'll let you say the word, sir."

Greene resumed shouting, which obtained the desired effect. All the unearthly noise seemed to be coming straight towards him.

Branches swayed and dark figures emerged through the bramble, barely visible in the last of the fading light. On his own hook, Cash had lit a torch. Instead of admonishing him, Wilkes ordered another private to do the same. Soon, more torches burst in flame in the other squads, as the leaders directed individuals to light them.

Large, hairy men, or apes, or *something* to that effect, emerged from the bramble. Confounded gasps escaped from the men of Unit Thirteen.

"Fire!" Greene shouted.

BOOM! The howitzer barked and fired the canister of .62 caliber balls into the wall of hair-covered beasts. All forty-two rifles thundered into them as well. The entire line of tall apes lurched backward, staggered by the withering gunfire. A second wave of beasts pushed past them, roared, and charged forward.

"Shotguns! Fire!" Greene shouted. I'd almost forgotten the gun, which we all carried on leather slings. Most of the rifles clattered to the ground as the men switched guns. Blasts erupted from our lines in a much more scattered fashion as the men presented them and fired at various rates. Most of the beasts screeched and turned back into the swamp.

With more joy than I'm proud to admit, I fired, reloaded, and fired my shotgun at a rate I'd never before experienced. It made me feel like some sort of avenging angel, laying waste to the enemies of God. I never even felt the need to draw the NCO sword at my side.

One of the beasts reached the line and bowled into Tomasini. The Italian blocked a swipe from a massive, clawed hand with his shotgun, but fell backward from the strength of the blow. Nick calmly stepped up next to the beast, placed the shotgun to its head, and fired. Its head exploded, and it dropped.

Another reached Van Benthuysen's squad, but the Scandinavian had fired his shotgun and already retrieved his rifle. He cracked one of the beast's arms back with the butt of his rifle, swung it around like an old hat, and drove the bayonet deep into the creature's midsection. The beast roared, grabbed the rifle with one hand, and punched Van Benthuysen hard in the side of the head with the other. The corporal staggered a bit, let go of the rifle, and collapsed to the side. Two more shotgun blasts dispatched the beast.

BOOM! The howitzer erupted one more time, firing another canister round at the central mass of beasts.

The big apes skedaddled as quickly as they'd charged. Only four had actually died on the soft ground, clear of the swamp. A few more lay dead inside the bramble, and most of the others limped away. I never got a good accounting of how many had come at us, but it was several dozen if it was one.

The strangest part was that some of the beasts shriveled into bones immediately. A couple dried up and their hair fell out, while one remained fully intact, just as it died.

"Anyone mustered out?" Greene asked. "Emile, you good? Leo?"

Van Benthuysen staggered to his feet with some help and gave an encouraging nod.

Dan Sonnier, our nurse, sprang about checking on all the injuries. I was surprised by how few we'd sustained, and none were serious.

"Tomasini and I are both fine, sir!" Van Benthuysen announced. "Rung my bell, a little, is all. Private Tomasini, you don't get to get huffy about Nick anymore, do you understand?"

"Not by a jug full, Corporal," Tomasini replied. He clapped a hand on Nick's shoulder. "Me and this here *Roman* are hunky dory."

"M Company!" Greene shouted, in a much more commanding voice than I'd ever heard him muster. "A lot of you have wondered as to the nature of this company. A lot of what I've done hasn't made any sense. If I'd explained before this very moment, you'd all have thought me mad, and maybe some of you still do. But you've just seen the enemy we're meant to fight! We're not like the rest of the Union Army, we're not fighting some misguided Americans with whom we're having a disagreement. M Company, or *Special Unit Thirteen,* was reformed to fight the evil that bubbles up when the world goes mad. Well, this country has gone mad, it's caught itself on fire, and now evil is coming out. We're going back into that swamp to hunt it down. If any of you can't handle that, you can go report to Lieutenant Cartter and nothing else will be said. Come with me into the swamp, and you will be now and forever more Marines of Special Unit Thirteen. So, anyone care to leave?"

Not a soul budged or, as far as I could tell, even drew a breath. After a long moment, I heard someone mutter, "I'd rather go in there than go to Cartter. These things die easy enough."

Scattered laughter rumbled through the company.

"Bully. Now. . . reload!" Greene shouted. Confusion reigned up and down the line as the men regarded their rifles, with bayonets attached, and their shotguns, unsure which to reload first. Even more apparent was their confusion at exactly *what* had just happened.

"Shotguns, men, just the shotguns, rifles will just be a damned nuisance in that swamp," Greene said. I gulped.

In the swamp? In the dark?

I noticed the men stood about with the same trepidation I had.

"You heard the Lieutenant!" I shouted. "Shotguns only, let's go!"

"And the rifles, sir?" Corporal Wilkes asked.

"Leave them, I say!" Greene said, frustrated. He stepped impatiently toward the bramble. "And keep those damned stocks on, I hope you all see why we need them!"

"Yes, sir, but we need to do *something* with the rifles," I said. Wilkes nodded his thanks to me, barely visible in the flickering torchlight. "The rest of the army will be running in shortly to find out what happened. We should stash the rifles under the bedrolls so that when our gun crew tells the late-comers we're chasing Rebs back into the woods, it's a bit more believable."

"Fine!" he barked. "Rifles under bedrolls! Hurry! They're making their escape. Follow me by squad as quick as you can, I'm going after them, by God! Sergeant, make sure the men all got their knives and a loaded shotgun."

"Yes, sir," I answered.

While I rushed to my tent, I heard him pass instructions to the gun crew.

"You two, what are your names?" he asked.

"Daniels, sir, and he's Meeker," the Acting Master replied.

"Daniels, Meeker," he repeated. "You reload and fire on anything that's not a man."

"And if it *is* a man, sir?" Daniels asked. Greene walked away as he answered.

"If they look like us, don't shoot. If they look like Rebs, shoot," he directed. Greene turned back and yelled at the company. "One more thing, men, anyone sees a woman all dressed in white, don't listen to a thing she says. Shoot her, if you got the sand."

A few of us nervously glanced around at each other in consternation.

Greene ran off toward the swamp and led in a squad who'd already formed. In the time it took me to stash my rifle and run back out, Greene and the squad had disappeared into the bramble. One more squad edged in after them. As I moved toward them, an Army lieutenant came running up, still working on the buttons of his coat. A few other soldiers tramped up behind him.

"What on God's earth happened over here?" he asked.

"Just a brief skirmish, sir," I said, as I saluted. "Nothing to make a fuss about, sir, we Marines ran them off and our lieutenant's leading a scouting party to make sure they don't come back."

"Well, do you need any support, Sergeant?" he asked. Before I answered, he continued, "And what are those things? They smell god awful."

He pointed at one of the few dead, putrid apes that hadn't quickly rotted away.

"Just some kind of animal, got scared out of the swamp by all the shooting," I said.

"That don't look like. . ." He gawked for a moment "But anyway, why am I asking you? Where's this lieutenant?"

"Like I said, sir, leading a party just a short ways out," I replied. "You're free to wait here for him to return, sir, but I'm on his orders to follow, and that's what I've got to do."

I saluted the lieutenant and ran to where the last two squads had collected.

Several squads already nervously sloshed their way into the swamp. Van Benthuysen looked at me as if awaiting confirmation that *this was really what we were about to do.*

"You sure you and Leo are all right?" I asked. Somewhere deep in the wilderness, a shotgun blast echoed.

"I said we're fine, Sergeant," he replied. "What in God's name are these things?"

"No idea, but it's what we're going after," I answered. "If you say you're fine, you're fine. Follow that torch. Head in Indian-style, one at a time, along the trail they used as best you can. Each man keep close to the man in front of you and the man behind you. Don't lose those torches."

Pride and instinct told me to lead the men in, but Greene had already done so. I decided my most prudent position was at the rear, as duty dictated someone ensure the entire company made it into the swamp and collected anyone who got lost. It felt cowardly, but I reminded myself it was necessary.

I touched my cross, said a prayer, and followed the last man into the swamp.

Moments earlier, my heart had pounded with the excitement of the fight, and the jarring of the cannon and gunfire. I'd felt terror at the sight of the wicked creatures, and then a rush of rapture as we beat them back.

As we tramped through the bramble and muck of the swamp, everything slowed down. My feet had become cold from being soaked and a chilled wind blew through the bramble. The stench, which I now identified with the beasts themselves, permeated the air.

The great chase devolved into a slow slog, through a swamp, at night, in the rain.

The rain, at least, was broken up by the low canopy of the swamp. We were all soon soaked to the bone, but most of us were able to keep our shotguns dry enough, or so we hoped. The torches, however, slowly died out as we went.

The trepidation remained as we wandered into the creatures' territory, stumbling through the dark and the thick, fetid growth. A waxing half-moon overhead illuminated things enough to see a couple men forward, but shadows dominated. I'd never felt so exposed or alone, even when I'd been on the open field at Bull Run, with everyone running off around me. In that swamp, those beasts could have come out of nowhere at any moment. We lumbered, loud and visible, into the abyss.

Periodically, the long, single file line would halt. Murmurs would work their way down the line about being lost, being stuck, having lost sight of the Lieutenant, or about having lost any sign of the enemy. Though discussion was limited in general, the men obviously avoided all mention of the nature of that enemy.

More than a few shotguns went off during the trek, fired at shadows by nervous marines. They were admonished by their corporals, but nothing could reduce the terror we all felt. It only increased as we heard the occasional growl or roar. Twice as we marched along, we encountered more dead apes, killed by preceding marines. Once, we found a dead alligator as well, stabbed half a dozen times in the head. The ape-beasts weren't the only danger in the swamp. Together, these proved that not all the discharges were unwarranted.

We suffered two injured marines on the trek. The first immobilized marine was Private William Horton, another Philadelphia man. I sympathized, as he'd jabbed his calf hard into the end of a stick. It was clear he'd be a burden if we were to drag him along as he requested. He was in Wilkes' squad, and the corporal had left him in place with another private. We passed another injured one, and I ordered him to make his way as best they could toward the makeshift Company Q. I assumed Greene lacked the knowledge that our numbers dwindled.

The other pervasive issue was the horrendous stench. Despite the fact I'd been raised to have an iron stomach, I constantly fought the urge to retch. Several times during the slog, a few members up the line lost the fight, which began a chain reaction of emptied stomachs down the line. Luckily, such instances affected the swamp little and changed the overall aroma not at all.

The passage of time and the distance we'd traversed became anyone's guess. At least a couple of hours must have passed. Our fear of the unknown became overpowered by exhaustion, cold, and the cumulative pain of every branch, every stumble, and every insect that impeded our progress. Gripes and complaints were stifled, but we all commiserated. At some point, my focus boiled down to putting one foot in front of the other, keeping up with Private Everett, the soldier in front of me.

My thoughts drifted back to Cassie Paul and that glorious kiss I'd received. Home came back to mind, and all the memories that came with it. As I jerked my shoes in and out of the muck, I wished I was there instead. In my mind, I envisioned a house, much the same as my parents, with Cassie baking a pie, and children running about playing. I sat by the fire, with a mug of beer in my hand, watching the children, and smelling a roast in the kitchen.

All at once, the bushes around us erupted with the roar of apes and the cracking of branches. Shotguns barked in response. The trap, which we all feared we would walk into, had sprung.

Casey Moores

Chapter 10: Escaping Darkness

Shouts, shrieks, growls, and blasts of gunfire sounded down the line ahead. I heard a splash in the muck behind me but had no time to determine its origin.

Hairy arms grabbed me from behind, knocking my shotgun from my grip. Everett turned and his eyes bulged at the sight of my assailant. He raised his shotgun, but gave an anguished look which expressed a fear of shooting me. I appreciated the sentiment.

I grabbed the knife in my belt and slid it out while something, which my nose told me was another ape beast, bit into my neck from behind. Thankfully, my leather stock protected me. I drove the knife as hard and deep as I could up into the elbow of the creature. As soon as it recoiled, I twisted and stabbed the knife even harder into the other arm.

With a roar, the beast reared its arm back and knocked me forward with a tremendous backhanded blow. My vision exploded with stars for a few moments. Everett blasted something behind me, but it was not my attacker. I reached about for my shotgun. Through my blurry, hazy sight I found the beast barreling toward me once more.

I slashed around defensively at the beast's arms. My knife and its arms danced about for a bit- it would swing,

I would slash, it would rear back, roar, and the sequence would repeat. When I sensed an opening, I shifted my weight and jabbed into the beast several good times.

It threw a wild swing at me. I ducked and slashed the arm as it went over. In doing so, I stumbled in the foliage and bumped my hip against my shotgun, which still hung from its cordage and was caught up in the branches. I dropped the knife in favor of the gun, desperately pointed it toward my attacker's face, and fired.

The gun bucked hard, and the beast collapsed sideways, dead.

Curiously, before my eyes, its hair seemed to fly apart, while its skin collapsed onto its bones and turned to powder. In the blink of an eye, its bones clattered down into the branches.

I turned about to find Everett's head cracked open, with another beast dying atop him. No one else was in sight, but I heard more firing and saw torches further ahead.

The beast atop Everett reached out weakly to grab my leg. It turned its head up slightly.

"Kurrrr. . . Oooe. . . Toooe. . ." the poor thing murmured. I pushed my knife hard into its ear with a squish and a crunch. It twitched and ceased moving. Then, it dissolved as the other had. I wriggled my leg out of its grasp and fumbled to reload my shotgun.

In the distance, I heard Greene shout, "Unit Thirteen, charge! Follow me! Charge!"

The call to charge forward echoed down the line as the corporals repeated it. The final shout lay far enough ahead of me, and I feared I would never catch up. My muscles ached, my head still pounded from the beast's backhand. My blistered feet protested every step. Nonetheless, I abandoned Private Everett's body and stormed through the swampy muck toward the sound of battle.

Truth be told, it was as much out of fear of losing the company and being alone than from an innate desire to do my duty.

One mud-sucking foot after another, I slogged into the moonlit swamp. I'd lost sight of any torches and wondered if anyone still carried them. However, the path of broken foliage and muddy tracks seemed clear enough, even in the poor light. All shouts had subsided, leaving an eerie silence. Concern mounted inside me that I might have lost the company, but I was encouraged by the occasional crack of a shotgun.

The remains of both the ambushed and the ambushers lay scattered about the path. One unidentifiable marine lay crushed under a log. At one point, I came across the crumpled corpse of Corporal Horne. His skull had been cracked and he was almost unrecognizable.

I counted a score or so of dead man-apes in various states of dissolution. Most appeared killed by shotgun fire, but several had knife wounds in their guts or necks sliced open. A marine seemed near death, but was still breathing in ragged gasps. I promised him we'd come back, hoping to comfort him. I knew full well he wouldn't make it and said a quiet prayer for him.

A good number of man-apes groaned and struggled. I dispatched them in the same manner as the first.

After another hundred yards or so, I heard the gunfire pick up again, not far ahead of me. A chorus of shrieks, roars, and howls followed. When I raised my head, I saw the flicker of torches and flashes of gunfire.

"Around me, Unit Thirteen! Circle up!" Greene shouted above the sudden cacophony. I realized I had not taught him the word "rally".

With renewed vigor, I surged forward and forced myself through the bramble, vines, and sludge. I found I could move quicker by stepping up onto the branches on each side, lurched in a precarious teeter-totter. It carried the risk of slipping face first into the muck, and made a tremendous ruckus, but that was no longer of any concern.

The flashes, blasts, screams, and howls swirled about in front of me like a great storm, something akin to that which had sunk the *Governor*. Another similarity to the event aboard the *Governor* was the presence of monstrous evil, but this evil was one which I could kill.

As I drew close to the battle, I stepped on a dead marine. I slipped and fell right on top of his shattered remains as I swerved to avoid him. The marine's head had been twisted about further than a neck was meant to twist, his dead eyes gaping open, his mouth fixed in a rictus of agony. I said another prayer and crawled past.

After I regained my footing, I found the remnants of Unit Thirteen Marines clustered together, facing outward. Apes charged in and out all around, some repelled by shotgun blasts while others crashed into the line, only to be stabbed and hacked to death by three or four marines working in unison. Our fine Lieutenant Greene was nowhere in sight.

A beast barreled through the foliage sideways into me and acted just as surprised as I was. It slashed at me with its overgrown, knife-like fingernails, but I ducked the attack.

I leveled my shotgun and frantically jerked the trigger.

It clicked uselessly, stopping but halfway down a bent firing pin. In the darkness, I hadn't properly aligned the cartridge.

The reeking beast pounded me in the gut, knocking all the wind from my lungs. I dropped the shotgun and fumbled for my knife. The beast grabbed me by my jacket, pulled me close, and wrapped a fur-covered arm around my head. I pictured the marine I'd just seen, whose head had nearly been twisted off, and imagined a similar fate was meant for me.

I jabbed the knife into the monster's side, the only target I could reach. The beast did not even twitch as it squeezed me tighter in its stinking, deadly embrace.

Fighting the inexorable pressure with futility, I closed my eyes as my neck slowly approached its snapping point.

A deafening blast shattered my eardrums from a foot away. The beast's death-grip slackened, and it fell, dragging me down with it.

"'Bout time you showed up, Sergeant, I could really use you just now," Greene said. He holstered his smoking Colt Dragoon revolver, with which he had just put a bullet through my assailant's head and pulled me free of the hairy beast. "Men seem confused when I shout at them to do this or that. If you could give them proper Marine orders to go on doing what they're doing, I think it would help."

"They seem to be doing fine, sir," I said. "But you should get in there as well, you're just as likely to get shot by them out here."

Greene had already disappeared back into the bramble. Cursing, I worked the bent-pin cartridge out of my shotgun and put another cartridge in, using much more care to align the pin correctly.

I struggled to my feet, for the millionth time that evening, and moved toward the cluster of marines with my free hand up. I checked left and right to make sure no man-apes snuck up on me.

Off to my right, I found a glowing white figure a couple dozen yards away. Curious, I paused and focused on it.

The figure was a pale white woman, dressed all in white, who glowed bright in the light of the half moon. The woman Private Cash had claimed to have seen.

"Madame!" I shouted. "You have to get away, Miss! There's a battle, it's dangerous!"

I later realized I'd forgotten the lieutenant's warning.

Honor dictated that I move to protect this strange, lost woman from the beasts who raged all about. I crashed through bushes and fought to get to her. A roaring man-ape materialized out of the bramble before me. I blasted it in the face, fumbled to reload, and continued toward her. Another cracked through bush to my left and I fired. The ape dropped, but still struggled, so I calmly reloaded and shot it again. It stayed down.

"Welcome, soldier." The voice was sweet and seductive. Milky white, satiny-soft, white hands cupped my raw, filthy chin. "Have you come to save me?"

Though there were no torches near us, she was illuminated by some mystic light. Light golden hair rolled into curls around her flawless, sweet face. Her lips formed into a tiny, blood red rose, which beckoned me in for a kiss.

Gorgeous, almond-shaped, icy-blue eyes peered into mine and reached into my soul. My heart warmed. Desire grew inside me in a way it had never done before. My jaw dropped open of its own accord and I nodded my head, awestruck.

"My great paladin," she said, almost as if she sang it.

Her white dress appeared so tight and smooth I wondered if it might actually have been white wash or paint. It clung to her in such a way which revealed every curve and detail of her figure. The neckline was so scandalously low that I could see the line down the middle of her gorgeous bosom. She heaved her chest rhythmically, and the tight dress strained, as if about to burst open. She twisted her legs and her hips shifted, which forced me to notice the line between her thighs leading up to a perfect "v".

I imagined marrying this woman, working for, feeding, and protecting this woman. The two of us lay on a rug in front of a fireplace and endeavored to create a family together. As my wife, she would be vigorous, insatiable, tender, caring. . . wonderful.

Somewhere, far off in the back of my mind, I got the sense that I had forgotten something very important.

"These men want to harm me," she whispered, and leaned close enough that I could smell strawberries, roses, and honey. The proximity drove me mad with lust. I yearned to grab her and be with her right there, in that moment. The only thing which held me back was a sudden anger toward those who would hurt her.

She cupped my chin lightly in her hands and gazed into my soul.

"They attack my guardians, and seek to kill me," she said. "Will you join my guardians and destroy my enemies?"

Desire morphed into rage, yet I found myself immobilized, caught in a cloudy haze of confusion. I knew the men she spoke of, didn't I? I arrived *with* her enemies, did that make me one? Had I come to attack her, or had fate simply brought me here so I could find her and be with her? If I had come to kill her guardians, would I need to make amends?

My hand went numb, and I lacked the strength to grip the shotgun. It fell from my grasp into the muck. My love for her competed with a whisper in the back of my mind. The whisper told me they were my men, and that I must keep faith in them.

"Kiss me."

She rolled the point of her tongue around her lips, inviting me in. Opposing sides of my mind screamed at each other. Part of me burned with desire, while the other part rejected everything about her. I did not budge and hated myself for my inaction.

"*Vrăjitoare!*" a familiar voice shouted, and the branches crashed and snapped to my right.

The angel in front of me screamed as a shotgun exploded into her midsection. Her face turned gray, her eyes turned sullen and black, and her teeth grew into sharp, black spikes. Similarly, black claws sprung from her fingertips, and she swept at the burly man. He spun out of the way and slashed in a figure eight with his knife.

Dumbfounded, I watched my beloved woman fight with a man I recognized from somewhere. Chowderhead Nick, I realized. The knife and the claws danced around each other with vicious, expert strokes.

Another man emerged from behind her and jabbed his knife into her side. She released an earsplitting shriek and flung an arm into the new arrival. Her powerful blow to the face sent him crashing back into the bramble. The first man, who I now recognized as Lieutenant Greene, stabbed her hard in the back.

The dark, ghastly caricature of a woman shouldered Nick away. Her long, skeletal arm reached over her shoulder, tore the knife from her ribs, and tossed it aside.

With a final shriek, she crouched low, sprang up into the air, and disappeared into the sky. The last I heard of her was a soft flutter of wings.

"Alex!"

Numb and dazed, I stared at the man who shouted in my face.

"Where did she go?" I asked. *She? Was it a she? Well. . . it* was, *but then it wasn't. Or, at least, it wasn't the same. . . Either way, where did that beautiful woman go?*

My gaze wandered up to the sky. *Something* had gone that way, but it wasn't *her*.

She would never leave me, she loved me. And she knew that I loved her.

Try as I did, I could not conjure the image of her face into my mind. It floated just outside the edges of my memory, like a butterfly I could not catch. As I dug around in my head for her, I found an unintended image. A cute, round face with hazel eyes and brown hair tied back in a bun.

Cassandra Paul, the girl who waited for me at home.

I grew sick inside with guilt.

Then, my vision exploded with stars for the second time that evening. Someone grabbed me by the shoulders.

"Sergeant Alexander Phillips, answer me, by God!" My lieutenant shook me violently as a follow up to the backhand he'd struck across my face. His pistol was holstered, his shotgun hung to his side, and he held his Mameluke sword, which was dripping with blood.

"Addison?" I groaned.

He chuckled grimly.

"She really addled your brains, didn't she?" he said. "That's the first time you ever called me that. Are you coming back to us or not?"

At that moment, I realized I was soaked and shivering. Somewhere in the distance, I heard someone shout repeatedly for Doyle. Tomasini crouched next to Nick and tended to four bloody scratches across the man's belly.

"Wh-who, or w-what w-was she, Lieutenant?" I whispered.

He peered intently into my eyes and frowned.

"Well, that's a little better," he said. He grabbed me by both elbows and pulled me along. "Come on, let's walk a little, get your blood flowing again. Tom!"

"Yes, sir?" Corporal Thomas Archibald, our quiet but intelligent marine from Maine, answered.

"How's that count coming?" Greene asked. I tried my legs, and a thousand points of pain surged up both. My body felt as numb as my mind, as if I'd been ripped, unwilling, from a deep slumber. I stumbled on the first step, but Greene held me up.

"Five more dead, sir," Archibald called out. "Sixteen wounded, all but four can walk, sir. Four unaccounted for- Private's Doyle, Garland, Johnson, and Parker. Dan's seeing to the wounded as best as he can."

"Thank you, Corporal," Greene shouted. "Now, Alex, where's that fine shotgun you were issued? Emile!"

"Yes, sir?" the Scandinavian shouted from elsewhere in the thicket. I felt around in the bushes for the shotgun I'd mislaid once again.

"Gather the wounded, carry or drag what dead you can, and take them and six healthy men back to the camp as pickets," Greene ordered. "Keep an eye out, Emile, there could still be plenty of them out there. Make sure everyone's reloaded."

"Yes, sir, Lieutenant!" Van Benthuysen replied.

"We win?" I asked.

"Yeah, Alex, we did," Greene answered. "Once that woman flew off, they, heh, well, I can't describe it any other than saying they sort of melted back into the swamp, and I am being literal. Not the strangest thing I've ever seen, but still…"

I saw Tomasini urge Nick to his feet, and the pair joined the march back to the camp.

"Alex, you should head back with them," Greene said. I stopped moving, shook my head, and tensed all my muscles, hoping to force them all back to life.

"No, sir," I said. I continued the search for my weapon. "Corporal Van Benthuysen can handle this detail as well as anyone. I'll help you search for our lost men. In the meantime, you and I need to talk. Do you know who she was?"

Greene dismissed me with a wave.

"So be it, but wait a moment," he replied. "Wilkes! Collect the rest of the company, we'll search for the other as a group."

"Yes, sir!" Wilkes moved off to do as ordered.

The main contingent of dead and wounded trudged off. I found my shotgun buried in the mud below me. I washed it out as best as I could but knew it would be useless until I could give it a proper cleaning. My faculties had mostly returned to me by the time the wounded detachment had left, and the search party was organized.

"You asked who she was, and I'm not entirely sure," Greene whispered to me. "I got a few ideas, but the closest answer I can give you is what you might call a 'witch', but even that's not quite right."

"What do you mean by that?" I asked. My emotions concerning the woman and the occurrence became a confusing mix of disgust, desire, and guilt.

"Well, a lot of those who you might think of as witches are just, well, free spirits," he said. "I have met women who live out in the wilderness by themselves, who are friendly enough." For the first time since we'd met, he blushed a little and gave an embarrassed half smile. "But who *polite society* would deem, well, *sinners.*"

"Can they possess a man's mind the way that...that that...*woman—*"

"Not at all, at least, not by any *unnatural* means," he said. "But what you saw, that is the proper witch of the Bible. That's the witch we fear, and for good measure. I imagine those beasts we fought were her creations, men she charmed and twisted to her purpose. Preserved them, too, which is why some of the older ones rotted up so quick."

I gulped as I realized that *I* could very well have become one of those *things*, had she had more time. Greene put a hand to my shoulder.

"Don't blame yourself," he said. "She's got an unnatural power. I believe she's made a pact with, well, to put it simply, a demon."

"Demon," I said, and the word drifted out of my mouth. "You said they were real. It still feels more like a nightmare. I still can't believe they're more than stories meant to keep children in line."

"Well, most are," he said. "And I've never met one myself. But a woman like that. . . she doesn't have the power she had without receiving it from something evil, a being who uses her to its own purpose."

"What would that purpose be?" I asked. He shrugged.

"Who knows?" he answered. "Gain more power, more control over mortal man? I've met some like her who just like to play with men. But it could be worse than that. I've guessed that something here has been trying to control men since long before anyone arrived from the Old World, just as there have been demons controlling man in the Old World for all of recorded history. And I wouldn't be surprised if some of those have come here to—"

"Lieutenant!" Wilkes shouted. He stormed up to us, breathing heavy. "We found a trail, the most promising one yet, with two trails of boot prints in the mud. We think two of them went that way, only. . . "

"Out with it, Lawrence," Greene demanded.

"It goes north, sir," Wilkes explained. "By my reckoning, too much further and we'll reach Secesh lines."

"Gather everyone up then," Greene said. "We'll head that way quietly, but in force. Let's make sure we see southerner pickets before they see us."

With Greene and myself in the lead, we crept through the swamp, slow and quiet, for about a quarter of an hour. My mind swam with guilt. I'd nearly betrayed the Company. If not by my action, then by my thoughts. I'd *desired* her so greatly that I'd actually considered killing the others. Worse, as I thought about it, visions of her features came to my mind. Her overall visage eluded me, but I could still see the woman's lips, her eyes, and the curves of her body.

With shame, as those images surfaced, I fought them back down and tried my best to conjure up Cassie. I had betrayed her as well. She was the girl waiting for me at home, the girl who wrote me letters to tell me of the goings on with my family and Philadelphia, and I had failed her.

A dim glow of campfires began to flicker in the distance through the bushes. We were, indeed, getting remarkably close to the enemy camp. I could feel the tension in our small party, and our pace slowed as we focused on moving silently.

When it seemed we were much too close to Reb lines, where we must turn back or be discovered, Greene stopped, turned, put a hand to my shoulder, and pointed forward. I peered ahead and found two figures crouched in the swamp a few dozen yards ahead, well illuminated by the Rebel campfires. Luckily, there wasn't a Rebel picket anywhere in sight.

Greene whispered an order to Wilkes and the others to return to the clearing and motioned me forward. Practically holding my breath, he led me on a careful crawl to them. I identified them as Private Melvin Doyle and Parker as we approached. Melvin tended to a wound on Parker's neck. At ten feet, they noticed us. Greene waved them towards us, and the four of us crawled our way out.

Another hour later, we arrived back at the clearing. I examined the wound on Parker's neck, where a swamp ape must have bitten him. He'd lost his leather neck stock. Greene demanded a report from the pair.

"Well, sir, durin' the fight, I t'ought I saw Parker here, just walkin' off," Doyle explained in his heavy Newfoundlander accent. "I find's him there, just sittin'. We's so close to the Rebs, I didn't know what to do."

"I see," Greene replied, and shot me a glance. "Parker, is it? Are you alright?"

"Yes, sir," Parker replied. His eyes darted about, as if searching for something. "I. . . um, sir, I thought I. . . but I, uh. . . I'm sorry sir, I guess I just got lost."

Greene clapped him on the shoulder again.

"Okay, well you're found now," Greene said. Parker flinched as Greene touched the wound on his neck. "There's why I make us all wear the stocks. Anyway, let's get back, we'll have our nurse, or a proper surgeon take a look at that."

Chapter 11: The Path

Dawn arrived during our march back through the swamp. More than once, Lieutenant Greene second guessed the path we took, but we eventually emerged right at our bivouac around midmorning.

I had not understood the state of our company until we emerged. Some of our marines were missing hands, limbs, or other parts of their anatomy. The men had faces covered in grime and gunpowder, with red, hollow eyes which stared into the distance. Some of those faces were heavily scratched up, and some lacked one or both eyes.

Lieutenant Cartter sat perched where our gun crew had been. The howitzer and the navy crew had left.

Cartter sprung to his feet. I pondered whether I'd attained a greater exhaustion than I had aboard the sinking *Governor.*

"Lieutenant Greene, nice of you to return!" he barked. As I looked around, I found most of the company had disappeared into the tents. A small triage, with an overworked surgeon, had formed in the center.

"Lieutenant Cartter, how may I be of service, sir?" Greene answered, as cheerfully as he could muster. "Might I inquire, sir, as to the location of our navy howitzer?"

"Supporting the attack, as you should be," Cartter said, and stormed straight into Greene's face. "I've heard quite a tale from your men. Something about a fight with some apes or some nonsense. General Foster of First Brigade has made inquiries into exactly what it is that the Marine detachment has been doing this past evening. If you were chasing Rebels, we should have received better word. I can plainly see there's been some kind of a scrap, but certainly not with *apes*! I say that's a bit too thin. Either way, you have failed in your duties, Lieutenant, and I plan to make a full report on your. . ."

He continued to bark his displeasure at Lieutenant Greene as I whispered a thought into Greene's ear.

"I'm sorry, Sergeant, is there something you would like to say at this time?" Cartter asked in anger. "I've a mind to put your entire company on charges, and if—"

"Lieutenant Cartter, if General Foster is displeased, then, if you would, please escort us to him and I will explain myself," Greene said. Cartter froze, and consternation grew on his face.

"I'm sure the general is quite busy right now, *Second Lieutenant*," Cartter responded.

"How is the attack going, *sir?*" Greene made the word sound like an insult, and I felt a twinge of pride.

"Stalled out, no thanks to the army's lack of Marine support," Cartter replied.

"Tell you what, *sir*," Greene said. "Take us to him, and we'll let you make the report when you get there. He'll want to hear what we have to say. But you'll need us along."

Cartter stared at Greene for a moment, looked at me, and then back to Greene. He licked his lips, smacked a mosquito on the back of his neck, and narrowed his eyes even further.

"I'll tell you what, *Second Lieutenant,* I'll take you to the staff tent," he said. "If you can't give me something good when we get there, and I mean some kind of heavenly wisdom, I swear by my mother I will have your entire company returned to chains, and I'll rip that rank off your shoulders myself!"

Sounds of sporadic rifle fire, interspersed with the occasional boom of a cannon, became audible as we marched along a central road toward the command tent.

"Lieutenant Cartter, is it?" Some rotund colonel, who never gave his name, returned our salute. "And what kind of information do you say you have?"

"Y-yes, s-sir," Cartter stuttered. I got the impression that Lieutenant Cartter had seldom addressed anyone above the rank of major. Aboard a ship, he'd surely interacted with a naval Captain. In any event, he seemed about to tremble with nerves. "As I, uh, I, I mean, uh, they, were, well, um. . ."

"Come on, Lieutenant!" the colonel shouted. "As you can imagine, we're a bit busy here, and we don't have the time to discuss where your missing marines were just now. This whole battle is stuck in a standoff because we only have one tiny little road to march up straight into the only three guns the Rebs have on this little island, with impenetrable swamp on either side. So, if you've come to file a conduct report or something, it can wait until after the battle."

"It's not impenetrable, sir," Greene said. He nudged Cartter. The colonel stared expectantly at the two lieutenants.

"Uh, yes, sir," Cartter said, and swallowed. He inhaled deeply, then continued. "My marines spent all last evening tracking some Rebs through that swamp, Colonel."

"Is that so?" the colonel asked. "Well, it has also been asserted that even if we were to get some men in that swamp, they'd be sitting ducks for Rebel pickets before they ever got out of it. What do you have to say to that, Lieutenant?"

"Colonel, sir, we found ourselves right up against their camp, sir," Greene said. "And we didn't see any pickets. I can't promise you that hasn't changed since the sun came up, but I can't imagine they'd watch by day what they didn't bother watching by night."

"Is that so?" a voice boomed from the tent in front of us. A stocky man with a single star on his shoulders emerged. He had a moustache which connected to a neatly trimmed beard which traced the sides of his face in the same fashion as General Burnside, our expedition's commander. Our entire group straightened and saluted as he exited the tent.

"General Foster, sir," the colonel said. "Beg your pardon, sir, but this is Lieutenant Cartter and, Lieutenant. . ."

"Lieutenant Greene, General," Greene said.

"Greene?" the general repeated. "You're not related to Captain John Greene, are you? Fought in the Mexican War?"

"My father, General, sir," Greene replied.

The general thrust his hand out to Lieutenant Greene.

"I'll take your hand, then." The two shook hands while the rest of us gawked. "I was at Molino del Rey, Lieutenant Greene. Hell of a job your father did there. Hell of a job. I can say with complete honesty I almost died that day, and I wouldn't be here if it hadn't been for what he and his marines did."

"I thank you, General," Greene replied. I noticed my lieutenant's eyes had taken on a blistering intensity.

"So, what's this business about the swamp, Lieutenant?" General Foster asked, clearly meaning the question for Greene. Greene nodded to Cartter. Cartter swallowed again, gave a slight nod in understanding, blinked, and responded.

"Sir, I am the commander of the Marine detachment for this expedition, sir," Cartter said. Foster adjusted his gaze and allowed Cartter to continue. "Sir, Lieutenant Greene here chased a group of Rebs into the swamp last night, sir, but was unable to make a full report until now. By his word, sir, that swamp is easy enough to traverse. Further, his company found themselves right up in the Rebel lines, with nary a picket in sight. It's his assertion, sir, that the Rebs would be easy to flank through that swamp, sir."

Foster shifted his gaze back to Greene.

"Is this true, Lieutenant?" the general asked.

"Yes, sir," Greene said. "I didn't think anything of it, sir, but when I made my report to Lieutenant Cartter here, he knew we should bring this information straight to you."

Cartter blanched and turned to stare at Greene.

"Excellent work, the both of you," Foster said. His gaze shot up and behind us. "Ah! General Reno! Jesse, get over here, we've got some incredible news."

A burly Brigadier General with a well-trimmed full beard sauntered up. A group of younger officers trailed behind him.

"General Foster, good day." He came to the group and returned our salutes. "Second Brigade is on their way, John. How would they best be employed?"

"Impeccable timing, Jesse." Foster nodded to our group. "These marines here have just reported that this swamp is not as impenetrable as we've been led to believe."

"Marines, you say?" Reno replied and shot us a suspicious glance. "Didn't hear we had many of those in this expedition."

"Well, I can assure you we do," Foster said. "In fact, we have a Lieutenant Greene here. Does that name sound familiar?"

"Good Lord!" Reno blurted. The newly arrived general took heavy stock of Greene. "Are you in any way related to the Captain Greene who saved our army at Molino del Rey?"

The contrast between Foster's recognition and Reno's was immense. My lieutenant seemed to become embarrassed and uncomfortable.

"My father, sir."

"I wasn't actually at Molino Del Rey, but I was involved in the other battles around Mexico City," Reno explained. "After we'd won, a group of us formed what we called 'The Aztec Club'. I dare say my friend Tom Jackson and I. . ." His voice trailed off a moment, a smile left his face, and his gaze dropped. Almost immediately, he regained his composure and continued. "Anyway, we heard some incredible tales of the exploits of your father and those Marines. Damn fine men, every one. Horrible loss that day."

"So it was, General Reno, so it was," Foster nodded. "Well, General Reno. . . as much as I'd prefer to light a few cigars and talk of such valiant times, I say we send your Brigade around the flanks, if what these men say is true."

"Right you are, General Foster," Reno continued to stare at Greene. "Lieutenant, would your marines do me the honor of leading Second Brigade?"

"No, sir," Greene said without a moment's hesitation. The response sat around our shoulders, like a dark cloud which threatened to strike us all with lightning. The generals were lost for words.

"L-lieutenant?" Cartter gulped. "You. . . the, uh, the generals, um, the attack. . ."

"General Reno, my marines spent the entire night, until this very dawn, marching through that swamp and they had a hell of a fight with the. . . *Rebels*, as Cartter here reported," Greene explained. "My company, sir, is played out and I will ask no more of them on this day."

The two generals regarded each other and held their breath. Cartter straightened, and he struggled to find any words.

"Sergeant Phillips and I, however, would gladly lead your men, General," Greene said. The entire group, myself included, exhaled in relief.

"Of course, Lieutenant," Reno said. "It is admirable you consider your men first. I would be honored to go into battle with you."

Foster clapped Greene on the shoulder and turned to the colonel. "Go pass orders, Colonel. Tell our commanders up there that we've got word they can flank the rebel army through the swamp. Second Brigade will go left. First Brigade is to make every effort to find their way through to the right."

"Yes, General," the colonel saluted and immediately waddled off.

Foster held out a hand to Lieutenant Cartter.

"Excellent work, bringing these men up here, Lieutenant," Foster said. "I'll ensure General Burnside knows of your service here."

"M-my honor, sir, General, sir," Cartter stammered.

"Good," Foster said, and retrieved his hand. "Now, make sure Lieutenant Greene's company is cared for and given every opportunity to recover. Then, head back to the ships and see to your marines, Lieutenant. Good day."

Cartter turned his gaze between Foster, Reno, and us twice. Finally, he saluted smartly, turned, and left.

Casey Moores

Chapter 12: The Battle

The concept of *tired* changed a good deal over the course of my life. As a child, *tired* came after a long day of doing chores, rushing out to spend hours playing in the streets with my friends, and an evening doing more chores. As I got older, *tired* came at the end of a long day toiling on the docks. When I joined the Marines, I found myself *tired* every moment of every day for the first several weeks.

After that, I became acclimated to Marine living and concluded I could never be more tired than I had already been. At Bull Run, I experienced an entirely new definition of exhaustion. I thought my Marine training had prepared me for battle, and I was wrong.

The day I spent marching, firing, running, and retreating at Bull Run, infused with an overwhelming sense of urgency, fear, thirst, horror, and desperation, had been a hell which no amount of training could have prepared me for. Even so, the Battle of Bull Run compared closer to my days in the streets as a boy than to the day I led the Second Brigade into the swamp at the Battle of Roanoke Island.

I'd awoken from a rocky ship having slept little, thanks to the whimpering of a sick lieutenant. We'd spent a long day on deck watching the ship scare off the Confederate Mosquito Fleet and silencing the few small shore batteries. At the *end* of that day, we'd unloaded, marched ashore, and built the camp.

Then, night's events in the swamp transpired as previously described. Midday that second day, without a moments rest, I found myself stomping back toward the swamp. Hungry, thirsty, and completely played out. The tireless Lieutenant Greene strode ahead of me, and the companies and regiments of Second Brigade marched behind us.

I'd spied Midshipman Porter commanding his six howitzers as we approached the point at which we entered the swamp. Acting Master Daniels and Flag Officer's Clerk Meeker spotted us as we trudged by and gave a wave, which Greene and I returned.

It set me to wonder what it was they thought of the previous night's events. The entire encounter still made little sense to me. I, however, had experienced unnatural creatures before, so to find more of them was not a tremendous stretch. I'd also been told by Lieutenant Greene that our mission lay in such a realm. Those sailors, however, had merely been men who manned a gun, knowing no other enemy than the Johnny Rebs, when giant apes charged us. They'd done their duty and stood with us, but I could only guess at their inner thoughts.

The six howitzers shot over the heads of First Brigade as rapidly as they could.

From somewhere I could not see, Rebel cannons replied. Rifle fire continued from both sides. I could tell which was ours and which was theirs by the tempo. Our regiments would fire en masse, as a line, in a great eruption. The Rebels, safe behind their earthworks, would fire individually in a constant, uneven rattle. Smoke billowed past us in great clouds.

Men screamed orders, screamed in confusion, and screamed in pain. Once, on our trek north, a single Confederate cannonball bounced past us and tore into a column who marched next to us.

Soldiers from First Brigade flowed steadily in both directions as we moved north on the road. Fresh companies moved forward, filled with a blend of eagerness and fear, to reach the front where they would line up and fire.

From the other direction, the injured and those assisting them wandered backed. These men were sunburnt, covered in smoke, filth, and dust, and looked as exhausted as I felt. Some limped, some clutched their chests, and some held their arms out at awkward angles. A few carried red-stained bandages around the stump of what had been a leg or arm, and a few carried bandages over their heads. Many clung to one or more wounded comrades, forming odd-looking creatures, shambling painfully along as disparate clumps of arms and legs. Scattered throughout the field were misshapen lumps of what had been men. Some were still, some twitched feebly.

Before we were anywhere near the front of the battle, Greene abruptly turned and disappeared into the swamp. I followed closely and endeavored to keep him in sight. The sounds of battle were muffled by the bushes but did not dissipate much.

As Greene charged forward, I found myself playing a part I'd played as a child. When we traveled through the city for gatherings or church events, my father would always set off at a great pace. Some of my siblings would keep up. My mother always lagged behind a good deal, and some of my siblings would remain with her. My role, throughout my childhood, entailed maintaining sight of my father while ensuring my mother maintained sight of me. In such a manner, I always felt it my duty to make sure our family successfully arrived at our destination together.

This was the role I found myself in as Lieutenant Greene stalked back into the swamp, taking no care to ensure the Brigade which we were meant to lead remained with us. It might seem strange that he was more difficult to follow during the day, with much less threat of attack by unnatural animals, than he was by night.

At night, I had followed the well-broken branches and well-tramped path broken by the several dozen marines who'd gone before me. Several had carried torches which were easy to discern in the darkness, even over a great distance. In the light, without a clearly trodden path, I had to do my best to catch what glimpses I could of his dirty, tattered, dark blue coat and, when I could not, follow the evidence of his passage.

Behind me, the companies of Second Brigade had formed into three rough columns behind me and tracked me as well as *they* could.

A hundred or so yards into the swamp, I found the path we had made the night before. As I broke onto it, I found Lieutenant Greene crouched and waiting calmly. He nodded his head left to indicate he would resume his trek. I looked back and searched for a moment until I found Second Brigade again.

Branches snapped back up the path, in the direction of our camp. Three soldiers, presumably from another company, stepped out onto the path. When they spotted me, they frantically raised rifles.

I dropped. Luckily, the branches kept my rifle out of the muck.

They fired. Near as I could tell, the shots went over my head. More soldiers spilled into the pathway, and they took aim as well. The soldiers following me recognized I was taking fire from somewhere to their south. Officers shouted orders and they raised their rifles toward the other group.

I pushed my hands into the air gently and raised my head to see. More soldiers had filed into the pathway, and they stepped forward tentatively. As I rose up, I shouted a greeting.

A line of rifle fire drowned my words, and I dropped my head back down again.

It sounds strange to me in the retelling, but I swear I could have gone to sleep as I lay in that muck. I certainly wished I could. Elements of the strange, beautiful woman returned to my mind. I attempted to overlap them with my recollection of the creature who'd sprung up and flown away in her place. I could not clearly remember any of those details, only that it had happened.

When the ringing in my ears faded and the smoke drifted past, I lifted my head again. A mere dozen yards away, I saw another rifle leveled straight for me.

"Shoot him!" someone shouted. I ducked again and forced myself as deep into the bramble as I could. Wood cracked in front of me, and I felt a tap on my cap.

"Stop shooting goddamnit! I'm Union!" I shouted.

"You got a gray uniform, you're a damned Reb!" I heard in reply. The nearest captain in my trailing company shouted a cease fire to his men.

"He said stop shooting, you idiots," Lieutenant Greene's voice echoed from the direction of the shooters. "He's just covered in mud, like I am. Now come on, Rebels are gonna figure us out if we make any more noise."

I poked my head up to find Greene standing next to the nearest Union soldier. He had pushed their rifle muzzle down, and he spoke softly to the company commander.

While the two company commanders sorted out their errors and regained their composure, Greene resumed his walk down the path.

I stood up and checked myself over. I was, indeed, coated in brown-gray muck that had dried to a dark gray. Heated as I was, I could hardly blame them. I dusted myself off as best as I could, glared angrily at both companies, and turned to follow Greene before I lost him again. Behind me, I could hear officers of various companies shout at each other, arguing over who should go first, over who shot at whom, and whether anyone had been killed or injured.

A little bit further down, the path narrowed. Greene seemed to have no trouble determining where it continued.

Another hundred yards or so down the beaten path, I found Greene crouched again, and peering out to our right.

"This is where we found Doyle and Parker," he whispered. I looked about and wondered how he could tell. I did not recognize a single tree or bush. Furthermore, though the sounds of battle had increased once again, I could not see any sign of the clearing the Rebel's defended.

Casey Moores

One of the company commanders came up behind us, followed closely by a major. Two lieutenants and three sergeants crowded in behind them.

"Right through there, sir," Greene said to them, though he glanced back and forth, as if unsure which was in charge. I nudged my head toward the major to help him out.

"Thank you, Lieutenant," the major said, and turned to the captain. "Captain Smith, you heard him. Get your men through this thicket quick as they can and form them up as soon as you're clear. When you're formed up, fire a volley, then shift left at double time to make room for the next company. Then reload, fire, and keep moving. Understood?"

"Understood, Major," Captain Smith said. Then, he turned to the lieutenants and repeated the orders. All, except the major, shuffled back to their company.

"Well, Lieutenant," the major said to Greene, "you've done your part and I'll tell my colonel as much. You're free to head back, we've got it from here."

"Hell, sir. . ." Greene began.

"Major," I mumbled, and both looked at me.

"Major," Greene repeated. "We came this far, might as well see it through. We'll stay out of your way, though, don't worry. Sergeant Phillips?"

"Sir?" I replied, just as confused by his use of my rank as by his insistence on joining the attack.

"Let's head further up, so we can stay clear of our Army brothers, and wreak whatever havoc we can," Greene stated. I suppressed an intense urge to shiver. More than being shot at by the Rebels or my fellows, I feared seeing *her* again. Despite what Greene told me, I did not want to learn whether she could enrapture me again as easily as she had the first time.

"God, man," the major said. "I'd heard you marines were crazy, but I can't imagine you're planning to go forward and take on the whole Reb army up there by yourself. If you are, just, please leave a few for us, all right?"

"I can't promise you anything, Major," Greene said, and motioned me along. "Please ensure no one else shoots at us."

"Looking the way you do, I can't promise *you* anything, Lieutenant," the major replied with a smile. "Just keep your heads down, is all I can suggest."

I saluted, which led Greene to do the same, and we trudged away.

Once we were clear of Second Brigade, my curiosity overcame me.

"Addison, what are we doing up here?" I asked. "Can't First and Second Brigade take it from here?"

"I want another chance to track any signs of this witch of ours," he said. I froze and felt myself go numb. He noticed. "Don't worry, Alex. I don't think she can control you anymore. I don't think she had time to. . .

Casey Moores

Well, I mean, men I've known who've been broken out of such a thing, well, uh. . . Hell, let me put it this way. If you ever find yourself convinced she's possessed *my* mind, I expect you to put me down right then. And I will do the same for you. Nature of this new business you're in Alex. Anyway, come on."

Not reassured in the slightest, I followed him, nonetheless. We picked our way forward until we arrived at the far back left corner of the clearing the Rebs held. As Greene searched for signs of the witch, I tracked the battle's progress. I could hear, but not see, the line fire of Second Brigade as they emerged from the swamp south of us. I could see, but not hear, the blue soldiers of First Brigade as they emerged, simultaneously by some miracle, from the far edge of the field. When I spotted them, they'd already lined up, and smoke erupted from sections of the line as I watched.

The Rebs, dressed in a haphazard variety of gray and brown, organized themselves and returned the volleys. They moved slowly, nervously forward. By the shouting and the poor discipline, I thought it obvious they were a good deal shaken by the arrival of the two brigades on their sides. I imagined they'd break at any moment, but, for several long minutes, they did not.

"No sign of her, dammit," Greene said. I'd forgotten his purpose and, at the words, took my own cursory glance around in search of any woman, or anyone in white. "Well, I suppose we should head back before we're discovered."

"But sir, the Rebs are about to break, I just know it," I said.

"How would you know that?" he asked.

"Because it's how we all looked just before we broke at Bull Run," I replied.

"You sure?" he asked, scanning around the field in front of us. "If they are, we'd get a good number of prisoners, I could ask some questions, right?"

"Yes, sir, you could."

"How quick do you think this'll happen?"

Instead of responding, I licked my lips, drew up my rifle, and aimed for the most important looking person I could find.

I fired.

The soldier three men down from my target jerked and fell backward. Then, he scrambled awkwardly back to his feet. He, and all the others, frantically scanned in our direction.

The entire group shouted and pointed while I reloaded. Rifles turned our way, but only a few fired. Most stood with dropped jaws, nervously clutching their rifles for comfort. None of the shots came anywhere near us.

"They're back here, too!" one of the Rebels shouted. "Damn Yanks got us surrounded!"

I reloaded as quickly as I could, crawled a few feet to my left, and fired again.

Before I took a third shot, the entire group tossed their rifles down and raised their arms. A wave of chaotic responses washed through the entire Confederate contingent. Some dropped rifles, some ran, and some fired in random directions. In no time at all, both flanking Union Brigades stormed through the lines and collected prisoners.

"Damn fine shots, Alex," Greene remarked. "How'd you know who to shoot?"

"Just lucky, sir," I answered.

Chapter 13: Tracking the Witch

For prudence, we waited a good measure before emerging from our hiding spot. Once all the firing had died down, we crawled out, dusted ourselves off, and remained as non-threatening as we could until some Union soldiers noticed us and realized we were on their side.

Nearly hallucinating with exhaustion, I nonetheless followed Greene around as he approached and questioned whatever prisoners we could find. There turned out to be a great deal of prisoners. Greene was not too subtle in his interrogations, he simply walked up and down the lines of prisoners shouting out questions.

"Where's the woman in the white dress?" he would shout, usually receiving half-hearted laughter or dejected grins in response. I suggested several times that we were not going to get anything out of them, but he did not relent.

"Damn witch up and left us," one mumbled. He looked younger than the others, and his gray not-quite-a-uniform wasn't as worn out. One of the others elbowed him and few gave him mean stares. However, as tired and defeated as they all were, none had the energy to do more.

"What was that?" Greene asked as he stepped forward and leaned in.

"Sir, I wouldn't get that close," warned one of the Union guards. Greene waved his hand dismissively.

"Who was she?" Greene asked the man.

The man peered up, his smoke-covered face a blend of apathy, anger, and fatigue.

"Just some old lyin' witch," he said.

"You hush up now," a larger, bearded prisoner rasped.

"What's it to ya?" the young man retorted. "We might coulda won, we'd been watchin' them bushes. But I heard tell that witch convinced our colonel she had 'em covered. But she just up and left us. Flew South for the winter."

"Boy, you don't shut that mouth I'll shut it fer ya," the glaring, bearded man growled. The two stared hard at each other.

"Let's not be starting anything," the guard said, muscles tensed.

"Look, this woman, whoever she was, sounds like she let you down," Greene said. "So, if anyone wants to see her come to justice on that account, tell me what you know about her, and I'll see it done."

No one spoke, or even made eye contact. Greene nudged the young man with his boot.

"S'all I had to say," the young Rebel said. "We coulda whupped you good."

Greene looked around. Relenting, he looked at me and nudged his head back toward the road.

He shouted a few more questions on the way back, but received no more replies. During the walk back, I observed several dozen more escaped slaves who'd emerged from the swamp on the east side. In contrast to the dismayed Rebs, these people all seemed excited, energetic, and happy.

My lieutenant paused to converse with them as well. The accent was just as hard to understand as the Rebel soldiers, but we learned they'd all been living there for months. The white woman had only arrived days earlier. The day the Union troops landed, they explained, she'd "pulled skunk apes outta da muck, 'sif dey always been 'dere." Unfortunately, none could tell us where she'd gone, other than South.

On return to the camp, Greene and I took stock of the wounded. We'd lost three more men since our departure, and another four were injured in such a way that they'd have to be sent home. Greene gave them some quiet words.

Finally, at the end of the longest day of my life, *Governor* included, I staggered into the tent and passed out.

The next few days passed in a blur. A flurry of reports came to Lieutenant Greene directly from General Foster, and correspondence arrived from Major Reynolds. He wrote letters in reply to the latter immediately, though he told me little of what they discussed. A couple days after the battle, reports came in about a naval battle further up the Sound, near a town called Elizabeth City. Another couple days past that, when the men of Unit Thirteen had largely recovered, we learned Burnside's troops had taken a town called Edenton. After that, it was said the whole area had been subdued. While the Union Army meandered about with no successes, the Navy and the Marines had deprived the South of more ports and tightened the noose a little more.

Personally, I spent every free moment I could reading letters from Cassie Paul. I tried my hardest to recall her face and, sometimes, it would come to me. As soon as it did, the image would drift back out of my mind and be overcome once again by the images of the white witch's features. In my dreams, the two blurred together, and then morphed into the winged demon I'd seen fly off. Sometimes the demon would remain to attack me, rip me apart, bite at my limbs, or pick me up and carry me away. With practice, Cassie's face became more available in my head, and the witch faded.

One might have thought our men would be downtrodden, angry, or confused by what they'd experienced. I actually expected a revolt that very next morning. In a strange turn, they instead came together. Where I was sure a bond had not existed, suddenly one did. They had pride in the unit and faith in each other in a way I would never have guessed.

Tomasini and Niculescu, in particular, had become the best of friends, with the former making a concerted effort to teach the latter English. Tomasini told a tale that Nick had been grabbed by his hair later on that night and nearly dragged off, had Tomasini not repaid his debt and shot the creature. As a result of the incident, both of them had shaved the hair off the sides of their heads as soon as they got back. It became the new fashion in the unit.

Cash had earned a reputation for fighting like the devil with the Bowie knife, and Doyle gained great respect for having snuck so close to Rebel lines in search of the lost and disoriented Parker.

During this time, random soldiers of various backgrounds showed up, with orders proving they'd been assigned to M Company. That remained the official title of the unit, though we'd taken the habit of calling ourselves Unit Thirteen. Some were regular Army soldiers from units bivouacked near us. Some were from the other Brigades. Most reported having seen something of our fight the night before the battle. Others explained they'd heard of the events and had told comrades they'd seen similar inexplicable things growing up. None seemed to know why they'd been re-assigned, but all had orders signed by General Foster himself.

The soldiers who'd been with us in the swamp promptly took it upon themselves to regale the newer members with exaggerated tales of what we'd done. I tried to redirect their cagey stories by leading drill and training with the knives and shotguns. We became quite the talk of the expedition when word got around that we not only carried the weapons, but were supplied with ample ammunition and powder with which to train.

As the company grew, Greene and I discussed making some of our privates into corporals, and a few of our corporals into sergeants. Emile Van Benthuysen, Tom Archibald, and Lawrence Wilkes were chosen to become sergeants. To keep me above them, Greene appointed me the First Sergeant. A formality, since I'd already been acting as such.

We awarded the rank of corporal to Sam Cash, Michael Clark, and Alan Conyers. Four of our new recruits had served as corporals in the Army and were allowed to maintain the rank.

I repeatedly informed him we needed more officers, and he wrote several letters to Reynolds. I can't imagine they had any officers to spare, but there was no harm in asking.

Several new wooden boxes were delivered as well. One contained more of the shotguns, powder, shot, and a smaller box of cartridges for my breechloader. The others remained a mystery, as Greene would allow no one else to touch them. On the one, and only, occasion on which he looked into them, I caught a glimpse of long, metal tubes. They looked far too wide to be gun barrels.

We also received a welcome shipment of replacement shoes and more leather stocks. I was simultaneously impressed and troubled that Greene had thought to order more stocks before we left. We had a need for them, as many had been chewed up or scratched off in our encounter in the swamp.

One day after the news of Edenton, we had a new arrival who proved to be the second most unusual person I have ever met.

A short, thin, soldier, too small for his uniform, strode brazenly into our tent, where Greene and I reviewed all the latest reports. I didn't give the soldier a second glance.

"Private, can I assume you are here to report in for duty?" I asked. He did not answer. Without looking up, I continued, "If you're here to join the company, just say so, and I'll get you on the roster and help you find a tent."

"I'm not here to join your company, but I am here to help it," he said, in a voice that sounded as if he intentionally made it deeper than it truly was. Perturbed, I looked up and prepared to admonish the young soldier. The words caught in my throat.

The young soldier's face, though smudged by dirt and smoke, was like porcelain. His light brown eyes were feminine. Before I reached a conclusion, she spoke.

"Bless your heart, Sergeant," she said in a thick southern accent. Greene's head snapped over to regard her. "Why l'il Addy Greene, I do believe I've set your Sergeant here all cattywampus at the sight of a lady in the camp."

Once the secret was out, I looked at her and wondered how I could ever have thought she was anything except a woman.

"Rest assured, Alex," Greene stated without looking up from the report in his hand, "you still haven't seen a lady in the camp."

"Addy, sometimes you make me madder than a wet hen," she said. "Now, are you going to introduce us, or not?"

"Please keep your voice down, Ellie, let's not draw attention to ourselves," he said, maintaining his flat tone. "Alex, please allow me to introduce you to the illustrious Elizabeth Octavia Beauregard, a highfalutin' debutante from a rich Louisianan family."

"Debutante?" she repeated, practically spitting the word in offense. "Is that all you think of me? Why, you and I have—"

"A freer spirit, you shall never meet," he continued. "In fact, this would be that other variety of witch I discussed."

"Oh, now you're just bein', well. . . okay, I suppose *that's* true enough," she said with a blushing smile. She extended her hand with the fingers down, as a lady would. "So. Alex, is it?"

"Yes, Miss Beauregard," I replied and took her hand respectfully. She half curtsied. I glanced back and forth between them and searched for words.

"Now, if we're all caught up, may I ask what it is you're doing here?" Greene asked.

"Well, Minty heard about this expedition, and knew there were a good number of coloreds down here," she explained. "*Contraband*, your big bugs call them. We just can't beat the notion that these people are property, no matter what. Anyway, I told Minty I'd come down and see what I can do."

"Which, dressed like that. . ." for the first time since her entrance, Greene looked at her and gestured toward her uniform, "is what, exactly?"

"Using my feminine wiles, of course," she replied, then frowned. "Which is not as simple as you might think. What I've done is pass around a camp canard that they're going to turn this island into a colony of freed slaves. Once they hear the men talkin' about it, your higher ups will start thinking that's what they're supposed to do."

Casey Moores

"Who's 'they', Ellie?" Greene asked.

"Doesn't really matter now, does it?" Miss Beauregard answered. "Long as the idea takes hold."

"As I said, Alex. . . *witch,*" Greene said.

"Now, Lieutenant Greene," I replied, "I understand the two of you know each other, but I will not have you speaking to Miss Beauregard in this manner. Moreover, sir, there is no way you can compare this lady to the, uh, the *thing* we saw in the swamp."

At these words, her eyes turned hard, and she jerked her head sternly back toward Greene.

"Addison, what does he mean?"

Greene looked at me, expressionless as ever. "Go ahead, Alex, tell her everything you saw that night."

I was apprehensive to tell the tale, because if it sounded crazy enough in my own head, it would, surely, sound worse to her. But Greene had told me to do so, so I told her everything I could recall. Truth be told, describing the events out loud helped me to reconcile the gorgeous, rapturous woman with the vicious, sharp clawed harpy.

"A woman in white," she said, letting the words drift out. "I'll have to get this written into my journal. I might come back and pick your brain again, just to get the facts right."

"Ellie here keeps a detailed account of every evil thing she comes across," Greene said. "Anyway Ellie, she seemed like a witch to me. A proper, demon-worshipping witch."

"Oh goodness gracious, you mean Kur Oto, I imagine?" she asked. "You know I've spent most of my life down here, and never heard hide nor hair of it. Plenty of stories of a white witch, though."

I dug into the fog of my brain, as I knew I'd heard the name somewhere.

"Doesn't mean it isn't real," Greene replied. "You believe just as much in this *Brotherhood* you're always on about. Much as I think they're a bunch of useless gentlemen who play with tarot cards and dance about in women's nightgowns, I'll grant they do exist. But, who do you think it is that they worship?"

"Well, you got me there," she replied. Then, she laughed. "It is a little funny though."

"What?" Greene asked.

"You think it's some kind of devil or something, and you want to hunt it and kill it. Just across this bay to the Northeast is a place called the Kill Devil Hills. I think it's just because a few ships have shipwrecked there, but who really knows how they name these things?"

"Well, I can't imagine she went there," Greene replied.

"Wait," I said, "you mentioned that on the ship, that name, right?"

The name still bugged at me, as if there was more to it I couldn't recall.

"Yes," Greene said. "I've found scattered messages that refer to the name over the years. It's my belief the name refers to, well, *something*, a demon perhaps, as I've said, that was here when Columbus arrived, and something that may still control things here. I wasn't too sure what our purpose was when I was given charge of this company, but it's become clear. *If* what I believe is true, then she may be the key to finding it. They had sent us south blindly, hoping we'd blunder across something, perhaps that sea creature again. In any event, we have, in fact, blundered across something worth chasing, and that's what we'll do."

"I'd say it's a ghost story," Miss Beauregard said, "but then, we have seen some strange things. I've just never come across it myself. Either way, you say you want to track down this *woman in white,* is that it?"

"Witch," Greene re-stated.

"Well, whatever it is, ghost story, or woman in white, or witch, there are only two places down here I can think to look for her," she said, with a hint of exasperation.

"And that would be?" Greene asked.

"Either the oldest, most haunted town in America, or the most magic infested," she answered. "Saint Augustine, in Florida, or New Orleans, the home of all dark magic in America."

"That's pretty flimsy reasoning," Greene said.

"Well, do you have any better ideas?" she asked. When we did not reply, she added, "plus I know for a fact that the Brotherhood is active in Saint Augustine. Tell you what. . . I'll round things up here and head there myself. By the time you find your way there, I'll serve her up on a silver platter."

"Hmmm. . . if there is something major influencing events down here," Greene said, "it does serve to reason it'd have a hand in one of the oldest towns in America."

"Didn't one of those Rebs say she *flew South for the winter*?" I asked. "Saint Augustine's south, right?"

Greene pondered for a moment and then set into a flurry of activity. He tore into the stacks of reports and letters he'd received. At length, he triumphantly pulled one out and waved it about.

"Well, Alex, it looks high time to get Unit Thirteen re-assigned," he said, with a smile.

"Sir?"

"Well, there's almost no chance the Union Army or Navy will make any move on New Orleans any time soon, of that we can be certain," he said, with a rare chuckle. Then, his eyes went wild, and his smile grew larger than I'd ever seen it. "However, the South Atlantic Blockading Squadron covers everything south of here, and Major Reynolds is still out there at Port Royal. It seems to me he's looking for something to do. As it is, he and the Marines there are just meandering around Port Royal, taking small forts and whatnot. I'll convince him, and he can convince the higher ups, that Saint Augustine is ripe for the picking. Then we can go have a look."

I nodded and acted enthusiastic toward this new plan. Deep down, I thought about how this would take us back through the area where I'd seen the sea creature, and that the plan entailed going after the woman who'd bewitched me. Though a part of me hoped I could regain some honor by then, a large part of me feared ever encountering either again. Shamefully, I hoped we would fail to convince the Big Bugs to re-assign us on such a flimsy hope.

If we were re-assigned, I hoped they would not agree that attacking Saint Augustine was a worthwhile endeavor. I'd never viewed myself as someone who would shy away from a fight, and had it been Rebels or even the skunk apes, I wouldn't have flinched. But I did not see how one could kill a sea monster or a witch who hypnotized men and flew away when she chose.

Chapter 14: The *USS Orion*

Lieutenant Greene wasted no time orchestrating our transfer to the South Atlantic Blockading Squadron. He once again involved Lieutenant Cartter, who was a great deal more amiable than before. Cartter escorted him back to the headquarters of the Brigade commanders, who authorized the move and arranged for a ship to take us south.

Miss Beauregard visited a few more times in the next few days, and then, without explanation, said she would meet us in Saint Augustine. How she planned to travel down the coast on her own I couldn't begin to guess, but it didn't seem my place to ask. She had, after all, found her way onto Roanoke Island without much trouble. By the time she left, it was a well-established fact in the camp that the escaped slaves would be formed into a free colony on the island. None outside our tent ever seemed any the wiser that a woman had walked among us. It made me wonder how easily spies could have wandered through the camp.

While we waited on the island, I received a handful of letters. Two were from my mother, the rest were from Cassie Paul. My mother's letters discussed the mundane goings on of my friends and family back in Philadelphia. They were a welcome distraction and made me think of home. I could not bring myself to open the letters from Cassie.

Just over a week after the battle, Cartter arrived with orders.

"Lieutenant Greene," he said to announce his presence. Greene and I rose with respect. His demeanor was softer than I'd seen it in all of our past meetings. "The reassignment has been approved, as I thought it might. Here are the orders. I am to tell you that you must keep them on your person at all times and destroy them if there's any chance of your loss or capture. As I give you these, Addison. . . might I shake your hand?"

Curious, Greene extended his hand to receive Cartter's.

"There's another thing I have been given the honor of telling you. You have been awarded the brevet rank of first lieutenant. Now, as I am directed, I can make no records and all orders for this company are to be burned upon reception. Thus, there will be no record of this, but you have my word it is legitimate.

"Whoever it is you are, and whatever it is your company is meant to do, I was clearly wrong about you and your men. Whatever it was that happened in that swamp, your actions the next day are, without doubt, commendable. Moreover, that you sought to share your success with me, well, I can't even fathom why you would do that. If our paths cross again, you'll receive every ounce of help I can endeavor to provide. Best of luck to you and your company, sir."

A few days after our orders arrived, we still awaited our transport, I took the opportunity to inquire about Miss Beauregard.

"Lieutenant Greene, sir?"

"It's Addison, for God's sake, I thought we resolved that in the swamp, and what is it?" he replied.

"Yes, sir. Might I inquire as to how you know Miss Beauregard?"

"You wait until now to ask me?"

"Well, sir, I didn't feel it prudent to ask in her presence, because I assumed if either of you wanted to tell me, you would have already," I explained. "And she always seemed to appear at the oddest times, so I never felt safe inquiring, but now she's gone, well. . ."

Greene set down the sheet of paper he had been reading. He sighed, sat, and looked at me.

"Yes, well, I suppose it's only natural," he said. "I should've told you about her sooner. I met her in Appalachia, when I was hunting devil dogs."

"Devil dogs?" I asked.

Casey Moores

"Yes, you know, um, *white devils* or *white things*?" he answered. Before I could ask further, he continued. "It was a hell of a sight, you must imagine, little southern belle like her, trekking through the woods with a rifle. Anyway, that's pretty much it, we just happened to find each other tracking the same thing. Remarkable woman, truly remarkable." With no warning, his eyes narrowed, and his tone became heated. "Now, I will not besmirch her honor by describing our relationship any further, I will not do it, I tell you, so do not ask."

"Yes, sir." Somewhat embarrassed by his unsolicited protest, my mind searched for a way to back out, and I promptly forgot to follow up any further on the term *devil dogs*.

"But I will tell you this, Alex," he continued. "Do not trust her. As I said, she is remarkable, and more than capable. I do believe her heart is truly on what you consider *your side* of this whole crazy affair between the states."

Crazy affair? You mean the war?

"But she is, at her core, dishonest," he said. "A bit of a rascal, you might say. I've seen her bluff the slickest politician you've ever met. I do not wish to be rude, and she's no bad egg down deep, but you must know. At times, if your aims and her aims are in congress, well then, she's a great ally to have. Unfortunately, her aims are all that matter to her, and as soon as they are at odds, you're nothing to her."

Sensing an unspoken, painful memory, I inquired no further.

A full two weeks after the battle on the island, we finally received word that our sixty-five-man company was to strike the bivouac and load onto the *USS Orion*. It was a 180-foot screw steamer with two thirty-two pounder guns and a heavy, twelve-pound Dahlgren boat howitzer. I learned from the crew that it was capable of just over eleven knots, which I found impressive. The howitzer was manned by none other than Acting Master Charlie Daniels and Flag Officer's Clerk Eddy Meeker. However, both had acquired Marine officer uniforms and the brevet rank of second lieutenant.

I learned that both had requested transfer to Unit Thirteen the morning after the battle, and their energetic midshipman, who'd written them a commendation, supported them. The request was forwarded directly to Lieutenant Cartter, as all such requests were, who rubber stamped them as surely as he did all others.

Relieved, I exhaled slowly after watching Greene salute the flag. We continued along the brow and approached the Quarterdeck. Normally, I would have remained with the company to arrange for the loading once we'd received permission to board. In this instance, Greene requested I remain with him to prevent him making a fool of himself, as he had when we left Hampton Roads.

As we approached the officer who awaited us, I perused the various ranks of those standing at the end of the brow and spied one with two gold stripes on his sleeve and gold leaves on his shoulder. The lieutenant commander was the highest-ranking officer to greet us.

"Gold leaves, two gold stripes, lieutenant commander, salute and request permission with him," I muttered under a low breath, with my head slightly down.

He stopped, came to a respectable attention, and drew his arm up, palm out, to salute.

"Sir, Lieutenant Addison Greene of the U.S. Marines, M Company, requests permission to come aboard!" he said. I relaxed some more. I'd make a proper officer out of him yet.

"Permission granted, Lieutenant Greene," the lieutenant commander said, as he returned the salute. "Welcome aboard. I am Captain Lucius Beattie of the *USS Orion*. If you would, please, follow me to my cabin, we have much to discuss."

The boatswain's mate finished piping the side, and then played a single "Ruffles and Flourishes".

"Yes, sir," Greene said, as he stepped aboard. He paused momentarily to regard me. "Sergeant, see to the men."

"Actually, Lieutenant Greene, I would ask that Sergeant Phillips accompany us."

The tone suggested it was not a request. That a ship's captain would both know my name *and* wish to converse with me was unusual. However, he was the skipper, so I obliged.

"Sergeant Van Benthuysen, see to the men," I shouted back. Satisfied he could handle things, I followed the two officers to the captain's quarters.

Inside, he motioned toward a couple simple wooden chairs, and moved to them. I did not sit, intending to wait until the captain did so. Greene followed my lead and remained standing. "May I offer a glass of whiskey?"

"We'd be honored, Captain," Greene replied.

Beattie poured three glasses, handed one to each of us, and sat. We sat as well.

"It is good to see you again, Sergeant," the captain said. "Seems we've both come a long way from the *Governor.*"

I choked on my first sip of whiskey at the surprise. He waited, gaze intent upon me, as I gave him a better look. He was somewhat familiar to me; I had not recognized as much when I first entered. I could not recall how I knew him. All at once, the memory of his face aboard the *Governor*, and aboard the small boat that recovered us at the end, returned to me. It was one of the sailors who'd leapt from the *Sabine* to the *Governor* to help secure us, and the boat chief who'd hauled us out of the water to move us to the *Sabine*.

"So, you do remember me," he said, and I reasoned he'd seen the recognition grow in my eyes. "And I can only presume you remember what we saw that night."

My shock must have been more obvious than my recognition a moment earlier. Greene looked at me and smirked.

"You seemed to think only you and Johnny Reynolds witnessed that, Alex," he said, and turned back to the captain.

"Sir, I feel I remember you wore a master's rank at the time," I said, desperate to change the subject.

"Yes, though I was promoted to Lieutenant almost immediately afterward," he clarified. "As we traveled on to Port Royal, I reported the, er, *encounter* to my captain. He brought in Major Reynolds, from whom I learned that I had not seen anything at all, much as he explained that you, who I saw staring at the beast, had not seen anything either. One month ago, I was breveted to lieutenant commander, given the *Orion,* and given some very detailed instructions as to how to support your company. Or, *Unit Thirteen,* rather, according to rumors. Very strange instructions, in point of fact. Or irregular, to say the least."

"Sir," I interjected. Both men looked at me as if I'd intruded, even though I'd been invited, given whiskey, and addressed directly. "I must be confused. I remember, when I first mustered with C Company, just before Bull Run, that a wooden schooner, named *Orion*, sailed south with our fleet, in the fall of last year, to be sunk with the stone fleet, to block ports in North Carolina."

"Very astute, Sergeant," Beattie replied, with a grin. He stared at me for a moment, as if searching for unexpected signs of intelligence, and took a sip of his whiskey. "That is, indeed, what happened to the last ship which carried the title *Orion*. This ship, you see, is not listed on the records, much as my promotion is not recorded in Navy logs. I am told that, although I must keep a proper log, that I am to destroy it if ever this vessel comes in jeopardy."

"I have similar guidance, sir," Greene said. "So, I hope we understand each other."

"We do, Lieutenant Greene," Beattie replied. "But my inquiries suggest that no one in the entire Union Army, Navy, or Marines had heard of you prior to the Battle of Roanoke Island. Almost every high-ranking officer, however, has heard of a *Captain* Greene who served in the Mexican War. Those who've heard of him speak in hushed tones, but tremendous respect. So, I ask you, how have you come to be an officer in the United States Marines?"

Greene finished his drink, took a quick glance at me, and then told the entire story. He began with his father in the Mexican War. Then, he made the same speech he had to me about the reality of monsters, demons, witches, and the like. Finally, he expounded on something he'd hinted at, but not directly told me.

"I've spent my life hunting these things down," he said. "Sergeant Phillips, you met that darling southern belle."

"Miss Beauregard, sir?"

"Yes, Miss Beauregard," he answered. "She actually grew up hunting them too. I know there's actually a good deal more Southern gentlemen than there are in the north that do so as well. Nonetheless, I was raised to know how to find, track, and kill the monsters that give most people nightmares."

"How is that even possible, Lieutenant?" Beattie asked. "Even were I to believe such a tale, which I am somewhat inclined to do having witnessed the creature when the *Governor* sank, however, I mean, how can one man like you, or even a group of men, do that and still be here to tell me?"

"It's fairly simple, Captain," Greene replied. "In normal times, you can find them one or two at a time, generally lost, fairly obvious in their actions, and overall, unguided. Think of it this way, a man can track and kill a single wolf, or a single tiger, or bear, even, if he's smart. But here's the issue, Captain. In times like these, they all seem to come out of the woodwork, band together, find leadership of one kind or another. When we open up and fight our wars, well, so do they."

"I see," he said. His expression became even more grim than it had been. "I've wrestled with it ever since that night aboard the *Governor*. Had Reynolds not confirmed that I'd seen, well, *something* unusual, to say the least, I would've thought I'd gone mad. I'm sure you, Sergeant, took it much better than I did. In fact, I saw what you did for those poor souls in the water. Much more than I could've mustered, and you have my commendation."

It was quite a relief for me to find myself in the company of someone who'd shared the horrifying experience. I yearned to discuss the matter with him, to ask if he knew what it had been, or whether he'd seen or heard anything about it ever since. At the very least, it would have been wonderful just to acknowledge the bond we shared, or, perhaps, to speak of the men we'd lost. However, he was an officer, and the ship's captain as well. It was not my place to command the conversation.

"Yes, sir," was all I said.

The conversation lulled, and we sipped our drinks to the sounds of the creaking ship and the gently lapping waves hitting the hull.

"Well, sir," Greene said, after some time had passed, "is there any word on my request? We find it necessary to get ourselves to Saint Augustine."

"Yes, well you're in luck on that account," Beattie said. "Before you'd even sent your somewhat curious requests to Reynolds, which he mentioned in his correspondence to me, our good Captain DuPont, who still commands the South Atlantic Blockading Squadron, made plans to capture some more ports in his purview."

"Wonderful news, sir," Greene said. "However, I feel there are some caveats forthcoming."

"Very astute, Lieutenant," Beattie responded. "For one, Captain DuPont has not shared his specific plans with me, as it has been made clear we are not a part of his command. I would guess he means to take Fernandina, and it follows he would try for Saint Augustine, but that is far from certain. For another thing, as I said, we are not under his command. You and I have the freedom to conduct our affairs as necessary, and that direction has likely made him somewhat irate and soured to our cause, which he must not fully know. To be honest, I sympathize with his position."

"Do you believe he would actively oppose our efforts, sir?" Greene asked. As I'd developed a sense for the man, I could tell Greene was growing heated.

"Only time will tell, Lieutenant," Beattie answered. "Though it may raise your spirits a bit to know that Major Reynolds still commands the large number of Marines assigned to the Squadron. I venture to say that will favor us greatly. In any case, I have prattled away at you long enough. I shouldn't keep you away from your men any longer. Oh, I almost forgot!"

Beattie leapt up and charged at a small chest on one side of his cabin. He flung it open and drew out a strange flag. Or, rather, a flag within a flag. It was primarily a plain crimson flag, and from one side that was all one saw. Stitched onto one side, however, was a tattered old silk flag. This was a slightly different shade of crimson, worn and faded in some spots. In the center lay an intricate gold dragon, such as I'd seen in picture books as a young boy. Below the dragon, the number thirteen had been stitched in white.

Greene rose and reverently floated to the flag. I saw moisture form in his eyes.

"It's beautiful," he said, and he reached out to put his hands under it.

I gulped in fear that the captain would admonish his rudeness, but Beattie made no mention of it.

"My father wrote letters which described the banner under which he marched, but I've never seen it," Greene continued.

"Well, with your agreement, Lieutenant Greene, we'll fly it below the colors, yes?" Beattie asked.

"Yes, Captain, it would be a great honor to me if you were to do so," Greene replied. He turned to me, eyes red, but face lifted as if in a dream. "Well, Alex, it looks like we finally get to operate under the appropriate banner of Special Unit Thirteen."

Chapter 15: Chasing Ghosts

O ur steam engine chugged away, belching smoke and noise, as we pushed south to Port Royal at as good a speed as the captain would allow. Captain Beattie later explained we were in a race to catch DuPont's Squadron before they departed, as it was unclear where they would head once they left. DuPont was particularly uninformative in his communications with Captain Beattie. If they left without us, we would be on our own to guess their objective. Greene suggested that they simply head for Saint Augustine, with or without DuPont. Beattie never replied. I can only guess that Beattie, though not directly under DuPont's purview, did not wish to act in the area of the Squadron's operational responsibility without coordinating with it.

I was amazed that Greene's "special authorizations" had gotten us this far. Although Greene did not seem to think so, I knew we would soon reach its limit. Surely, not every officer in the Union Army felt indebted to Addison Greene's father.

In any event, our race south had begun. Greene was slightly better adapted to sea travel than before, enough so that he came up on deck after a few days. This miraculous event occurred so that he could introduce another new invention. With my help, he'd drug up one of the long, heavy crates that contained the long metal tubes.

"Archibald! Clarke! Tomasini! Niculescu! Report to me at once!" The entire company, and the crew of the *Orion*, were caught off guard by such a formal call. The four men handed off their duties and appeared before us. Unsurprisingly, the rest of the company and most of the crew drew their attention to our small group.

Greene dramatically opened the simple wooden crate. Inside were four long, metal tubes with openings cut out at one end. At the open end, there were also two-toed spades, to grab the ground, and, at the other end, there was a block with large screw plates on the sides.

"Gentlemen, I have selected you four to be the rocket squad of the Company," he said. "You will be under Lieutenant Daniels' supervision as part of our artillery contingent. Have any of you seen rockets before?"

All four shook their heads to reply negatively, though I saw a few of the numerous onlookers nod their heads and smile in recognition.

"Okay, well, I'm going to show you how these work. If you don't want to kill yourselves or waste the very expensive rockets, I'm going to need you to pay close attention. Is that understood?"

"Yes, sir!" all four shouted. Removing two long stakes, Greene attached them to the blocks by means of the screw plates. Attached correctly, they spread into an inverted V; the forelegs of the whole contraption. With the forelegs set against the rail and the spade pressed against the deck, he pulled a shorter, closed tube out. This had a rounded cone at one end, and three small, curved metal plates welded inset to the other end, sort of like a miniature, three-bladed pinwheel.

He placed the smaller cylinder inside the cut out of the larger opening, at which point it was apparent the rigid pinwheel fit into the groove at the end, near the spade.

"With the forelegs and the base claw secure, you place the rocket into the launcher tube, like this," Greene said. "Then you insert a piece of fuse, and fire."

He slid in a piece of pre-cut fuse, grabbed a torch, and lit the fuse. The deck of the ship became dead calm as it slowly burned its way into the rocket. When the fuse had burned in with no immediate response, several exhaled in disappointment. Then, there was a high-pitched hiss and the rocket shot out through the tube at an incredible speed, spinning so fast I could hardly tell. It flew a couple thousand yards out into the sea and exploded low over the water.

"All right boys, I got four more rockets to spare," Greene said. "I want each of you to fire one, so you know how it goes. Then, we'll save the rest. Unfortunately, you'll have to learn how to aim them real time. But then, the sorts of things I expect we'll fight, we'll probably be kinda close anyway."

All four men, and just about everyone else for that matter, had grins from ear to ear. Apparently, they'd only heard "rockets", and, once again, missed the part about "sorts of things I expect we'll fight". Personally, I wondered what the things would do to an evil, black sea monster. The kind I'd seen on the exact same route on which we were embarked.

I'd be lying to say I didn't let my gaze drift to the water. As always, I found only fish and sharks.

There was only one other bit of excitement on the way to Port Royal.

"Aye, what's that?" Private Meier shouted. He was on the port side, amidship, staring and pointing at something. Several crewmen and marines turned to look. A few spyglasses peered in the direction. No one could see what he pointed at, myself included. At length, Conyers, the winner of the Whitworth rifle and Meier's sharpshooter partner, strolled up next to him. The two conversed, and Meier pointed some more. Finally, Conyers showed recognition and got excited as well. Then, Midshipman Sullivan, one of the crewmen, confirmed a sighting with his spyglass. He called for the captain, who then called for Greene. As Greene and I approached, the steam engine quieted a good deal and the ship slowed.

"Lieutenant, get all your men below deck," Beattie directed. "And have someone take down that banner of yours."

"Yes, Captain," Greene replied. "But, sir, may I ask what's going on?"

"It's a blockade runner," Beattie said, "Returning from Europe, headed to Charleston, no doubt. We'd lose too much time if we gave chase, much as it *should* be my duty," he cast narrowed eyes at Greene, "but it'd be futile anyway. I've another idea. *If* it's bigger, faster, with more guns, which is likely if they've crossed the Atlantic, it must see a solitary Union ship as a potential prize. Honestly, being alone, I've actually wondered whether the Confederate Navy might give us trouble. In any event, if the captain of that ship assumes they have more men, I'm guessing they might get a little bold. But they won't be counting on your marines."

"Well, isn't that a dirty trick," Greene said, as more of a statement than a question.

"I've seen them do worse more than a dozen times in the last year," Beattie replied. "I suppose you'd have me do the honorable thing and fight a losing gun battle?"

"I see, Captain," Greene said, sounding a little morose. "Slowing to lure them in won't delay us too much, will it?"

Beattie stiffened, but before he could dress Greene down, Greene shouted, "Sergeant Archibald! You and the rocket squad on deck, one tube each, and stay low!

Conyers, Meier, you too! The rest of Unit Thirteen get below and arm up. *Fully armed*, men!"

At this, Beattie smiled and turned to shout orders to his crew. By that time, all among the crew knew that the men of Unit Thirteen carried shotguns and Bowie knives in addition to their rifles. If any Rebs attempted to board the ship, even if their number matched ours, they would be in for a hell of a fight.

"Daniels, Meeker," Greene continued, "load that howitzer with grape and cover her up as best you can! Conyers and Meier grab that Whitworth, you four lay low with the rockets and stay ready."

As directed, the men disappeared below deck. Archibald, Clarke, Tomasini, and Niculescu emerged a short while later, each with a loaded tube, fuses already installed. They stayed low and dragged the tubes to the port side railing. While laid out below the railing, they set to attaching the forelegs, but remained careful to keep themselves and their rockets low. Conyers and Meier came up as well, carrying the Whitworth rifle. I directed the men on deck and confirmed Greene's orders were followed. Greene, who'd armed himself, returned to Beattie's side. Once all was set, I joined the two officers.

"She's turned, all right," Beattie said, getting animated. "I believe she's making a play for us. Okay, well, if she's seen us, moving too slow will give up the game. Ahead three quarters! Two points starboard!

That'll make it look like we're running, but still let them close with us. I'll bet we could match them if we went full."

Thus began the contradictory pursuit of a Union gunboat by a Confederate blockade runner. It makes more sense when one considers the *Orion* was a fourth-rate ship, while the Rebel ship was likely third or second. As they closed, Beattie informed us she did have four guns to our two, and that she was large enough that her crew surely outnumbered the *Orion's* standard crew.

Excited as he was, I became quite the opposite as time passed. Though I'd grown up in a port and spent a lot of time on boats, the only naval engagement I'd seen was when the North Atlantic Blockading Squadron had engaged the Mosquito Fleet near Roanoke Island. That had hardly been an engagement at all. The fleets had simply traded a few shots until the Confederates ran. It had also occurred in the tight confines of a bay, not the open ocean. Hunkered down low to remain out of sight, I nearly fell asleep.

"Here it comes, men, look sharp!" Beattie cried out, almost gleefully. "She'll fire a warning shot in a moment; I know it. Then we'll act the hopeless crew and strike the colors. Greene, ready your men, quietly, as soon as we slow."

"Yes, Captain."

The runner did, indeed, fire a warning shot a few minutes later. Beattie ordered the flag lowered and the engine to idle.

"She's taken the bait," Beattie said. The closer the ship got, the more relaxed his demeanor. An excited, happy captain would have ruined the surprise. He gave a low toned, continuous update of their progress, and voiced estimates of when they would close with the *Orion.* Unexpectedly, he straightened and shouted, "Something's spooked them! They're turning off, they're giving it up! They've fired! Everyone down!"

One cannonball screamed past our starboard, but the other crashed through the railing and burst through two men on the deck as if they were paper.

"Engine all full!" Beattie shouted. "Well, we might have been lying to them, but they fired at a ship that had, by all signs, surrendered."

I wondered why we didn't turn to return fire. After a moment's thought, I realized we would lose that battle, and the captain knew it. We might escape, but they'd give us several good shots before we got away, whereas our cannon would remain useless. Even the howitzer was on the main deck.

"Lieutenant, the rockets," I said.

Greene jumped to his feet. "Rockets, to the aft! Someone get them a torch!"

Three of the men hesitated in confusion, but Archibald sprang up and hauled his launcher and the single rocket to the aft rail of the ship. The others caught on and trailed behind. Archibald placed the forelegs down, did his best to aim, secured the rear spade, and reached for a torch. He lit the fuse as the other set up.

The rocket hissed out and shot across the sky. For a long moment, we all stared at it slack jawed. It went out toward the blockade runner and flew well over the top of it. Niculescu and Clarke were dumbfounded and chewed their lips. I surmised they were working out how to adjust. Tomasini, however, crouched, put the tube up on his shoulder, and pushed the back of the tube up off the deck.

"Nick, light it!" Tomasini shouted. Before Niculescu could get the torch, Archibald touched the fuse. Tomasini's rocket fired straight toward the runner and struck it just port of the bow. Our crew cheered.

"Clarke, Nick, get to it!" Greene shouted. The other two rocket men remembered themselves and imitated Tomasini's technique. Clarke's shot dug into the water, just short of the runner. Niculescu's shot struck the central smokestack, which burst apart. Flame burst upward in a brief flash, and then the smoke ceased. Another cheer went up on the *Orion*.

"Get them more rockets!" Beattie shouted. Greene shouted in agreement, and Wilkes, who'd just come up, turned about and went back to get some.

The blockade runner lurched to starboard and slowed. We pulled well away from it as its crew unfurled its sails. It did not fire on us again.

"Well, Captain," Greene said, cool as ever, "would you prefer to keep toying with them, or shall we be on our way?"

The machinations were clear on Beattie's face. Our ship captain was torn between pursuing a wounded enemy or fulfilling his obligation to Unit Thirteen.

"Two points to port!" Beattie bellowed. He waved a dismissive hand to Greene.

We continued on our way south without any further incidents, aside from poor weather.

Chapter 16: Chasing DuPont

We were slowed in our passage to Port Royal by poor weather. It was not quite the storm that sank the *Governor*, but I was still greatly unnerved. On March 1ː, we arrived in Port Royal to discover DuPont's fleet had departed the day prior. Though Greene wished to press south at all haste, Beattie informed him we required re-supply.

While the crew and the company labored to affect our replenishment, Cash and I handled a few specific deliveries, courtesy of Major Reynolds. Crates set aside for M Company included enough muzzle loading shotguns to arm our new members, as well as a few more breechloaders and several cases of cartridges for them. Another case contained more Hale rockets, and yet another contained more Ketchum grenades.

News came in that the Union had beaten the Rebels in Mill Springs, Kentucky, and taken Fort Henry in Tennessee. The land battles got a great deal more press than our successes along the coast.

A letter from Reynolds also awaited Greene. It nearly threw him into a frenzy, though I restrained him until I could get him to our cabin.

"Well, Alex, this may be our last shipment of things for a while," he said through gritted teeth. I hadn't seen him so livid before that moment. "It seems that there is an effort underway to spoil Johnny Reynolds' good name. Moreover, Captain DuPont is, as Beattie suggested, wholly against the operations of this company. Now, our orders come from higher than either of them, but Reynolds believes DuPont will do whatever he can to hinder us and will do nothing whatsoever to aid us."

"Well, sir, it was only a matter of time before one of the Big Bugs decided we were an unnecessary indulgence," I said. "I mean, look at it from their perspective. They generally can't know much about us. There are a good number of higher officers who have a sense of what was done in Molino Del Rey, but those who have no knowledge of it must resent the notion that *something* happened, but they cannot be told. Truth be told, there are only so many men who served there, and there must be plenty more who did not. Hell, DuPont, is Navy, and probably has almost no knowledge of what happened, and if he does, it's simply something that marines did while ashore, no more or less deserving of merit than Chapultepec."

"Pig-headed mules," Greene said. "I see your point, but it doesn't mean I have to like it."

"Either way, sir," I said, "it doesn't change things all too much. We're as well armed as we ever were, even if it's all we'll get for a while. In the meantime, let's not let it distract us from our real job."

"Yes, of course," he grumbled. "Though there's still no word on any offensive against Saint Augustine. If DuPont's planning something, he's doing it without Reynolds' knowledge."

"Well, then let's head down, link up, and if we don't get the answer we like, we do as you suggested," I said.

"Which was what?" Greene asked me.

"Take it ourselves," I said. "My dad told me something, just before I shipped out. He said 'son, whenever you find yourself in the thick of it and something needs doing', remember that it's better to beg forgiveness than to ask permission.' Now, the whoopins he gave me when I was younger indicated the opposite, but either way, that's what he told me. I think it applies here."

Greene's anger dissipated and he broke into a laugh. "Yes, yes, it just might."

After another day, we broke south to Fernandina to catch up with the South Atlantic Blockading Squadron. Our first communication with the fleet was an order to support and attempt to head off Rebels who'd abandoned the defenses at Fernandina. DuPont informed Beattie that an attack on Saint Augustine would take place as soon as the area around Fernandina had been pacified. Though I know Greene yearned to demand Beattie ignore the orders and take us south, he wisely bit his tongue.

For several long, uneventful days, Captain Beattie received orders to travel this way and that, such that we ran figure eights all around the Cumberland Sound. At first, we believed we were supporting the assault on Fernandina itself. On March 5, we learned Fort Clinch and Fernandina had been taken the day prior. This repeated with St. Mary's Island, which was taken with a few shots of grape and canister, as well as Simon's Island, Brunswick, and Jekyll Island, which had all been abandoned. As these operations progressed, Beattie informed us they were all taking us further from Saint Augustine, as opposed to closer.

In the afternoon on March 10, Greene received a message from Reynolds.

"Well, it seems we'll still be supply limited from here on out," Greene said, as his gaze traced the lines down the letter. "He's in an all-out shouting war with the paymaster of the *Wabash*, who was supposed to be responsible for the Marines. Reynolds reports that the Battalion is being deprived of all the basic necessities. He wonders if this is some reaction to all of the outlandish requisitions that have been approved on our behalf."

He set the letter aside.

"I am starting to worry about Johnny's health. Word is, he got all heated and ordered some marines to swim to their boarding ships when they loaded up to come south, and yet more rumors that claim he's inebriated more often than not. It may be true, or it may be the powers that be are attacking him as a means to disband this unit. On one hand, I'd feel a bit of guilt if he's reaping some petty punishment for supporting us as he did. On the other hand, there's no point worrying about it. Let's be grateful for what we've gotten, and make sure we put it to good use. No more live fire training, we'll train by dry fire. And make sure the men know we gotta make every round count from here on out."

"Sir, we might have an advantage Major Reynolds doesn't have," I said. "If we make requests through Captain Beattie, we might be more likely to at least get the more usual type of supplies."

Greene smiled.

There was a knock at the cabin door. I opened it, and we both snapped to when we discovered Captain Beattie on the other side.

"Yes, of course you can use me to requisition whatever you need, within reason," Beattie stated. "The doors on the *Orion* were not particularly thick. But that aside, I've got some, well, *interesting* news. I've received orders to return to Bay Point. However, I have also received *word* that DuPont has sent a few ships south to take Saint

Augustine. A few days back the *Keystone State* tried to find its way into Saint Augustine, but couldn't thread through the sandbars. However, the *Wabash* and the *Mohican* are down there, looking for a way in."

I expected Greene to bark back in anger. Instead, he spoke with dignity and respect.

"Well, Captain Beattie, you have DuPont's orders, and you have my request," Greene stated. "Do you find yourself in a dilemma, or have you made a determination?"

"You know, and I say this in confidence, but I have a sense that DuPont's getting snippety about the press Burnside has received up North, where there's almost no word of his successes down here. I'm betting he's trying to shore up his accomplishments in a bid for admiral. Were he to allow Special Unit Thirteen a part in taking Saint Augustine, he'd be restricted in what could be reported to the press. I imagine he wants to avoid that circumstance.

"Well, anyway, the order was passed via semaphore, the 'wig-wags' as you say," Beattie said. "Standing as I was on the starboard side of the ship, looking into the setting sun, it's always hard to sort out all those flags and whatnot. I feel my safest course of action would be to maintain my course until I receive better clarification. Looks like I've chatted enough, I've got to get back to running a ship. Good day."

As he left, I saw a frown grow on Greene's face.

"Haven't we been tracking north this whole time, chasing DuPont's ghosts?" he asked.

"Yes, sir," I replied. "However, he said we was watching the sunset from the *starboard* side. He was telling us we're headed south. And I'd venture to guess he means to avoid giving DuPont any opportunity to send any more messages."

Greene did not light up, but did cheer up slightly.

"They'll still have the town before we get there, and any hint of our mark will be gone," he said. I nodded in grim agreement.

Late afternoon the next day, Commander Christopher Rodgers greeted our longboat when we stepped onto the wharf in Saint Augustine, as well as Captain Doughty, commander of the *Wabash* Marine Guard.

"Welcome Lieutenant Greene," Rodgers said, after salutes had been rendered about. "I have orders from DuPont that I am to give you whatever assistance I can while you conduct yourselves in the town. Please let me know what I can do, and it will be done."

"Thank you, Commander," Greene said. "I will do so, sir."

"Now I must advise caution in your pursuits, Lieutenant," Rodgers continued. "Though the town leaders, such as Mayor Bravo, have been welcoming and hospitable, a good number of the women in the town are downright hostile. I'm fairly certain the Saint Augustine Blues, that's what they called the town's Secesh defenders, only left last night. That's why I've got the 7th New Hampshire Volunteers going ashore to guard the city. But, as I said, not everyone here is all too friendly. Watch yourselves."

"Yes, sir, Commander," Greene replied.

By Rodger's orders, we had a mere eight men with us, and Greene left four Marines, under Corporal Clark, to guard the boat. The lieutenant, Cash, Parker, and I set off to explore the city.

Behind us, longboats hauled in the volunteer regiment.

At this point, I will admit, we were lost for ideas. We conjectured that if our white witch had been in the city, she would have left before it was taken. However, we had no other leads, so we walked off as if we had a plan. We passed some beautiful hotels around the central square. The square itself was devoid of people; whoever had received Rodgers had disappeared back to their homes.

At the northeast corner of the square, we found Tolomato Street, which led us to the Tolomato Cemetery. Greene had the notion that such an old cemetery might provide some kind of direction. The sky got dark as we meandered about in a confused fashion wondering exactly what might serve as a clue.

"Someone's coming," Private Cash reported calmly. I heard the clatter of boots on the cobblestone coming up the road toward us from the square. Through the gaslight, a large figure developed, which then resolved into a pretty southern belle in a large yellow dress with red flowers and white lace trim.

"Addison!" she shouted, as she stomped up toward us, both hands holding her dress up so she could walk. "Bless your heart, you just march to your own drummer, don't you? I said I would be here waiting for you. I don't suppose you could have spent any more time looking around the square, you had to go and make me come charging up this road when I heard talk of some northern fools, who were wandering about in a cemetery, didn't you?"

To be honest, I only caught half of the words in her accent, which was much thicker than I remembered.

"Oh, Ellie, my dear, I know how much you love cemeteries. I figured if I waited around one long enough, you'd find me," Greene said. Cash gasped at the response. Parker simply returned his rifle to his shoulder.

"Well, aren't you just a peach?" she asked. "Come on now, let's get inside where we can talk. Too many things listening here. My friend Clarissa has a house just back on the square. Come on."

We followed her to a house which was, as described, on the square. Greene ordered Cash and Parker to remain outside as a guard. I briefly considered how scandalous it was to be two men calling on a house with two women at such a late hour.

Clarissa, we discovered, was a mouse of a woman who'd recently been widowed. She did not explain how, and we did not think it prudent to ask. The house seemed unnaturally cool to me, a sharp contrast to the warm air outside.

"So, Addy, how was your trip? You sure took your sweet time getting here," Miss Beauregard said. Clarissa quietly brought some tea in for us, and I thanked her. She quietly floated back out to leave us alone with Miss Beauregard.

For no reason I could discern, I suddenly felt very light-headed. I thought the tea might help, but it was still too hot.

"Dammit, Ellie, just tell us what you know," Greene replied, agitated. "Is she here? Or anything else that you find unusual?"

"Well, I will tell you one thing, you're sure lucky that you didn't show up before the other Union soldiers did," she said, and began to blow softly on her tea to cool it.

"Why's that?" Greene asked.

"The Saint Augustine Blues would have still been here, had you arrived first," she said. "There's almost a thousand of them, and they would have made short work of your company. But they all scampered as soon as they saw those other ships sniffing around the sandbars."

"Huh," I said. "Sir, Captain DuPont must have known that, maybe he was just trying to clear the way for us."

"Well, regardless of his intentions, it's left us nothing," Greene grumbled. "Isn't that right, Ellie? You'd have told me by now if there was anything for us to find here, and you haven't."

"There you go again, Addy, guessing at my ways," Miss Beauregard said. "And I do believe she was here. The Brotherhood, too."

Visions of the woman leapt into my mind unbidden. For the first time since I met her in the swamp, I could see her angelic face clearly. My dizziness worsened. I set my tea down to avoid spilling it.

"Was?" Greene said. "Dammit, out with it, Ellie, tell me everything."

"Well, since you asked so nice. . . When I arrived, the Blues, that was the militia here, seemed awful worked up over something. They were in a big mess of running about, making all kinds of preparations. Turns out they were getting ready to up and leave, as they did."

A soft buzzing noise developed from somewhere in the house. I looked to the others, but they did not comment on it. Miss Beauregard took a sip of her tea. I thought to do the same, but my stomach turned a little sour, and I decided to give it a moment to settle.

"That doesn't mean anything, they could have just figured out the Union Navy would come down here eventually," Greene said.

"Yes, but I heard tell around town, at just about the same time, people started talking about seeing ghosts here in Saint Augustine. Now, there have always been rumors of such in this town, but there was a great deal of talk, specifically about a ghostly white woman, who came about at night, and stole the hearts of men who were out by themselves."

"Why didn't you start off by telling me this?" Greene asked.

The buzzing noise increased, and I detected a horrible smell.

"Why Addy, I'm trying to paint the picture for you, I can't just lay it all out at once," she replied. "But fine, I'll cut to the chase. The Blues haven't gotten far off, and I believe they plan to come back and make a fight for the town."

"What makes them think they can do that?" Greene asked.

"If they thought they could make a fight, why didn't they defend it?" I asked, though it pained me to speak.

"Because of your ships, Addy," she said. "Even on the other side of the sandbar, they know you boys could blast away at their town. It also gives you somewhere to run to when they attack."

"So, what, do they have a plan to deal with our ships?" Greene asked.

"I believe they do, Addy," she answered, "the Blues themselves were braggin', just before they left the town, that they'd be back as soon as The Brotherhood and their *guardian angel* had dealt with the ships."

"She's here, and she's got some plan to take out our ships?" I asked. Then, I retched and almost lost my stomach.

The buzzing and the stench became unbearable.

"Beg your pardon, sir, Miss Beauregard, but don't you two hear that. . . or smell that?" I asked, doing my best to avoid further retching.

"What are you—" Greene started to reply, but at that moment Miss Beauregard dropped her teacup and fainted back against her chair. Greene rushed to her. "Ellie! Ellie!"

He glanced around in a panic. When his gaze moved to the broken teacup, he announced, "She's the only one who had the tea, isn't she? Go find Clarissa, that friend of hers, if she's still here. I think we've been played for fools!"

Though still dizzy and feeling sickly, I staggered through the house. Greene remained with Miss Beauregard.

"Miss Clarissa!" I searched the kitchen and the dining room and found no sign of her. As I thought about it, we'd heard nothing of her since she'd brought the tea. I climbed the stairs. The buzzing increased, as did the stench. I fought through the fog in my head and searched the bedrooms above. I soon recognized the noise and smell came strongest from the master bedroom.

I opened the door to the closet and vomited. I found the dead, fly-and-maggot-covered corpse of a mousy little woman. Clarissa, if that's who the corpse was, had been dead for days.

Chapter 17: To the Ships

"The boats!" Greene cried, when I'd explained what I found. "We've got to get back to the boats!"

"Sir, what about Miss Beauregard?" I asked.

"We'll have the volunteers look after her," he replied. "She's alive, but there's no time. We might be too late already!"

He ran to the door, and I followed. Cash was alone outside.

"Sir, Parker's disappeared!" Cash said. "He said he heard something, but before I could stop him, he turned a corner, and he was gone. It was just a couple of seconds, sir!"

"We'll find and deal with him later," Greene said. "Let's get back to the long boat! She'll be somewhere near the ships!"

"You mean, we gotta warn them, right?" I asked.

He shrugged.

As we ran through the square, Greene spotted a group of the New Hampshire Volunteers, and instructed them to see to Miss Beauregard. We raced down Treasury Street to arrive back at the wharf. I feared our four marines might not be there, that perhaps the white witch would have gotten to them before we did.

Thankfully, they awaited us at the wharf, and the three of us piled in. A nearly full moon had arisen overheard by then. In the moonlight, we rowed our way up the Matanzas River, past Fort Marion, and toward North River. The ships, unable to maneuver through the sandbar, awaited further out.

We pushed ourselves through the water as quickly as we could. I saw something float to the top.

"Oars in!" I shouted, and frantically secured my oar inside the boat. Greene did the same with his, as did the other two who manned oars. We sat in silence and searched the water.

"What was it?" Greene asked.

I thought I had seen one of the tentacles, with which I was horribly familiar. However, I saw no more signs, and again began to doubt my sanity.

"I'm sorry, sir, it must have been my imagination getting the better of me, I think we can—"

Something bumped against the boat and all of us jumped. Black tentacles emerged from the water on all sides. The beast of my nightmares had returned.

Without awaiting orders, each of us drew our large knives, chopping and stabbing at the giant, black appendages. The tentacles responded by thrashing and swinging about, nearly knocking one of the new Marines, Smith, I believe, into the water. Clarke pressed a shotgun against one and fired. The tattered remains of the tentacle retreated. Greene fired his heavy pistol into another tentacle, and it recoiled as well.

He used the brief moment to throw open the chest he'd ordered we bring along. He tossed hatchets around to us, which greatly aided our fight against the thrashing creature's arms. Two of the others found enough time and room to grab their rifles and shoot.

With a strong whack with the hatchet, I found I had the space to bring my shotgun to bear as well. Before long, it looked as if we had the upper hand. Between the hatchets and the sporadic rifle fire, it never again gained a good grip on the boat. On the other hand, we were not moving. I wondered whether we or the beast would give out first.

All at once, the tentacles snapped back into the depths. Some of the men reached for their oars, but Greene stopped them.

"Reload, and be ready, men, it'll be back at any moment, I expect," he said. We did as told, each with an eye on the water around us. Reloaded and ready, we waited. The water lapped softly against us, the only sound for several long moments.

It emerged with a great eruption of water on our port side, with its tentacles all together in one bunch.

"Shoot it, men, get me an opening!" Greene shouted. We blasted away as one, and the buck of the massed fire nearly tipped the boat. The inky sea beast threw its tentacles wide. In that moment, Greene tossed one of the grenades against a mass of limbs. The deafening explosion knocked us all back against the edge of the boat. Repulsive pieces of black flesh splattered over us. A great wave smacked against the boat, and Samuel Cash pitched over backward into the water.

The shattered remains of the beast sank back beneath the waves.

I caught sight of Cash's hand below the water and snatched it before he sank away. I almost went in myself, but Clark and one other grabbed hold of me. Trusting them, I heaved Cash up until he could reach the edge, and then I helped him all the way into the boat.

"Oh Gods, thank you, Sergeant, I thought it had me," Cash said, as he spewed seawater back into the river. Something bumped against the boat. I assumed the creature was back, but then I saw a shark's fin move quickly away from us.

"It'll be back soon, reload and let's get moving!" Greene shouted. We grabbed our oars and rowed for all we were worth out toward the ships.

We heaved the oars in unison to Greene's call for several long, grueling minutes. We cleared the sandbar into the open ocean, where the *Orion* waited not much farther out.

My eyes were drawn to a brilliant glow on the beach to our south. To my amazement, I spotted the white witch, as beautiful as ever, standing serenely a mere hundred feet away. Instead of the uncontrollable love and lust I'd felt at Roanoke, I experienced a blend of fear, disgust, and anger.

The moonlight and her glow were sufficient for me to see that one of the hairy beasts stood beside her. By the accoutrements, I could tell it wore one of our uniforms. A soldier with a rifle stood on her other side. He, too, wore a US Marine uniform, though there was not enough light to identify him.

"Guns!" Greene shouted, with no explanation.

The creature emerged in a great splash on our starboard side with a great flurry of tentacles. Two slapped hard against me, knocking the shotgun from my hands and throwing me backward. Another grabbed my left leg as I tumbled. The other marines on the boat blasted their rifles and shotguns into it. I held onto the boat for dear life with one hand while I drew my knife with the other. With a wild scream I stabbed as hard as I could into the cold, rubbery flesh that held me.

Out of the corner of my eye in the bright moonlight, I saw another grenade fly past me and toward the monster.

"Down!" Greene yelled. I had no ability to do so, but I shoved harder with the knife and curled myself into a ball.

An explosion thundered and the boat pitched high on a sudden wave. Were it not for the tentacle which held me, we would have capsized.

The tentacle released me, and we watched the last few flailing limbs of the creature sink below the water.

"Row, men, row!" I heard a voice call from somewhere behind us. It was Captain Beattie, urging us on. We manned the oars once again, beating the sea into foam with desperation and fury.

"Come on, come on, we're almost there!" Greene shouted.

An oar was torn from my hands. Though the others continued to row, the boat stopped, as surely as it would if we had gotten stuck on sand or a reef. We readied guns once more. Sheer, silent terror lingered.

Tentacles snaked up the end of the boat and another creature pushed itself up onto the boat with us. It bore no scars or injuries, and I reasoned it was a new creature. If there was more than one, there was no telling how many there were.

"There's two, one at each end!" Beattie called out. Most of us fired at the aft creature and then swung and stabbed at it.

I spared a glance back at the other end and spotted Greene, readying to use another grenade directly onto the creature at the bow. The blast would have killed him instantly. Fortunately for him, but unfortunately for us, it was knocked from his hand and fell into the water.

Several loud shrieks pierced the air. Something exploded against the side of the aft beast. As I realized it had been hit with a rocket, something much greater slammed into its side and tore it away from the boat. My mind caught up to the deafening sound of a cannon.

With our end clear, the boat pitched down towards the bow. That creature, still clinging to the front, leveraged it down to force the bow under the water. Its purpose was immediately clear, it meant to dump the lot of us into its waiting maw.

Private George Thompson, one of those who'd watched the boat with Clarke, dropped, bounced, and landed in the creature's arms.

Greene tossed his last grenade straight into its mouth. It swallowed the object down.

Nothing happened.

Thompson screamed as the beast pushed him into the rows of teeth. They pulsed up against him, as I'd seen before. With a loud crunch, Thompson went silent.

All of us clung to the boat and could no longer spare a hand to shoot at it. Two more rockets exploded against its side, but it hung stubbornly to us, awaiting its meal.

My hand was just about to slip when the creature expanded and released all of its tentacles. It gave an enormous burp, which sprayed teeth, parts of Thompson, and partially digested fish all over us. It went limp and sank. The boat dropped flat against the water.

I saw several more fins dart toward us and submerge just before reaching us. The sharks, I realized, feasted on the dying creatures. I found the thought gave me a strange comfort.

"Get back to it, we're almost there," Greene shouted. "If there's three, there could be hundreds!"

I heard the collective gasp of the other marines on the boat at the implication.

We bumped against the *Orion,* and I found a hawser they'd dangled for us to grab hold of. The others secured their weapons, hatchets included, and climbed up. While they did, I told Greene that the witch stood on the beach. He spun, searched, and saw her.

"Corporal Conyers!" Greene shouted.

"Yes, sir?" echoed from above.

"Shoot the woman on the beach!" Greene ordered.

An enormous tentacle, far larger than any of the others I'd seen, rose up and wrapped completely around the boat.

"A kraken, Alex! I told you! I told you those others were small ones, didn't I?" He pointed, smiled, and laughed, as if he'd just settled some great joke.

"Go, sir, go!" I shouted to Greene. I fired my shotgun into it, but it didn't even flinch.

It pressed so tightly to the boat that the boards began to crack. Thankfully, it seems uninterested in us. I climbed up, tight on Greene's heels. The boat fragmented into splinters beneath my feet. As I climbed, I discovered more tentacles attached to the sides of the ship. A truly gigantic creature lay below us, such that might break up and swallow the entire *Orion*.

On deck, all hands raced about in a frantic maelstrom. The massive tentacles did not search for men, they all hung tightly to the ship itself. The beams of the ship groaned and creaked with infuriation. Beattie shouted an endless stream of orders to attack them with all means available.

The 9-inch gun barked, and one tentacle recoiled for a brief moment. Rifles, shotguns, and pistols fired. Greene ran to Conyers and Meier, reiterating his orders to shoot the witch. Then, he ran below deck.

Our rocket squad had found four sailors to light the rockets. Using the shoulder fire technique Tomasini had come up with, the four lined up at one railing and fired as one at a single tentacle on the opposite railing, with little initial effect.

Daniels and Meeker, with a team of sailors, wrestled to work the howitzer as well, firing upon the same tentacle as the rocket squad.

"Fire!" Daniels shouted. The howitzer boomed. A moment later, Daniels cursed. "Dammit, canister's worthless. Let's try the grapeshot!"

I stopped hacking at one of the tentacles to catch my breath. I looked up to see Meier focused on the beach with a telescope while Conyers fired the Whitworth Rifle. They both cursed and Conyers reloaded.

Once again, I noticed shark fins dancing about, a short distance from the boat.

"Chum!" I shouted.

I searched the deck for Beattie, found him, and ran to him.

"Captain," I said in huff. "The sharks! They attacked the other three when we'd injured them. If we dump chum and whatever else we can on the creature, maybe they'll attack it too!"

He shrugged.

"Nothing else is working, we might as well try it," he replied. He grabbed a collection of sailors and sent them to collect whatever shark bait they could find.

Greene re-emerged, with Van Benthuysen helping him to carry another crate of grenades to the deck.

"Marines, come and get 'em," he shouted. Every man of Unit Thirteen, myself included, ran up to grab a grenade.

"Toss them between the great arms, men, get the armpits if you will," he said. "And careful! Don't kill yourself."

As he said the last, one of the privates tripped as they ran toward the edge. The grenade tore a hole in the deck and launched his mangled corpse over the side.

"Dammit, I said be careful," Greene repeated, a morose dread in his eyes.

Water lapped over the edges of the railing, and I realized the boat had been dragged down to the water line. In moments, we would be submerged, and it would all be over.

I discovered the rocket squad and the howitzer team had nearly severed the tentacle they'd focused on.

Conyers whooped a cry of elation, which I assumed was from a good shot. A moment later, he froze. Then, he collapsed to the deck. Blood trickled from a hole in his head.

Meier screamed with rage and grabbed the Whitworth from his dead partner.

Sailors all around dumped chum and buckets of fat, blood, fish, and the like all around. The circling sharks burrowed into the sides of the creature.

Boards in the center of the deck cracked and splintered. The ship was not far from buckling altogether.

"I got her!" Meier shouted. "By the Dickens, I got that white strumpet, but good!"

Tears formed in his eyes as he looked down on Conyers.

"That was for you, Alan."

I heard a great, but distant, eruption of cannon fire and the *Orion* lurched sharply starboard. Two large cannonballs tore through the air overhead.

The *Wabash* had pulled up closer to us and had fired a broadside into the kraken. I'm not sure how many of the

Wabash's forty-two guns hit the monster, but all the massive arms on that side of the ship released.

The ship dipped into the water on the starboard side as only those tentacles held on. Water washed up over the side. I was certain the boat was about to capsize.

All at once, the tentacles dropped away. The ship bounced up and swung violently to port. I went into the air and nearly flew off the ship, but Van Benthuysen caught me. A few others were not so lucky, and I'd just taken great care to ensure that sharks filled the waters around us. The crew of the howitzer lost control of it, and it smashed through the railing, taking a sailor with it.

The ship settled. The crew collected themselves. Beattie shouted orders to take roll and check the ship for damage. After I'd thanked Van Benthuysen, I directed him to account for Unit Thirteen. While I took a moment to catch my breath, I let my gaze drift out to the water between us and the *Wabash*.

Tiny pockets of churning water lined the side of the *Orion*, where the sharks feasted on whatever sailors and marines had gone over. Some screamed when they surfaced, some thrashed about in a desperate, losing battle. Some of the sailors on decks threw out ropes, but none were saved.

Further out, in the space between the two ships, a much greater maelstrom convulsed about. The enormous kraken writhed in agony as it was set upon by dozens of sharks, perhaps as many as a hundred. The thrashing beast drove fast toward the *Wabash*, and I feared the beast meant to take down its more powerful tormentor. The rows of cannons would be almost useless engulfed in the creature's arms.

The *Wabash* poured another broadside into the water as it closed. A couple more shots tore across our deck, but didn't hit anyone and no one felt the need to curse the *Wabash*. After the great blast of cannon, the enormous beast stopped in place. It lurched about for a moment, and then surged south as if looking to escape.

"Hell of a sight, isn't it?" Greene, who'd appeared beside me, asked. "Never thought I'd see one of them this close. *Hoped I wouldn't*, I suppose I should say."

"Why doesn't it go deeper under?" I asked. "It would be safe from the cannons there."

"I think that's your doing, Alex," Greene said. "The only part that isn't getting chewed up by sharks right now is the part above water. But now it's realized it's in a wicked state all around."

I turned to look at him. His face was covered in black powder and blood trailed down from a gash on the side of his head. His left arm was scorched black. He leaned awkwardly to his left and had his right knee slightly bent in pain.

"You look to be in a wicked state yourself, Addison," I said.

"You're one to talk, Alex," he replied. "Besides, we won. It's a great day. Or night, I suppose."

My gaze returned to the base of our ship where the shrieks and churning had ceased.

"Not for them," I said. "It was my bright idea to collect all those sharks in here, and all those men are dying horrible deaths for it."

His hand shot to my jaw and forced my head to point toward the flailing kraken, which crawled away from ships.

"Your bright idea is what'll be the end of that thing," he said. "This ship would've gone down, and the *Wabash* and the *Mohican* might have as well. Those sharks would've had a much finer feast then, on all of us. And then the Blues would've come back in and killed or captured our whole contingent in Saint Augustine. And then, knowing how successful she'd been, that witch would've summoned that beast, and all its little baby beasts, to go take on more of our fleets in other places. She could've opened back up all these ports we've been taking, the blockade could have crumbled, and the war would be lost.

"All those other ships in the Union Navy don't have *us* on board. They might not have Hale rockets, they might not have Ketchum grenades, but, even if they did, they wouldn't have Special Unit Thirteen on board. They don't have a dragon fighting on their decks," he pointed back to our moonlit flag, with the golden, Chinese dragon proudly flapping about in the wind, "and they don't have a man like you to lead them."

"What do you mean? You're the officer." I said, confused. "Hell, even Daniels and Meeker rank above me, now."

"Horse piss, Alex," he replied. "You've been the true officer in this company since long before I joined it. All I've done is given these men the right tools and pointed them in the right direction. You're the one who leads them."

We watched the fading sea battle in silence while I considered his words. Ever since we'd left Hampton Roads, I'd envisioned having a chance to find and fight the beast I'd seen aboard the *Governor*. I'd never imagined there were more than one and despite what Greene had said, I'd never pictured them being any larger than that first one I'd seen. I had, however, dreamed of defeating them and had thought that doing so would have brought me great elation. As it was, I felt no different.

"What's more, the creature will not be back, and that's on you," he continued. "That ship over there could've wailed away as it did, but the creature could've just slunk away and licked its wounds. But instead, you drew those sharks in, emboldened them, and helped give them a taste for it. Those sharks are gonna hound it all the way back to hell. Could take days, damn it all, it could take decades. But that thing will not be back to bother us, you mark my words, Alex. And that is all on you. Those men died doing their duty, and we will honor them for it. Whatever guilt you have over what happened to them had better be matched against the knowledge that your actions defeated the greatest creature I've ever heard of. Well, you, Conyers, and Meier as well."

"Wait, what?" I asked.

"One of them, or both of them, got a shot on that white witch of ours," he said. "You do remember she had a part to play in this, right?"

I felt myself go flush with both embarrassment and anger.

"Of course not, you miserable—"

"Easy, there, Sergeant," Greene smiled. "Anyway, I figure she was either the one calling the beast or knew how to draw its attention, maybe even controlling it, and possibly protecting it somehow. If it hadn't been for those two sharpshooters, we might still have a fight on our hands, you never know."

"So, did they get her, then?" I asked. "There were two soldiers with her that I saw." Conyers' fate returned to my consciousness. "Oh lord, Alan. . ."

He tilted his head. "Yeah, something got him, one of those two soldiers, maybe, but we gotta find out what. Plus, both Alan and Paul seemed to think they got her."

"Well, what are we waiting on, then, let's go get her!" I said.

"I was hoping you'd say that," Greene said. "I was afraid you might be played out again. I wasn't sure if you'd have it in you to go chasing her down."

Casey Moores

Chapter 18: The Hunt Resumes

Greene, Meier, Cash, and I rowed out in the moonlight toward the beach where I'd seen the witch and the soldiers. It was difficult to determine where, exactly, they'd been. Earlier, I'd spotted her because of her brilliant white glow. That the glow was gone meant that she was either dead or departed. I assumed the latter, as I did not truly believe she *could* be killed.

After we pulled up on the shore, it did not take us long to discover the two soldiers I'd seen. Neither were covered in hair, as I'd thought one had been. Both were former men of Unit Thirteen. One was Private Josiah Garland, who'd disappeared in the swamp on Roanoke. The other was Private John Parker, the same who'd left us the night prior.

Garland was dead, shot clean through the neck. He was pale, as if he'd been dead for days. His rifle lay loaded and unfired by his side.

Parker lived, though he'd been shot in the gut and gurgled blood. His rifle *had* been fired. We crowded around and knelt beside him. Meier stepped close and leaned down.

"You shot Alan, didn't you?" Meier reached forward to grab Parker, but I held him back. He looked at me with pure hatred in his eyes. "You know he did, Sergeant. He was the next best shot after us and Clark. And he had a witch working with him. You look me in the eyes, Sergeant Phillips, and you tell me he didn't shoot Alan!"

"We know he did, Private," I answered. "And he'll pay for it. Hell, he'll be dead in a bit and that's probably by your doing, if it makes you feel better. But he knows where she went, and we'll get that out of him before he goes, understand?"

In a huff, Meier snapped his head away and stormed off.

"Yeah, I shot him," Parker said in a weak voice. He formed a numb smile. "He was tryin' to kill my love, my sweetheart. She told me he'd do it too. She even put herself between us and the bullets that came for us. She tried to save us, but Alan shot us anyway. Didn't get her, though, try as he did."

I grabbed his collar.

"Why, John, why'd you do all this?" I asked.

His eyes took on a crazy look and his smile widened.

"You know why, Sergeant, you know why."

Meier stomped back up. "What's he mean by that?"

Greene put up a soft hand to hold Meier back.

"I mean, your Sergeant here loves her as much as I do," Parker said, and gurgled a spot of blood. "Don't you, Sergeant? She told me you did, she told me you were sweet on her, and why not? But she didn't love you like she did me, she told me that too. I was the only one that was worthy, she said. Garland over there, he was turning into one of those swamp beasts 'cause he wasn't worthy, but I was. We were gonna—"

He choked, spat, and groaned in pain.

"It's what she does, men, she addles your brain," Greene said. "Makes you love her; makes you want to do anything for her. In fact, your Sergeant Phillips here is the only one she couldn't turn."

I looked into Greene's eyes when he said this. Guilt grew inside me at the lie. I wanted to shout that I'd succumbed as well, that she'd entranced me, that if it hadn't been for Greene, she would've taken me too. Greene's look told me I should not do that, that the men needed this lie.

Meier and Cash stared at me in awe, and I said nothing.

"She's coming back for me, you'll see," Parker mumbled.

"Where'd she go, John?" Greene asked.

"She knew you'd be coming for her," Parker said. "She swam out into the sea, like a beautiful mermaid from one of those stories. But she'll be back to save me."

"I hate to tell you this, John, but she's not coming back," Greene said in a soft, soothing tone. "We killed her monster, and she's headed off again to sow death somewhere else. You're going to die soon, and you won't see her again."

"That's not true!" Parker snapped and followed it up with a bloody cough. His voice lowered to a near whisper and his gaze turned distant. "She's coming back for me, and she's gonna be my wife! She's got a mansion waiting for me in the Crescent City. I'll be a wealthy gentleman, with her on my arm. I'll drink wine, and eat roast every day. . ."

His words trailed off and his chest settled.

After waiting a few moments, Greene gently brushed his hand over Parker's face and closed his eyelids.

"Let's get these two back, so we can give them a proper burial," Greene said.

"Go boil your shirt, are you crazy? These sons of bitches?" Meier shouted.

"Dammit, Private, you will show our Lieutenant respect, or I'll whip you to kingdom come!" I shouted back. To be true, I wasn't all that sure myself that I agreed with Greene. I simply couldn't stand Meier speaking to him that way. "Look, I know you're fit to be tied, but let's hear him out. Lieutenant Greene, sir what do you mean by it?"

Greene, in his usual manner at moments like this, took his time to respond. He stood up, gave a great sigh, and looked at Meier with sad eyes. Then, he pointed at the dead man at his feet.

"John Parker here, and Josiah Garland over there," he said, and pointed to our other lost Marine, "were killed by that witch, not by themselves, or by you. She did this, and we'd all best remember that. These were our men,

men of Special Unit Thirteen. They fought and bled alongside us, and now they've died doing the job we're asked to do. One of the dangers of our job is unnatural, devilish witches like the one we've been tracking. Evil so great it can steal your mind. This," he pointed to Parker again, "could have happened to you, and don't tell me otherwise, because I don't rightly know if it couldn't happen to me. I've seen great men give into it. These men would never have been in a spot where this could have happened if we hadn't set out to do what it is we do. *This* is the danger of going out to fight the great evil we go out to fight. They died fighting it just the same as George Thompson, same as everyone we just lost fighting that sea monster, same as everyone we lost on Roanoke Island. The same as your friend Alan did. So, you see, if we don't honor *these* men, then we don't honor any of them. We keep faithful to each other, even those who succumb to these devils. We're telling everyone else that she killed them, because, in truth, that's exactly what she did. She robbed them of their faculties and forced us, forced *you*, to kill them. We'll bury these men at sea with the same honor we give everyone else who dies in this company. Do you understand me?"

Fighting back the water in my eyes, I nodded in agreement. Cash nodded as well.

Tears streamed down Meier's face, and he turned his head, ashamed.

"Yes, sir," he said.

"Good," Greene said. "Let's get to it."

The *Orion* was much worse for wear, but still seaworthy. She needed patches where the *Wabash* had hit her hull. They also shored up her insides with lumber, but I can't imagine the ship would ever be quite the same.

The *Mohican*, who'd missed the entire thing, loaned us a replacement howitzer. Commander Rodgers solicited sailors and marines from both ships to replace those we'd lost. When more volunteered than we needed, he selected the recruits himself. All those aboard the *Wabash* knew our purpose firsthand. Those aboard the *Mohican* had seen the distant battle, seen the aftermath, and heard tales from the *Wabash*.

Although Rodgers made it very clear that none were to write about the incident, in neither letters, journals, nor ledgers, he was incapable of suppressing the rumors. The crazy tale of the event would surely become popular scuttlebutt.

However, I realized afterward there was no need to fret over loose lips. While all messages and dispatches were to avoid any mention of our company or its activities, any reports by our many witnesses were, to a man, dismissed as the ravings of liars, lunatics, and swindlers. Once again, we were a camp canard and nothing more.

After seeing to all the injuries, recovering what lost we could, and paying respect to our fallen, Greene and I took a longboat back to the small city of Saint Augustine to inquire towards Miss Beauregard. We found her in the hospital. Though pale and weak, we were told she was recovering well.

"I have to say I'm greatly surprised to see you alive, Ellie," Greene said. I caught his gaze and gave him a stern look. Reluctantly, he added, "And relieved, of course. Naturally I'm relieved to see you alive."

I smiled at his addition.

"Though I have to say I'm not quite sure *how* you survived, Ellie," Greene said.

I rolled my eyes in surrender. I might have made an officer of Lieutenant Greene, but I would never make a gentleman of him.

"Death is too scared to come after me, you rest assured," Miss Beauregard replied, with a frail smile. Her gaze dropped. "I'm still rather embarrassed I couldn't tell it wasn't my Clarissa. Poor woman. She must've been dead for days before I got there, and I had no idea. How'd she even know to expect us?"

"That witch can fly as a bird, swim as a fish, make herself look like another woman, and mesmerize men," Greene said, and I clenched my fists. "She can go anywhere and find people to tell her what's going on.

She had two of our men under her control, one of them was with us the whole trip. For all I know, she flew up as a seagull and talked to Parker. Or, as we figured, she was down here with a plan, and we blundered into it with no better reasoning than 'Saint Augustine is a really old city'."

"She had a plan either way, sure enough," Miss Beauregard said. "And you boys handled that well enough, I hear tell. She must be all riled up right now. So, what're *we* fixin' to do?"

"Well, *you* are staying here until you're better, Ellie," Greene said.

"Oh, I'm not piddlin' around here, I'm hunky-dory," she replied and straightened herself up. "If there's fun to be had, you ain't leavin' me here. That dog simply won't hunt. So. What do we know?"

"Well, Parker said he and her were to be married and that they'd live in the Crescent City," I said. "'Course, the first part is balderdash, I'm guessing that's what she tells any man who falls for it. But I don't know what 'Crescent City' means."

"New Orleans," Greene supplied.

"Yeah, my hometown," Miss Beauregard said. "Might be it's time for me to go home. Oh, can you imagine what it'd mean to The Railroad if the Union were to take that city? Lord, Minty would be right jubilant if that would happen."

"You've mentioned Minty before, who is that?" I asked.

"Harriet Tubman, a good friend of mine," Miss Beauregard replied.

"Well, it's a trap, either way," Greene said. "And the Union Army's not taking New Orleans any time soon, anyway."

"What do you mean, a trap?" I asked.

"*Living in a mansion in Crescent City*" Greene quoted. "A woman like that doesn't need to give details like that, does she? She addles men's brains, and they do what she wants, isn't that how it works?"

"I suppose," I said.

"So, she supplied that little tidbit just so we would hear it," Miss Beauregard said. "She wants y'all to go lookin' for her there."

"And while you and I both know how easy it is to sneak in or out of that city, we can't exactly go in with a Company of Marines, can we?" Greene said. "It'd be suicide, even if it weren't a trap."

"You said the Union Army wouldn't be taking it any time soon, but it's exactly what the Union Navy wants to do," I said.

Both gawked at me as if I'd spoken Greek.

"That's what these squadrons have been doing," I continued, "or haven't you been paying attention? From the onset, we've been taking ports, trying to block them off from their shipping. That's the whole reason they got blockade runners in the first place is because we set up a blockade."

Greene continued to stare.

"Goddammit, Addy, you sure are smart when it comes to witches and demons and whatnot, but you're not worth a hill of beans when it comes to this war, are you?" I asked. "We've been cutting them off from the start. The Navy aims to take any city it can, and I'll bet you my boots they've got plans to take New Orleans."

"Yes, Alex, I understand that," Greene replied, sounding offended. "Why do you think I read all those reports they send me? They've got a Gulf Blockading Squadron, and that is something they'd *like* to do. But they got no way to do it, not by a jug full."

"Well, the least we can do is go see, isn't it?" I asked.

"Well, yes, of course, Alex, that is what we're going to do, as soon as I can get DuPont to release us," Greene grumbled. "I just don't see what good it'll do. They're not going to attack, you'll see, and we're not going into a city full of Southern soldiers, even if we can sneak in."

"Well, then, I best get ready to go," Miss Beauregard said. "Once again, even though it's a long way, I'll be there faster than green grass through a goose. My mother's old hairdresser, a woman of a great many talents, might know something about your white witch. In the meantime, while you sort yourselves out, if you would both please remind all your Yank brothers not to go sniffing around outside the town? The Blues are still out there, and while they won't find the muster to attack the town now their 'guardian angel' is gone, they can sure as hell cause a great bit of mischief everywhere else."

Casey Moores

Chapter 19: The Prussian

Departing was not as simple as we would have liked. For one thing, Beattie demanded several more days to get the *Orion* ready to move. Beyond that, it took a couple more to gather the supplies to make the voyage. Above all, Beattie was adamant to acquire both the approval of Captain DuPont and an escort for the journey around the great Florida Peninsula. When Greene inquired how quickly we might be able to contact Captain DuPont, we learned the man had been aboard the *Wabash* the entire time. It was, Beattie explained, his flagship.

In retrospect, this should have been obvious.

We were a bit confounded to learn this, as I would have imagined the man might want to meet the Union's monster hunters, since he had just seen a fight with an actual monster.

It was not until the nineteenth of March when we were finally summoned to the *Wabash* to meet with him. Even then, we received permission to board from the *Wabash's* duty officer and waited on deck for more than an hour. At that point, we met with Captain Rodgers (still a Commander by rank) who gave us a brief thanks for our "grit and efforts on that most peculiar night". We stood around on deck for another hour after that before we were escorted to Captain DuPont's quarters. During this whole time, I must remark on the great restraint displayed by my Lieutenant Greene. I spent the entire time fearing he would go into a conniption fit, yet he remained calm and quiet.

We entered the quarters and were directed to seats by the master, who did not introduce himself. DuPont sat at his desk, writing a dispatch, and did not acknowledge us at all when we were shown in. He had intense, intelligent blue eyes and a bushy mustache that wrapped around to an equally bushy beard under his chin.

Greene looked at me once while we waited and I put out a low, calming hand. Thankfully, he interpreted my signal to remain silent and still until addressed.

Sometime later, DuPont gave a great scratch at the parchment at which he toiled and sat up.

"Master Lang!" he shouted.

The master who'd shown us in dashed through the door.

"Aye, sir?"

"Have this sent at once to Lieutenant Budd on the *Henry Andrew*," DuPont ordered.

"Aye, Captain." The master retrieved the letter and disappeared.

DuPont directed his gaze on us and remained silent for more than a minute.

"I had wondered what it was this unusual detachment was meant to do," DuPont said.

Greene cleared his throat and opened his mouth to speak, but I gave him a short nudge. We had not yet been asked a question.

"I'm always suspect of those who I'm told to give *whatever support and courtesy the situation allows*," DuPont continued. "And my situation, when you arrived, was heavily devoted to *my* charge, which was shutting down as many Secesh ports as I am capable of holding. I appreciate that you felt some need to come down here to Saint Augustine, but I can scarcely imagine a fourth-rate ship and a handful of marines would have scared off the thousand or so rebel militia who held it."

We stared in response. I might have blinked.

"Now, obviously, the nature of your business has come to my attention, but I remain confused as to what your Marine Company would have done had it not been for a few broadsides from my flagship, which most certainly would not have been here had I approved your request to travel here on your own."

I could sense Greene tightening up. God bless him, he didn't budge.

"And now, with no reassurance whatsoever that those creatures, whatever they were, will not return, I find a request that you be released to join Captain--excuse me, that's *Flag Officer* Farragut in the Gulf Blockading Squadron."

Greene shifted, and I swear I could hear him screaming inside his own head.

"However, it seems you did little to deal with the beast that we could not have done without you," DuPont said, "and General Tom Sherman has raised a complaint that we are poorly utilizing his land forces. While I feel we could secure the area entirely with marines, especially those of your mettle, it seems I must succumb to the general's wishes. So, despite the fact that I've ordered the entire Marine Battalion under Major Reynolds to come south to guard the city, I'll have to send them away again as soon as they arrive. A shame, seeing as John Reynolds is a good man, and now I've got him sailing back and forth to no purpose. In any event, it would furthermore be seen as a sign of good faith for me to send your mysterious company away as well."

Greene opened his mouth, but DuPont preempted an interruption with a sharp, dismissive hand in the air.

"To that end," he continued, "there are several ships passing through, led by the new *Unadilla*-class gunboat *Pinola,* set to join Flag Officer Farragut. These should provide you safe passage on the way around the peninsula."

Greene and I glanced at each other. He'd calmed entirely. His lips parted slightly, but he still did not speak.

"One last thing, Lieutenant Greene," DuPont said. "I'd heard the incredible tale of Captain Greene at Molino Del Rey, but assumed it was mostly fictitious. I now suspect the tale might be true. If it is, I hope you will live up to his legacy."

He scratched out a signature on another letter, folded it and held it out.

"Here is a generic order assigning you to the Gulf Blockading Squadron," he said, and handed it to Greene. "That is all, you are dismissed."

Without either of us having said a single word, we stood, saluted, and left.

In a curious twist, on the twenty-second of March, after days of urgency and restlessness, Greene suddenly wished we would wait one more day. For one thing, we learned a contingent of sailors had been ambushed near the town of New Smyrna, well south of us. Greene wondered aloud whether any unearthly means had been involved and wished to investigate. Also, Reynolds and the Marine Battalion were expected to arrive within the next day.

Unfortunately for him, Lieutenant Commander Beattie and Lieutenant Crosby, captain of the *USS Pinola*, chose that day to inform us that all ships in the flotilla were prepared to depart, and that to delay would tempt poor weather. Greene had little say in the matter as he'd spent the previous days goading them into the exact action they were taking.

During the voyage, we received word of other happenings in the war. News had trickled in about a great victory in Tennessee, which had happened back in February. One of our generals, named Ulysses Grant, had taken Forts Henry and Donelson, demanding "unconditional surrender" of the forces there, which we all rejoiced to hear. However, everyone in our neck of the woods found it disheartening to hear the journalists call them the "Union's first great victories", as if everything we'd done up and down the coast counted for nothing.

Another piece of news was that two incredible new ships made of iron, one Union, one Confederate, had fought each other right near Hampton Roads. As the story went, the Rebels had raised the burned hulk of the *USS Merrimack* from the harbor at Newport, covered it in iron plating, renamed it the *CSS Virginia*, and wreaked havoc across the Union fleet at Newport News. The next day, the Union Navy's own ironclad ship, the *USS Monitor*, arrived to meet it. According to reports, the two had shot at each other for hours until, finally, the Rebel ship had retreated. The lot of us marveled at what iron-covered ships might mean for the future of naval warfare. For our part, we openly wished we'd had such a ship to fight the sea demon.

Early into the trip, the Captain of the *Pinola* invited Beattie and Greene to his ship for dinner. I accompanied them on the trip over, but, naturally, was expected to linger on deck while they drank and ate. I received a lot of inquiries from the small group of marines on board, as well as from some of the sailors, over what had happened at Saint Augustine. I frustrated all of them by explaining I was under orders not to discuss the matter.

Greene and Beattie emerged from the dinner heavily involved in a great discussion with an older gentleman who was not in uniform.

"Al-, uh, Sergeant Phillips, may I introduce you to Julius Kroehl," Greene said as we joined up. He had taken on the liveliness that told me he'd found someone he considered useful. "He's a Prussian, who was an artilleryman when he lived in Berlin. Correct me if I'm wrong, Mister Kroehl."

"No, please, you are doing a fantastic job," the Prussian said.

"He is assigned here as a submarine engineer, if any of you know what that means," Greene continued. "Pretty remarkable man. He has been a photographer and was an engineer for the Crystal Palace in New York. He was, at one point, to be a Union Army captain of pontoniers, but that regiment never mustered. He has some incredible ideas about an underwater ship."

"Ja, a *Unterseeboot*, or undersea boat," Kroehl said. "I'm not sure the military applications would be any more tremendous than, say, a hot air balloon at this stage, but it will be excellent for discovery and exploration."

"Oh, I'm sure we'll find some use for it," Beattie said. "And I say we'd better get moving on it before the Confederates come up with their own."

"Agreed, Commander," Greene said. "In any event, Mister Kroehl here has been hired mostly for his knowledge of *explosives*, specifically underwater explosives. He is to clear the Mississippi of torpedoes and support an attack on New Orleans in whatever manner he can."

"Explosives, sir?" I repeated.

"That's right, uh, Sergeant," Greene said. "And I've secured permission from Captain Crosby to bring him aboard with us, so we might pick his brain. I'm thinking Tomasini and Niculescu might be a perfect pair to learn what he knows. We can always find another couple men to use the rockets."

Greene left the "apprenticeship" to Kroehl open to volunteers, but strongly encouraged Tomasini and Niculescu to do so. Melvin Doyle was the only other volunteer. I must admit it was a little comedic to see the Prussian conversing with an Italian, a Romanian, and a

Newfoundlander. I can hardly imagine how any of them understood each other.

Kroehl was dismissive of the Ketchum grenade. He agreed it was a simple design, but opined that it would have a great chance of failure and be easy for the Rebels to catch and throw back. The Prussian found it hilarious when we pointed out the irony of the name "Ketchum". He joked the two armies might one day make a game of it.

The Hale rockets gave him great interest, and he wondered aloud if he could engineer something similar. This would have been tremendous, as most stores of the rockets had become barren as no one on either side had taken to producing them.

Despite my best efforts, word spread about our unit and its purpose. We found that certain items would mysteriously arrive on board with instructions notes that said, *<item> has been lost at sea, please ensure it is put to good use.*

We received barrels of gunpowder, boxes of shot, and even, astonishingly enough, a second howitzer. This gift let us expand the artillery contingent, with Daniels in overall command. He and Meeker each took charge of one howitzer and had dedicated Unit Thirteen Marines to man them. Archibald remained in charge of the rocket squad, in which Privates Edwards and Williams had been assigned to replace Tomasini and Niculescu.

The flotilla made a brief stop at Fort Taylor in Key West for supplies. Much as I'd heard grand stories about the Caribbean, I found it was not much more than bugs, sand, moisture, and heat, as well as a near constant breeze. The island had a small settlement around the Fort and a sizable fleet that seemed to have little to do. The sailors there confirmed they did next to nothing, aside from praying to avoid yellow fever. During the short stay, it occurred to me that it was, perhaps, the closest I'd ever been to the sort of place where pirates may have operated, in the olden days.

I'd dreamed of such things and played at being a pirate as a young boy in Philadelphia. We had always been told of the heroic exploits of the Navy and the Marines, but several of us always wanted to be the pirates as it sounded like a lot more fun. In the end, of course, I grew up and enlisted as a Marine in the precise hope I would hunt actual pirates. I'd never had the opportunity and, with my newfound purpose, assumed I never would.

At the start of April, we arrived at Ship Island. Dozens of ships lay anchored all about and thousands of troops were massed all about in bivouacs, the largest collection of troops I'd seen since Bull Run. I immediately recognized that such an immense force could only be intended to capture New Orleans.

I thought Greene would be thrilled to hear the news.

"I can't see how it does anything for us," he said. When I detailed my thoughts, he'd waved me along to search for Captain Beattie. We stomped along the deck, and he kept his voice low. "I've been thinking on this, and I should've discussed it with you sooner."

We passed down a hall toward Beattie's cabin. At this point, it was a standing order that Greene spoke with the captain whenever he wanted. He gave a solid knock on the hatch and an aide announced us.

"I'm not sure if it *is* in our best interest, after all, if the city is taken by the Union before we, um, go *hunting* there, as we say," Greene explained.

"Addison, come on in," Beattie shouted. We went into the room and sat. "I assume you're here to discuss the enormous assault force we have gathered here. Imminent attack on New Orleans, I suppose you've already guessed."

"Yes, Captain," Greene said. "But I'm still a bit lost as to the best way for our little company to proceed. This white witch we've been stalking has, as we've discussed, quite clearly set a challenge for us to meet her in the city. So, here's the issue I've been chewing on these past days. If the Union takes the city, we'll have to race in with the vanguard in a desperate attempt to locate her before the attack forces her to fly, or swim, or whatever, off again.

Casey Moores

Worse, I fear she may be setting a trap for the entire Army, or Navy, sorry, I'm not sure what I call both together. A trap, nonetheless, much as she tried setting at Saint Augustine, but this time with much grander designs. It could be a disaster if we can't head her off beforehand."

"Let me stop you for a second, Addison," Beattie said. "Let me discuss the options of approach, with specific respect to the West Gulf Squadron's plans. Lake Pontchartrain is entirely unacceptable for the attack. It is assumed that we'd need to push past numerous batteries, which would force a major naval engagement. That could include Confederate ironclads, and it *would* necessitate a land assault south to the city proper, against which they would be well-prepared. Once a land force moves away from Pontchartrain, the Navy could no longer support it, and the assault would be prolonged and very costly. So, Butler and Farragut, our respective Army and Navy commanders here, won't do that. Neither should *you* try to do that, as it would be obvious and suicidal. Any other land approach would be even worse."

"So, Captain, it's to be up the Mississippi, then?" I asked.

"Very astute, Sergeant Phillips," Beattie said, and he regarded me with a curious eye.

"Wait, how is that any better?" Greene asked and shifted in discomfort. "That's a long, windy way up that river to New Orleans. They could line the way with guns and block the river up with a handful of boats."

"You're thinking like a hunter, Addison, or an irregular. . . you're thinking about what *could* be done," Beattie replied. The captain looked back to me with the sides of his lip curled. "Sergeant, what do you think?"

"Well, sir," I responded, and I paused to parse my words. "There *is* a lot of river, but the Rebels only have so many men and guns. If they're that heavily ready for an assault from Pontcha-, uh, well, the lake you mentioned, which anyone with half a brain would be, and they'd also be covering a few other less likely approaches, so they'll be spread thin. Even if they gave up all the rest of it to line up the river, they'd still only have so many guns in one place while we'd have at least as many on all these gunboats shooting back. As to river boats, if the Confederate Navy ever makes any kind of showing in a stand-up fight against us, I'll eat my hat. I imagine they'd mass it into one spot and try to hold us there. If we break through that, our ships sail right up into the city itself. As soon as we put that many cannon in the middle of the city, it doesn't matter how many troops they've got there, we'll be able to tear their guts out. Pardon me, sir."

"Exactly, Sergeant," Beattie said with a chuckle, "and well said. We assume they'll try to hold us at Fort

Jackson and Fort St Phillips, which is quite a ways from the city, but the last good defensible spot. We get past that, any Confederates on the riverbanks will be nothing but gnats. As to ships on the river, they might cause us some trouble, but we'll beat them, just as you said."

"Fine," Greene said with clear irritation, "but that doesn't solve *our* problem. How does all that help us get into the city without having to fight our way through the entire complement of Southern forces all by ourselves?"

"Well, knowing all this narrows our options, sure, and I do concede it will be tricky," Beattie said.

"Sirs," I said. "There would be some opportunity, wouldn't there? If we could time it well, if we could put ourselves near the front of the fleet when everything goes in and get ourselves in among all the chaos, we might be able to catch her."

"That sounds too much like we're hoping to get lucky," Greene grumbled. "But for now, I suppose it's the best we got."

Chapter 20: Breaking the Chain

"**O**f all the miserable, no account ideas you've had, this one tops them all, Alex!" Greene shouted over the constant roar of cannon and mortar fire. We watched, helpless, from the deck of the *Orion* for the occasional flashes of light to see the progress. From the deck of the *Pinola*, Kroehl and Doyle struggled with wires and explosives on one of the small partially-sunk hulks, to which the Rebels had attached a chain that blocked off the river.

Preparations had continued for more than a week after our arrival. During that time, we learned the plan, as we'd guessed, entailed driving up the Mississippi and past the defenses. There, the Navy ships would threaten the entire city with their guns and an assault would be well supported and impossible to defend. In mid-April, the massive fleet steamed into the mouth and up the Mississippi.

There was little resistance until we reached the two forts. Both forts were built in the modern star-shaped fashion, constructed of red brick, and reinforced with logs and sand that could soak up bombardment. Fort Jackson was closer, south of a bend in the river, and its guns commanded the entire bend. Fort St. Philips lay on the opposite bank, further up the river. Its guns point straight down the river, where ships would have nowhere to hide. The chain stretched across near Fort Jackson, at a spot where both forts would be able to focus their fire. The crew of the *Orion* told me there were more than a hundred guns between the two, more than enough to blast the fleet to pieces.

For several long days, a small flotilla of mortar rafts attempted to pound the forts into rubble. Several days along, scuttlebutt said Rebel prisoners told us the mortars had nearly destroyed Fort Jackson. However, it still kept up a steady battery fire on any boats that steamed up to take a look. Beyond that, the chain remained.

Captain Farragut must have become impatient with the mortars, because he'd directed the *Itasca, Pinola,* and *Kineo* to attempt to break the chain. We went along to help, under the belief that as soon as the chain broke, the fleet would sail up the Mississippi, punch through the small Mosquito Fleet the Rebels had collected, and into New Orleans. If we got there quickly enough, we could track down the white witch and stop whatever plan she had concocted before our troops piled in. That was the hope, at least. Greene remained pessimistic.

"While I still have no better plan, I'm inclined to agree with you on the futility of this endeavor, Lieutenant," Beattie shouted. While the rest of the *Orion's* crew and Unit Thirteen fought to maintain the gunboats position and to fire the guns as steadily as they could at Fort Jackson, the three of us stared at the *Pinola.* "Damned fool's letting his ship drift too much against the current. If the wind picks up at all—"

As if goaded by his prophetic words, a gust blew past us at that very moment. The *Pinola*, now perpendicular to the current, could not maintain its position against the hulk where Kroehl had laid the explosives. In the flash of a rocket from Fort Jackson, we saw both Kroehl and Doyle watch, helpless, as the wires to their explosives pulled away and snapped. Both leaned against the rail and grabbed hold, as if they contemplated jumping out after their rigging. They did not. Across the water, we heard Kroehl unleash a stream of what I assumed to be Prussian cussing. The chain would not be blown apart with explosives.

The *Pinola* chugged slowly past us, heading back down river in defeat. Doyle shouted to us as they drifted along.

"Wires came loose, sir, we couldn't blow the charges!" he said. He threw his arms up in frustration.

"He's going to have to go back a few hundred yards before he can turn around to make another go of it," Beattie said. He scanned around, and then perked up and pointed. "Well, they've got the right idea!"

Greene and I snapped our attention to where we pointed. The *Itasca*, another new *Unadilla*-class gunboat like the *Pinola*, had anchored against another hulk and unloaded a team of men with picks and hammers. They attacked the hulk and the chain with fervor.

"Master Dawes, ahead quarter, one point starboard!" Beattie ordered. He turned to us. "I'll bring us in on the other side. Sergeant, get your Marines ready to help, at the double, man!"

I gave Greene a quick look, and he nodded with a slight smile.

"Unit Thirteen!" I shouted. "Axes, hammers, hatchets, whatever you can find, then form up on deck! No guns, just the tools!"

Beattie brought the *Orion* up to the hulk, where we tossed hawsers to the *Itasca*'s work party. I led a detachment from the company onto the hulk, directed some to take hold of the hawsers, and put the rest of us to work attacking the chain. The group of us got into a steady rhythm of powerful swings and cracks against the chain and the hulk. Though I didn't consider the source, the sky lit up more often so we could see our work.

Time seemed to stand still as I focused on the work at hand. My muscles ached in protest and my shirt soaked through with sweat, but by no means would I allow the men to see me let up.

One by one, we broke through the restraints on the chain, and then, finally, one of the men from the *Itasca* cracked through the chain itself. A great holler of joy swept through the team and the crews of both ships.

"Come now, back aboard!" I heard Beattie shout. "We've got to get clear before they sink us!"

At that moment, I realized the cannon fire from the fort had picked up its intensity. It seemed every gun on the south bank had focused on us.

"Flame rafts!" the duty officer shouted. We turned and saw a group of burning rafts drifting down the river toward us. The Rebels had tried sending such boats at our fleet before as they had low enough draft to get over the chain. Most had still gotten caught on the hulks or the bank and the few which had made it past had done little damage. These, however, looked to be coming straight at us.

"Mister Daniels, Mister Meeker, see to them!" Beattie ordered. "Marines, aboard now before we leave you behind!"

I grabbed a hawser line, gave my own frantic orders, and swore at the slowest moving men. Howitzers and rockets lashed out at the flame rafts, sinking one. Braced against the hulk, with the hawser wrapped around my arms as tight as I could make them, I continued to unleash a stream of imaginative profanity at Unit Thirteen. One by one, they jumped, climbed, struggled, and were hauled aboard by sailors onto the *Orion*. At long last, I was all that remained.

The pull of the ship overcame me and tore me from the unstable platform. With my arms wrapped into the hawser, I sucked in a deep breath of air and splashed into the river.

Casey Moores

Once again, my mind constructed an image of the larger of the evil creatures reaching up to ensnare me. I knew that the ones we'd faced were over a thousand miles away. I knew that the largest was most likely dead. I also knew, however, that our mark was suspected to be nearby, with some sinister plot to finish us all. Good sense would say she might have similar beasts in this river, waiting to swallow some poor Marine sergeant. I had also been told there were alligators in the river.

My lungs had started to beg for air, my hands burned against the rope, and my arms were nearly pulled from their sockets as I was hauled from the water.

I collapsed onto the deck of the gunboat and spat to clear my mouth of the putrid river water. While I regained my senses, I heard Greene arguing with Beattie.

"We're going the wrong way, you fool! New Orleans is that way!" Greene said. Beattie walked away from him as if attempting to escape, but then stopped and spun about.

"Yes, *Lieutenant*, but the river is still full of those fire rafts, and torpedoes as well, beyond which is the Confederate river fleet, which we know contains at least one ram ship," Beattie responded, leaning in and stabbing his finger to point up the river. "Meanwhile, *every single gun* from that fort and the next fort after it will be trained on us. We're still in the same pickle as if we'd tried to storm in by land, Lieutenant, we'd be fighting our way through all the Confederate forces by ourselves. What do you think our chances would be?"

"But what about this great fleet, Captain?" Greene replied. "I thought that when we broke this chain that his whole fleet would storm up the river to the city. Didn't we place ourselves here so that we would be at the forefront? I apologize for being short, Captain, and I understand that this ship needs to withdraw at this instant, but we'll still turn around and continue in shortly, will we not?"

"Lieutenant Greene, that will be the decision of Captain Farragut," Beattie answered. "I sailed up here in hope there would be a bigger break and that Farragut would be prepared to sail up the river immediately. If you look around, you'll see I was mistaken in that belief. I now realize Captain Farragut is right to proceed with caution. As things stand now, if I were in command of this fleet, I would take another day or two to better organize the fleet."

I stumbled to my feet, sopping wet and dripping, and staggered toward the pair.

"Alex, goddammit, where have you been?" Greene asked. "*Captain* Beattie here tells me that, although we've broken the chain, it might still be days before a proper assault proceeds up the river."

"Makes sense, sir," I said, "and there's our opportunity."

"What?" both officers asked.

Casey Moores

"Assuming we can find our way in some other way," I said. A chill ripped through me, and I shook.

"Explain, Sergeant," Greene said. Both men stared at me as if I'd turned into one of the ape beasts from Roanoke.

"Well, the chain's broken," I said. I fought the chill and straightened up.

"Thank you, Sergeant, but—" Greene began, with a dismissive wave of his hand.

"The *Pinola*'s on fire!" shouted one of *Orion*'s lieutenants. We flew to the rails to see. The *Pinola* lay stuck against the far bank, covered in flames. I could pick out the shadows of sailors rushing about with buckets, in a desperate fight.

"Good lord, if it reaches their magazine, they'll be blown to pieces," Beattie said.

"Kroehl is on that ship!" Greene said.

"And Doyle too," I replied in admonishment. He looked at me and gave an embarrassed nod in agreement.

"Hard to port, bring us alongside them!" Beattie ordered.

"Didn't you say they are about to explode?" Greene asked.

In a low, chilling tone, Beattie replied, "I said they *might* explode. If we get there before they do, perhaps we can avoid that fate. If we arrive after, we can rescue their survivors."

"And if we arrive *as* they explode?" Greene asked.

Beattie tilted his head and shrugged.

When we drew up alongside them, Beattie cheered and noted they'd gotten the door to the magazine closed. Whoever had done so had given them the time they needed to douse the flames. Our two ships escaped down river, away from the flame rafts and Fort Jackson's guns.

Once safe, the officers regrouped, and we resumed our discussion.

"All right, Sergeant, you were saying?" Greene asked me. "So, the chain's broken, but we're not attacking yet. How does that help us?"

"The Rebs are gonna know the game's up, sir," I continued. "City's gonna be a mess. If Captain Farragut wants to take his time and do this right, we have until he decides to sail up this river to make our way in and do what we need to do."

A cannon ball exploded close behind us. Everyone on deck flinched, except the three of us. Greene formed a smile and locked eyes with me.

"Captain Beattie, would you please take us to Barrataria Bay?" Greene asked.

"Barrataria Bay?" Beattie snorted. "There's miles of swamp between the closest I can get you and the city. Even if you can find the way. . ."

"I know the way, Captain," Greene said.

Greene and I looked at Beattie in triumph. Beattie glanced back and forth between us.

"Okay, then," Beattie said. "Okay. I'll still need to get permission from Captain Farragut and General Butler."

"Understood, Captain," Greene said. "If you would, please see if you can find out when they plan to attack."

"If that's all settled, sir," I said. "Then please excuse me. We need to make sure our men get as much rest as possible before we set out."

Chapter 21: Lafitte's Trail

"**A**nd I tell ya, this gunner's mate was top rail, I say," Doyle told us the story of his time on the *Pinola*. "I t'ought, well we all t'ought, the flames'd get into the magazine, and we'd all be done for. But that man, he runs into the magazine, on his own hook, see, and he shuts himself in with it. Can y'imagine? Flames everywhere ya can see, and this one, he *runs into* where all the powder and shot and everyt'ing is stored, right into the Devil's teeth ya might say, and, just. . ." Doyle straightened and spread his hands apart with great drama. ". . .closes the door. I's ready to jump, I was. We all were. And there was no way to know, not by a jug full, whether simply closing the door would've stopped it. Which means he shut off his only means of getting out, ya see? Saved the ship, he did. Saved us all."

"Did you get his name?" one of the others asked.

"Fearsby, or Frisbee, or somet'ing like that," Doyle answered.

"Hey!" someone called out from the next boat forward. I turned to look and saw them motion their hands down, and they pointed behind them to the trees. We were leaving the Bay and entering the swampland around it. It had taken a full extra day to receive permission from Farragut to separate from the fleet. Captain Beattie had created the premise that our mission would serve as a diversion and that, even if our cause was doomed, it might help to cause a panic in the city and convince the general in charge to withdraw. I hoped the first part wasn't true, whether the other part was or not.

Even after receiving permission, the trip to exit the Mississippi and circle back around to Barrataria Bay carried us into the afternoon that day after the chain had been broken. We had no word on when the Navy planned to sail up the Mississippi to New Orleans, and Greene's impatience took on a life of its own.

"All right, men, we're into the teeth of the Devil ourselves now, let's quiet down," I ordered.

As we rowed half a dozen longboats in a narrow waterway out of Barrataria Bay, we did all we could to remain as silent as possible. I don't know if we needed to bother, as the frogs, crickets, birds, owls, and myriad insects created a hell of a racket. I'm not certain anyone outside a hundred yards would have heard us fire a volley. The mortar and cannon fire at Forts Jackson and St Phillip hadn't let up, we'd heard it until we left the Bay, but there was not the slightest hint of it where we were, only a few miles to the west.

I did my best to keep my eyes, and my mind, off the putrid, brackish water and what might have been in it. For all I knew, the witch swam beneath us, summoning every swamp creature she could find. For all I knew, we were blundering into the very trap she'd set for us.

Reason told me there were countless miles of swamp, and that, even if she had been a bird or a fish or something, finding us would have been near impossible for her to do. Reason told me that, but my heart told me otherwise. I spent the whole journey ready to grab my shotgun at any moment and reminded the others to be ready as well.

I could only imagine that the rest of the company stayed on edge as well. Our two major experiences had been in a swamp and in the water. For several long hours, we drifted slowly through both.

Greene sat in the lead boat and directed our passage. I could not fathom how he knew which of the many random, interlocking routes through the swamp to take. To me, every tree, fallen tree, and stump looked that same as another I'd just seen. Every other waterway we passed by seemed to reappear a short while later- the same view, repeated endlessly. We had departed late in the morning, and the evening approached. However, it was that Greene found the way. I knew there was no way he would find the way in the dark.

"Do you think the Lieutenant might be lost, Sergeant?" Cash asked me.

"Go boil your shirt, Sam," I replied. "Out of all of us, he's the only one who might *not* be lost. You better pray he isn't, or we may spend the rest of our days in here."

I was in the third longboat, with Meeker behind us and Daniels in the sixth, which was last. We'd left behind all overt accoutrements that announced us as Union soldiers, aside from our coats, of course, which we'd have to settle later. We'd also left the rifles behind to keep from standing out, so we carried only our shotguns, carbines, knives, axes, and swords. Each boat carried two small barrels of powder and a few boxes of shot. Those of us with special cartridges had only what we could carry. The only one to keep his rifle was Meier, who said he'd be damned to leave the Whitworth behind. Greene allowed it.

Knowing we had a shortage of firepower and assuming we needed them more than they, the officers of the *Orion* had supplied us with every sword and pistol they could find with cartridges to match. Thankfully, it meant that most of our sergeants and corporals had one of each. They'd only had a couple hours to familiarize ourselves with the pistols before we launched, but it was better than not having them.

Our final gift from Beattie was the ship surgeon, a Marylander named Jack Shilling. From his reaction, I deduced he had no part in the decision.

None save Greene had any idea how we would find our quarry. Although he and Miss Beauregard had claimed the witch left the clue about New Orleans as a trap for us, I did not mention such to the men. It would definitely have led to an immediate mutiny. Unfortunately, I didn't believe he knew what awaited us there. I found myself forced to put my full confidence in whatever plan Greene had, though I felt guilty that I hadn't fully told the men what might await us. It ate at me.

"I swear we're being watched," Cash remarked.

A low whistle from the boat ahead of us caught my attention. When I looked up, I saw Clarke pointing off into the trees and bushes. In a low voice and with a hand beside his mouth, Clarke called, "The coloreds are a freeman's militia. Greene says they're letting us pass."

Curious as to what he meant, I stared off into the foliage. I nearly jumped when I discovered a colored man holding a musket, still as could be, no more than ten feet away from us. He squatted next to a bush and stared at our contingent. I repeated the message to the rest of the boat and gave instructions for the last man to tell Meeker's boat.

We saw a great many more of the men or, possibly, the same men several times, before we came to a great embankment of black mud where Greene and the next boat up had pulled ashore.

Greene met me as we pulled up.

"Glad the militia found us, I'd followed Lafitte's trail about as far as I knew," Greene said. "And I'd have been totally lost in the dark."

Confounded, I raised an eyebrow. He *had* almost gotten us lost, if not for dumb luck.

"Lafitte?"

"Pirate, a few years back," Greene said. "Saved the city from the British, according to the residents."

"And you led us in here, knowing you could only get us so far?"

"Get the men off for a spell, and gather them up," Greene said. "You and I have some words to give them, and some work to do. In the meantime, set them to covering their coats with the mud."

The order got passed around and, although there were a few grumbles, the men proceeded to darken their coats with fetid, black mud. In the trees, I discovered another group of armed colored men at the outskirts of the embankment. Most of them watched outward, only a few gave us the occasional glance over their shoulders. Greene came to me after a few minutes and asked me to gather the men up.

"Keep to your work there, men, we can't go into a Southern city looking like Northern Marines," Greene said.

A large number smiled at that. A few kept working, but most stood still and awaited his words.

"You men are a part of what the Marine Corps calls 'M Company'," Greene explained, his voice loud enough for all to hear. "But I hope you all know, by now, that our true title is Special Unit Thirteen." He pointed to one of the newer recruits. "Can you tell me what we do, Private?"

The private turned pale and panned his head around at the others.

"Sir, we, uh, we fight sea monsters, sir," he said. Some of the others chuckled.

"That is one thing we have done, yes," Greene said. He pointed to Van Benthuysen. "Sergeant, can you explain what it is we do?"

Sergeant Van Benthuysen straightened and projected confidence. "Lieutenant Greene, sir, we fight the monsters our enemy employs against us."

"That's closer to the mark, Emile," Greene said. Some of the newer men gasped. Greene looked at me. "Alex, what is it we do?"

"Sir, the short answer is that we fight monsters, yes," I said. "Per your words, Lieutenant, evil, and *monsters,* as we say, are always out there, but they're rare, unique even, hard enough to find that they're tall tales, fables, and scary stories for kids most of the time. But they come out of hiding when there's a big war. They collect, they're mustered up by the Devil or who knows what. It's our job to track them down and nip them in the bud."

"That's right, Alex," Greene said. "Our enemy is not the Southerners, per se. It seems the ones we're hunting are doing what they can to help them out, but our fight is specifically with that evil, not the South directly. Now, can you tell me what we're doing here?"

He pointed to another new hire.

"Uh, sir, this is just where the generals sent us," the Private said. A few men laughed. Greene pointed at one of them.

"What do you think?" he asked.

"I heard we tracked those sea monsters from Saint Augustine here, sir." Some nodded their heads, and some shook their heads.

"Paul?" Greene asked, looking at Meier.

"Parker told us she'd be here," Meier replied, with a chill in his voice.

"Who?"

"The witch."

Gasps and grumbles emerged all around. A few muttered their disbelief, some went pale in shock, but a few stood like statues, knowing the truth of the matter. I hadn't realized the men had been so torn on the subject.

"That's right, Paul," Greene said. "The white witch, who raised those swamp apes to send against us in Roanoke, who commanded those sea monsters against us in Saint Augustine. The one who turned Parker and Garland against us and made them shoot poor Alan Conyers. She can fly like a bird, she can swim like a fish, and she can take over your mind if you let her.

"Just like Paul here said, Parker gave us a message that we'd find her here. Now, here's the problem that we haven't told you. She gave us that message, through Parker. She wanted us to come here to her. She's got a trap waiting for us and, I'll be honest, we're walking right into it. But, before you all get huffy, let me tell you we'll do it on our own terms. We'll figure out her game, and we'll beat her. Whatever it is she's got planned, it's probably just as much to break our attack on the city as it is to break us specifically. But we're not going to break, are we?"

"No, sir!" a large number replied, but not all. I'd voiced to Greene my concern about the men not knowing what we faced. He'd laid it all out, and I was greatly relieved.

"Sir!" shouted Wilkes. "I've gotta ask something, sir. How are we to know she didn't take Sergeant Phillips as well? Enough of us saw him there, on Roanoke, just standing there, doing nothing."

The blood drained from my face. It had not occurred to me that some men might have wondered what happened to me that night.

Van Benthuysen made a move toward Wilkes, with rage on his face, but Greene stopped him.

Shouts, both for and against me, erupted throughout the group. Even the fresh fish seemed to opine one way or the other. Men started to shove each other. I feared the company might become too wrathful to handle. The militiamen out in the trees took notice and watched us with concern.

As the ranking sergeant, I knew I should be the one to break up the row before it happened. However, seeing as I was the cause, I found myself frozen.

"That's enough!" Greene shouted. He'd drawn his pistol, but pointed it to the ground. He was still as relaxed as ever. The fighting ceased. With his free hand, he pointed at me. "This man is your commander. I know I was given the job, but I'm really just your guide. I just happen to be the one who knows the most about what we're doing. But, you all know damn well I don't know a thing about being a Marine, or an officer, outside of what this man has taught me."

"Now, I know some of you saw, and probably all of you have heard, what happened on Roanoke Island. Let me tell you what happened. That woman, this white witch we're chasing, well she took Parker and Garland like that," he snapped his fingers. "Blink of an eye, a few soft words, and they were jelly in her hands. But your sergeant. . .well, Alex, why don't you tell them?"

Fear and anger battled within me. I feared they might be right, that she might still have some control over my mind. I feared they were right not to trust me. However, from somewhere else inside me, rage boiled up. As much as I knew they had a right to wonder, I was enraged that they did.

"It's as he said, men," I said, fists clenched, muscles taught. "I didn't know who she was, or why a woman like her was there, so I went to see if she needed help. Oh, but in that moment, when she spoke, she became the loveliest woman I'd ever met. Somehow, I believed in an instant that we were destined for each other, that she was an angel sent from heaven just to make my life perfect. She's powerful, that's all I can say. Stopped me in my tracks."

"See! She bewitched him!" someone shouted from the back. I didn't recognize the voice. A few murmured in agreement, while some shouted to let me speak. I raised my hands to quiet them.

"But then she asked me to do something," I said. "She said I should set to killing all of you. She told me that you all wanted to hurt her, and that I must defend her by killing you. As beautiful as she was, as charming as she was, as much as I truly desired for her to be mine. . . I mean, Lord help me, she even made me forget my sweetheart, back in Philadelphia. But she asked me to take arms against you, and, well, I couldn't. . . I just, I *wouldn't. . .*"

"I was there, and Nick too, and Tomasini, you saw," Greene said. "While we snuck up on her, I heard her promise him the world. I heard her tell him to turn against us all. He didn't budge. Easy enough for any woman to steal our hearts, right boys?" A large number chuckled. "But a witch, with the Devil's magic? She turned poor Parker and Garland against us, so much so that Parker, completely possessed by that witch, killed

Alan Conyers. But she couldn't beat Alexander Phillips. This man, the *true* leader of Unit Thirteen, kept his faith in us, and I'm going to keep my faith in him. Leo, what do you say?"

Greene shot Tomasini a look.

"I didn't see or hear much, sir, but Nick did," Tomasini said. "Nick, what'd you see?"

"Sergeant, good, yes," Niculescu said. "*Vrăjitoare*, uhh, the weetch, she. . . no!"

He waved his hands apart outward.

"Nick says the sergeant's top rail," Tomasini said, and he turned to look at me. "Sergeant Phillips, you are the finest man in this company, and I got a dose of hot lead for any coffee cooler what says otherwise. You have my faith, Sergeant."

"You have my faith, Sergeant," Niculescu said as well.

"Our sergeant pulled me straight out of the mouth of those sea beasts," Cash shouted. "Same ones that ate poor George Thompson. You have my faith, Sergeant."

"You heard it, men," Greene said. "We're going to keep our faith in him. Moreover, we're going to keep our faith in each other. Remember that, above all. We will always be faithful to each other, we will stand together, and we will keep our honor. Remember that, and she cannot beat you. She cannot take your mind."

I looked around. There were no more arguments and no more disagreement. None cast suspicious glances toward me.

"All right, then," Greene said. "If that's done, then I'm assigning your Sergeant Alex Phillips to lead us into the city."

I blanched, but held my bearing.

"With the help of our new guides. These men are with the First Louisiana Native Guards. Free colored men who," he put up a hand to forestall protestation, "Muster for the Confederacy. Now, now, before you all opine on the matter, let me explain. Our circumstances make for strange bedfellows, as they say. First of all, they are men of New Orleans. That is their allegiance and this peculiar matter between the North and the South is of no concern to them. They know that something is rotten in their city, something wicked and evil, and they know we are here to fight it. So, they are going to get us into the city. From there, we'll be on our own.

"Well, that's done. Now, let's check each other's coats one more time, make sure we do not, in any way, look like Union soldiers. Because we're about to sneak into a Rebel city, dodge whatever trap has been laid for us, and we're going to kill this witch."

A dull roar of approval emerged, just as quickly quieted by the sergeants and corporals. Greene smiled and nodded to me.

"All right, you heard him," I shouted. "Check your coats, check your arms, and load back up!"

As the men gathered themselves and prepared to rebound the boats, Greene clapped me on the shoulder.

"I think you give me too much credit, sir," I said in a hushed tone.

"I don't think I give you enough, Alex," Greene said. "With God as my witness, this will be your company soon enough."

Chapter 22: The Crescent City

When we resumed our trip toward the city, the Louisiana Guard supplied each boat with two men as guides. One stood at the front and gave hand signals to the other, who sat at the back and steered.

"Captain Louis Golis," ours said, to introduce himself. His last name was pronounced "go-lee". His accent was a strange sort of rough, guttural French, but he enunciated his words better than most men I knew.

I will admit, it was a great surprise to learn the colored man who guided us was an officer. I did not think such a thing existed. During the trip, however, I learned most of the officers in their militia were colored. Captain Golis assured me that their high-ranking commanders, who were not colored, had no knowledge of our machinations.

He shifted in discomfort and glowered at me every time I called him "sir".

I pried into why he and all the others would join a cause that sought to maintain the enslavement of their kind. He explained that his family had been free for generations, that they had been successful in New Orleans and considered one of the more prominent families. When the war started, a call had gone out to protect and defend the city, and it had been his duty, and the duty of all the others, to keep the city safe.

"It is the same duty," Captain Golis explained, "that put me in this boat with you, tonight. The city will fall, and, maybe, we can hope, there will be no fight. Even now, General Lovell knows he will lose his forts down there, and he's moving troops and guns out of the city as fast as he can. I do not think he will surrender, but I do not think he will fight. But there are others, the Brotherhood, and I think they will fight. You will fight them, which is why we bring you to the city. That is what Madame tells us."

"The Brotherhood, sir?" I asked. "Madame?"

He shrugged. That was all I could get from him.

We rowed the line of longboats through the labyrinthine channels of the swamp. For the first couple hours, there was no moon and we paddled in near darkness. Yet, the militia guided us along with confidence. A waning half-moon arose at about the same time we saw the first dim lights of the city.

After gliding past a tall levee, we emerged from a canal onto the Mississippi itself. We'd appeared, almost as if by magic, in the heart of the city. Endless rows of docks stretched into darkness along the opposite bank. The water was so calm I could barely tell that it flowed.

"Sir, are we in the city now?" I whispered.

He whipped his head around, and his eyes burned straight through me with anger. His finger flew to his lips and pressed hard. With trepidation, the captain searched up and down the docks. At length he calmed, but pressed his finger to his lips once more before he returned his attention to the river ahead.

After his silent admonishment, I realized I could hear a great number of distinct voices from across the river, though I could not see well enough to determine the sources. With shame, I remembered how well the sound carried over calm water.

It was unnecessary, but I repeated the gesture for the benefit of the other soldiers in our boat.

We followed the southern bank for a while and crossed just before a massive right bend. With expert precision, our two militiamen led us up against an empty, gas lit dock. As I scanned the dock, light spread over our boat from the opposite direction.

"Hey, boy!" a gruff, Southerners voice called out. "What you got goin' on over there?"

Every head on our boat snapped over to look. A solitary confederate soldier stood on the next dock over with a lantern in his hand. As my eyes adjusted, I could make out sergeant stripes on the arms of his gray jacket.

"Don't say a word," Golis warned me in a whisper.

Captain Golis' eyes went wide, and his demeanor softened, as if he'd transformed into a curious child.

"Yessuh, sorry suh," he said. "Suh, I's jus' takin' dese soldiers up da street, suh. General Lovell wanted us to move some soldiers to protect General Beauregard and Senator Slidell's wives in case da Yanks come 'fore we can get dem out. I's jus' doin' what I's tole', suh."

"General Lovell's orders, you say, boy?" the sergeant asked.

Golis nodded, still wide-eyed and looking scared.

"You, there, you the one in charge of this group?" the sergeant asked, looking at me. I stood, almost lost my balance, and nodded. He smirked as I stumbled. "Okay then, boy, you take 'em to go watch the women."

"Yessuh," Golis said.

The sergeant walked away and led a small group of soldiers down a street, away from us.

"We should have a little time before another patrol comes," Captain Golis said, his voice once again deep and commanding, his bearing stiff and noble. "Let's move before these morons have a chance to think twice."

"Yes, sir," I replied. He glowered at me. I waved my men off the boat.

My group of marines gathered on the dock as the next boat drew up. Golis left the boat under the care of the man who'd steered. While more boats pulled up, Golis led my contingent away from the docks, across a street, and across a great square. He took us toward a tall, white building with three black spires. We crossed the street and turned west along the large, drab mason building that sat next to the cathedral. As he led us through a great entryway with a heavy iron gate, I discerned the purpose of the building.

"Sir, is this a prison?" I asked.

"It was," he replied. "But no longer. It was a barracks for soldiers, but they left this morning. There is more than enough room for your men."

"Well, sir, I do not mean to argue, but is there any better place?" I asked. With only one way in or out, it was the perfect spot for someone to lay a trap. I found myself losing trust in the captain.

"No, Sergeant, there is not," he said. "No one will be looking here, and no one will think anything of it if they find men here. Anyway, there's fresh bread in there, I got a cook inside with a few pots of jambalaya."

I had no idea what that was, but I did not ask.

"Captain, I mean no disrespect, sir, but I'm not crowding our men into a prison where they'll be easily trapped if the Conf-, I mean, the *other* Confederates catch wind of us being here. It's not that I don't trust *you*, sir, but this is, it's just. . ."

"Problem, Captain?" Greene asked, as he approached from behind with his group.

"No, there is no problem," Golis answered, keeping his eyes on me. "Your sergeant wonders if a prison is the best place to keep your men. I assure him it is. Madame has said this will be a good place."

"You hear that, Alex?" Greene said. "If Madame Laveau says this is a good spot for us, then it is a good spot for us."

"But, sir—"

"This will do fine, Captain," Greene said to Golis. "And thank Madame Laveau for me, if you would."

"Laveau?" I asked.

"I don't know about you, Alex, but I'm played out," Greene said. "Captain Golis, sir, you and your company have my great thanks for getting us here safely."

Golis nodded, though he maintained his stern expression, almost looking as if he were in pain.

"Bon, get some rest," he said. "Tomorrow, Miss Beauregard will meet you in the Cathedral when it opens."

"And you, Captain, what are your plans, sir?" Greene asked.

"We've done our part, Lieutenant, it's all on you now, *comprenez-vous*?" Golis asked.

"Yes, Captain, sir, I understand," Greene asked. Without another word, the captain stalked off, collecting his men as he went.

"My, do I smell a jambalaya in there somewhere?" Greene asked. "I tell you, Alex, they got the finest food in the New World in this city."

It might have been my terrible hunger, but I soon learned he might have been right. Jambalaya turned out to be an unusual blend of rice, meats, vegetables, and spices. Though I could not identify everything in it, it was delicious. The company cleaned out the cook's pots in no time.

After gorging myself on jambalaya, I verified the men had set themselves up in an orderly manner and set a watch schedule. I checked around the entire prison to see if there were any other doors or gates. There were none, as it was a very old style of prison. I found no windows, save a few at the top with thick iron bars all across. Even if one could pry the bars out, there were no ladders and we'd foolishly not brought any rope. It would not have surprised me if it had been built sometime around the founding of the city. After reconnoitering, I joined and stood the first watch myself.

"Sorry for all the fuss and subterfuge, Addy," Miss Beauregard said, as she led us down various streets and away from the river. "But I can't exactly have some rough looking soldiers come calling on John Slidell's wife, now can I? Can you imagine the scandal that would be? And you boys are certainly pretty rough looking right now."

It had taken some work to rouse Greene from his slumber, and he remained groggy as we trekked through the city. Miss Beauregard had been waiting in the Cathedral, dressed in a fine, billowy blue dress with pink flowers. She rushed us out as soon as she saw us and explained that we were her escort, and that we should act the part.

We still wore our dirt-covered coats, and they still didn't show much blue. We only carried our pistols and knives, so that we'd be less noticeable.

I saw a sign that read Burgundy Street as we made a right turn. After traveling several blocks on it, she directed us to a door in a narrow alley.

"This is the servant's entrance, again, I hope you don't mind," she said, seeming to be more embarrassed than I thought was warranted.

We walked through a kitchen where a collection of colored servants were cooking, cleaning, and generally rushing about. They stopped abruptly, bowed their heads, and cleared a path for us as we passed through. I noticed some gawk at our outfits, but I wasn't sure whether that was due to the dirt caked on them or the underlying color.

"Is there any coffee in here, Ellie?" Greene asked.

"Well, you're quite lucky, Addy, there's not much in the whole city but I told Mathilde to make sure she had some."

"Mathilde?" Greene asked.

"All in good time, Addy, we'll make introductions shortly," she said. We left the kitchen into a hallway, and she pushed us into a cloakroom.

"Change into those, if you wouldn't mind," she said, pointing to two sets of clean clothes laid out on a table. We both changed into gray trousers and cream shirts, presumably to be more presentable to the ladies of the house.

Once changed, she led us further down the hallway, which led to a grand foyer with a great staircase winding up to the second level. Just before the staircase, we went through French style doors into a large sitting room. Two women in expensive dresses sat on couches. They looked similar enough to be related, with dark hair, brown eyes, and prominent noses. One had a round face with puffy cheeks, while the other had a long face. The long-faced one was much paler than the other and seemed frail.

By their austere expressions, I got the impression they disapproved of our presence. A large, well-dressed colored man stood against a far wall. He stood tall and erect, with a blank expression as if he were a statute. I guessed his purpose was to protect them from us.

"This is them?" the round-faced one sneered.

"Yes, Mathilde, this is them," Miss Beauregard replied. "May I introduce Marine Lieutenant Addison Greene and Marine Sergeant Alexander Phillips?" She turned to us and gestured toward the round-faced woman. "Addy, this is Mathilde Slidell, this is her house, and her sister, here," she pointed to the other woman, "Caroline Beauregard, who's my cousin-in-law. They are the daughters of the Deslonde family."

"I am honored to meet both of you fine ladies," Greene said.

"Madame Slidell, Madame Beauregard," I said, with a respectful nod of my head. I had not the courage to ask, but I wondered if Caroline Beauregard might be the wife of *the* General Beauregard, one of the Rebel generals who'd led troops against us at Bull Run. The thought that such might be the case made me consider the strange turn of events that had led me there.

"Would they like any sort of refreshment?" Madame Slidell asked.

"Well, Addy here said he'd be very grateful for some coffee," Miss Beauregard said. "Alex, would that work for you, too?"

"I would much appreciate it, Miss Beauregard," I replied, with another nod. Madame Slidell rang a bell, and a short, wide-eyed servant came to receive the order.

"So, you say they're here to deal with the Brotherhood?" Slidell asked. In a dramatic fashion, she turned her head to look out the window. "I don't see how that's our concern. Moreover, wouldn't that be bad for the cause, with which both our husbands are closely tied? The Brotherhood is on *our* side, are they not?"

It occurred to me that I still didn't know who the Brotherhood was, but it didn't seem my place to ask just then.

"The Brotherhood is on *their own side*, Maddy," Miss Beauregard said in a huff. "And I thought I had told you that Madame Laveau claims the Brotherhood means to do something horrible."

"*Madame* Laveau!" Slidell spat. "That old hairdresser? You're taking your orders from her now, then?"

"Look," Miss Beauregard said, "this city is going to fall one way or the other and you know it—"

"No, we do not," Slidell retorted.

"—Even General Lovell knows it," Miss Beauregard continued, unperturbed. "Troops and guns and horses and whatnot are all fixing to skedaddle. This city is lost to the Confederacy until someone's *husband*," I noticed her glance toward Madame Beauregard, "finds the time to come take it back. When he does, I wish him a great victory, I truly do, but right now the city is done and the Brotherhood, from what I hear, have some crazy plan to burn the city so the Union can't have it."

"That may be," Madame Beauregard said, speaking for the first time and in a wispy voice, "but what do you want from us?"

"Word about the goings on of the Brotherhood are scarce as a hen's teeth," Miss Beauregard said. "I was hoping you might have some idea where they might be meeting up these days. That's it. Point these boys in the right direction and help me save your city."

"No reason to get all bowed up," Madame Slidell said. "If you want to send these boys to their death, that's fine with me. Only, no one knows where they all meet up, anyhow."

"Well, all I'm asking is that we talk about it," Miss Beauregard said. She took a seat in an ornate chair by one of the two large windows. "No harm in that, now is there?"

I wondered if we were meant to sit, but Greene did not budge. The servant arrived with two china cups, full of coffee, set onto two small plates. I could only assume they could have offered cream and sugar, but they did not, so I did not ask.

The three women chattered on for the next couple hours while we stood by, silent. They gossiped about all the comings and goings of various families. They discussed the scandals concerning which members of which families had been seen with which members of other families. Interspersed throughout, I heard them mention the abandoned properties of northern families. Some had been broken into and looted by the "rougher elements" of the city, some had been carefully protected by General Lovell, and yet others had become barracks for Confederate soldiers. A few had even been gifted by the mayor to loyal Southern families.

At no time, during the entire discussion, did any of the ladies reference us in any way. I also noted that they never discussed the witch we sought. Greene and I simply stood there, knees and feet aching, while they prattled on about the wealthy families of New Orleans. I found it necessary to shift from time to time to avoid letting my legs fall asleep, but I also tried to do so as little as possible so that I would not appear to be fidgeting.

"All right, then," Miss Beauregard stated, "I think that gives us a good place to start."

Not a single word had been spoken which seemed in any way related to our mission.

"I thank you ladies for the fine hospitality," Greene said with a slight bow. "Please, don't trouble yourselves on our account."

I bowed as well, but remained silent. Miss Beauregard rushed us out of the sitting room and back to the cloak room. The two ladies did not acknowledge our departure.

"Probably best you remain in the trousers I gave you, but put your coats on," she said. "You gentlemen are going to take me on a tour of the city, see if we can find a sinister looking spot."

"I don't suppose we could get something to eat, Ellie?" Greene asked, and I was glad he did. The cook Golis had supplied had been baking bread when we'd left. We'd had nothing of sustenance except the one small cup of coffee.

Casey Moores

"Oh lord, I'm so sorry," she replied. "Come on, let's fill up those breadbaskets. Normally we're a lot more hospitable down here. . . well Addy, you know. . . but today you *are* the enemy in a city that's about to fall."

Chapter 23: The Search

"All right, Ellie, I'd like to start with the Henderson, Wilmot, and Anthony residences," Greene said as we left through the servant's door. I recognized the names from the conversation, but could not recall any details about them.

"Sir, is there a chance we can stop by to check on the men?" I asked.

"No time, Alex," Greene replied. "We wasted an enormous amount of time just getting here. There's no telling when Farragut's sailing in here, and we've got to stop whatever it is the Brotherhood is planning before the Union Navy arrives."

"This way," Miss Beauregard said, and led us up a street, further away from the water.

"Addison, that's another question that's been sitting with me," I said.

"Well, just look who's getting all familiar," Miss Beauregard said, and she cast a smirk in my direction.

"You're wondering why we're chasing down the Brotherhood, whose importance we have not explained, when we've spent all this time chasing your witch," Greene said. I chilled at his use of the word *your*.

"Yes. You made a great speech about how we were going to get revenge for Conyers, and Parker and

Garland as well, in a way," I said. "I thought stopping her, by whatever means, had become the purpose of this company. I thought—"

"Our purpose is, and has always been, to fight the evil that pokes its head out when the world's gone mad," Greene said. "That's what you told the men, isn't it? And you were right, because that's what I told *you*, isn't it? Before now, even I only knew of the Brotherhood through rumors, but if they're the evil that Madame Laveau is worried about, then that's the evil we've got to face. And I'll bet my hat our witch is involved somehow."

"But if we have no idea what she's up to, how are we to know what kind of trap she's set for us?" I asked.

"We can only solve one crisis at a time," Greene said.

"I declare, you two squabble like an old married couple," Miss Beauregard said. "The first house is up this way."

She turned us up a wide street, which was lined with impressive mansions. Confederate soldiers raced about on horses, in wagons, or marched in formation. Few citizens seemed to be venturing about in the chaos. Thankfully, no one gave us a second look.

"Last question," I said.

"Oh lord, I hope so," Greene replied.

"Madame Laveau?"

"Yes, I should have discussed her with you more before we came here," Greene answered. He grimaced and took a moment to think. "She's a local, well. . ."

"She's a Voodoo priestess," Miss Beauregard said.

"Voodoo?"

"Yes, Voodoo," she repeated. "Here's the Anthony House."

My inquiry ended as we inspected the mansion. The mansion had been identified as one of the abandoned northerner estates that might have been commandeered for the purposes of the Brotherhood.

As we approached, we witnessed Confederate soldiers stomping in and out of the house. They carried out all the furniture, fabrics, lamps, paintings, clothing, and anything else they could get their hands on. The Confederacy was appropriating the property of their northern enemy before they vacated the city.

"Well, I don't think they'd be in there," Greene said.

"I'd ask if there's no decency, but I do suppose there *is* a war going on," Miss Beauregard said with a sigh. "There are another half dozen or so houses up this way. I can't imagine we'll have any luck, but, perhaps, if one of them is not being looted, that might be a sign."

We hustled past the bedlam of the Anthony House and continued.

"Madame Laveau?" I repeated. "Voodoo?"

"Oh yes, Voodoo is sort of the local religion down here," Greene said.

Casey Moores

"Some think it's a sort of magic," Miss Beauregard said. "Whatever it is, Madame Marie Laveau always seems to know what's going on in the city, and a lot of the coloreds treat her as a sort of spiritual leader. She does seem to have horse sense, and she's never led me astray. I figure if we could find her just now, we wouldn't be piddlin' all over town looking for a needle in a haystack."

"You say she's never led you astray," Greene replied. "And I've had the same experience, thus far. Hell, I took it on her word that we put our company in a secure place, despite Alex's objections. But if she's dealing with forces from the other side, well, it doesn't matter if she has a heart of pure gold and wits to match. She'll pay the price someday, you mark my words."

Neither of us had a reply, and the conversation ended.

For hours, we wandered up and down the streets of New Orleans, focusing on the places the ladies had discussed. We examined abandoned homes, markets, schools, theaters, and even a couple of old, rotting cotton mills. We went along the entire north bank of the river, looking for any empty shops or warehouses. Some places had soldiers rushing about in a panic; barracks which were being vacated. Some had been abandoned. Those took more time as we searched them for signs of activity. A few of the great mansions had new owners. Those, Miss Beauregard assured us, had been deemed unworthy of attention by the sisters. Greene seemed unconvinced, so I suggested we could return to them if we found no better candidates.

Around midday, we snuck back into the kitchen at Slidell's house for some vittles.

In the afternoon, we explored a few more mansions and edged westward through where the banks and exchanges were located. We saw a prison that was still in service and appeared normal, as well as a couple active orphanages that Greene expressed interest in. None showed any signs of sinister activity.

We'd circled back to the waterfront in the early evening, moving along the docks toward the Old Prison where we'd left the company.

"So that's it, Ellie?" Greene asked, disheartened and choleric. "Those are all the ideas you and those fine southern ladies came up with?"

"That's all of them," Miss Beauregard replied. "I suppose, as you said, Alex, that now we'll have to go back through the Yankee houses that were gifted away. Good chance we'll rile folks up if we don't play it just right. I say we head back to the Slidell House, grab a root, and call it a night. Maybe I'll pick those ladies' brains some more on those families that have found themselves a mansion."

"I'll be happy for us to sit out of that conversation, if you don't mind," Greene said to my relief. "Are those really the only two orphanages in the city? Just one for boys, one for girls?"

"Well, there's a much bigger one further out, way off in the outskirts, moved there years ago when they found themselves with too many girls," Miss Beauregard said. "But it's miles out, you were rather specific we were looking *in* the city, weren't you?"

"Yes, I was," Greene replied. "Whatever it is that someone's doing, it only follows that they'd do it inside the city if they wanted to wreak havoc on the Union Navy. Besides, I don't think we have the time to trudge all the way out there to take a look."

"You said *moved*?" I asked. Both stopped walking.

"You did say that, Ellie, didn't you?" Greene asked. "Moved from where?"

"Oh my, I did, didn't I?" Miss Beauregard replied. "Well, I'm talking about the Poydras Asylum, an orphanage for young girls, but they got too big and moved to a much bigger estate out in the country a little before the war."

"Where was this?" Greene said, animated.

"Just back yonder, between Lafayette Square and Tivoli Circle," Miss Beauregard said. "At Julia Street and Saint Charles. The Campbells own it now and built a mansion in place of the old West Indies style home. But then Mr. Campbell, who's a surgeon, headed out with the Confederate Army. Come to think of it, Caroline and Matty mentioned no one had seen Mrs. Campbell or her four children- no, five, they just had a baby- for some time."

"Dammit, Ellie, that's it, I know it!" Greene said and turned about to march back. "We were just there!"

"Lieutenant Greene," I said in a tone which was *not* deferential. "The company is just up this road. We will check on them, *sir,* and then we will go take a look."

He spun back to regard me, rage on his face, but said nothing for a few, long moments. His look drained away, he nodded, and a slight smile grew on his lips.

"Quite right, Alex, quite right," he said. "Moreover, we may as well take them with us on this one. It's the place."

"How can y'all be sure?" Miss Beauregard asked. "It's just another building, same as the others we've seen."

"It's the place," Greene said. "An abundance of young virgins, centered in the city, transplanted just before the war. I'll sell the devil my soul if some number of those girls never made it to the new orphanage."

"But Poydras House is a good place, that's taken good care of those girls for decades," Miss Beauregard said, sounding offended. "And anyway, the Campbells just completely rebuilt it."

"I don't dispute that," Greene said. "And I'm sure the new Poydras House still is. But the forces we face take pleasure in corrupting the good and, actually, the fact it's been rebuilt makes me even more suspicious. Great opportunity to hide something nefarious in a reconstruction. And the fact they haven't seen that family. . . they're either complicit, hostages, or dead."

"Ma'am, may I ask what yer doin' out and about with these Yanks?"

I hadn't heard the man approach and, by their shocked expressions, the other two in my party hadn't either. A bearded, gray coated man walked towards us from an alleyway with a rifle leveled at us.

"Yanks?" she replied with indignation and a smile. "Heavens to Betsy, no, my good man, I appreciate your concern, but these men are my protection. Can't be too careful with the Union on our doorstep. I know our boys will whup them something fierce, but you know how crazy folk can get when there's a fight nearby."

"I would say that lies do not become a Southern lady, but we all know the truth of that particular matter, don't we?"

The voice that spoke those words ignited both lust and rage within me. The honeyed voice carried a much more sinister undertone than it had when I'd encountered her in the swamp. The witch stood in the dark shadows of an alleyway between two shops, yet she glowed with the same unnatural light I'd seen before. Though my memory told me I'd found her beautiful, she now seemed as pale as a corpse and just as appealing.

Greene ripped the rifle from the soldier's hands and drove the butt back into the man's face with a loud crack.

"Ellie, run for it!" he shouted. He spun the rifle in his hands and pointed it at the witch. "Alex, get her into the prison!"

As he fired point blank into the woman, I pulled my Navy pistol out with one hand and grabbed Miss Beauregard's arms with the other. She shrugged me off and broke into an awkward run along the docks and shops toward the square where the old prison lay.

I hesitated for a brief moment to see what the shot had done to the witch, but Greene ran into me and shoved me along. Other than the new black hole in her midsection, she seemed unaffected. She formed a grim smile and stayed in place.

"Come on, you fool!" Greene shouted. I heard the stomp of boots behind us as I broke into a run.

The sound of gunfire pierced the air and we charged up the street.

"Left, up Toulouse!" Miss Beauregard shouted. Looking ahead, I found the reason. A group of Confederate militia had collected in the great square south of the prison.

Greene's Colt Dragoon pistol barked, a sound I'd come to recognize.

Miss Beauregard let out a piercing shriek and stopped running. As I approached, I found her clutching her side and trying to limp forward. I ducked under an arm, wrapped my arm around her, and carried her up Toulouse Street. Greene caught up a moment later and propped himself under her other arm. Within a few short steps, we lifted her off the ground and raced onward.

We turned on Chartres Street and found our way clear to the prison entrance. Musket fire ceased as we turned the corner on our pursuers. Greene and I found a steady cadence and picked up our pace.

The metal gate of the prison's stone archway had been blasted from its hinges, but a blockade of furniture, wagons, and barrels now lay across the entrance. As we closed on the barrier, I noted, with curiosity, that no enemy troops or cannon dwelled anywhere near the prison. I understood the reason even as I accepted that escaping inside was our only option.

"It's Lieutenant Greene and Sergeant Phillips, don't shoot!" Greene called out. "And we've got an injured woman here, help us out!"

Shots rang out from the square and zipped by us as Greene and I pushed Miss Beauregard over the makeshift barricade. My feet slipped twice on loose material, and our hands wound up in places that would have horrified me in any other circumstances.

I heard footsteps from behind announce the approach of our pursuers.

A shotgun appeared over the top of the barricade and blasted over our heads. Greene and I heaved Miss Beauregard up with everything we had. Finally, she was grabbed from the other side and hauled over. We scrambled over as well.

"I'll be honest, Alex, I didn't think we'd make it," Greene said, as we collapsed on the other side.

"I'm still not sure we will," I replied. "I'd say we found the trap, and we just joined the company in it."

Casey Moores

Chapter 24: The Siege

Before I'd caught my breath, Van Benthuysen announced "Here they come!"

I saw that Dr. Shilling and Dan Sonnier had taken Miss Beauregard and carried her back to safety.

A deafening burst of volley fire, followed by a chorus of war cries announced the Rebels were charging.

"Just like before men, stay low, keep your cover, don't shoot 'til you know you're gonna kill a man!" Daniels shouted.

Just like before. The phrase made me wonder how long the fight had been going. It was obvious it preceded our arrival, which meant we'd intentionally been allowed inside. I pushed the thoughts aside and checked my pistol.

Greene and I had come over the center of the barricade. I saw Van Benthuysen, Daniels, and a dozen other men stacked against the sides. Two other groups of marines knelt in two ranks a few dozen yards back, angled apart from each other to the sides of the entrance. Meeker led one, Wilkes led the other.

"Fire!" Daniels shouted. The call was repeated by Van Benthuysen, who stood and fired his carbine. The men on the sides rose, took aim, and fired. I crouched up and found a target, but he took a shotgun blast in the face before I pulled the trigger. I re-aimed at another and fired. A shot zipped through my hair, and I dropped to reload.

The wood of the barricade rumbled and shifted. A Rebel soldier leapt over the top and crashed down onto me. I narrowly avoided being stabbed by his bayonet, and we locked into a tight scrap. I let go of my pistol, but he kept one hand tight to his rifle as we wrestled on the ground. I grabbed the rifle to keep him clubbing me with it, and reached for my knife. He gave me a hard knock in the face, but I freed my knife from its sheath and buried it into his ribs.

He released the grip on the rifle. I left the knife buried in him, snatched the rifle with both hands, and cracked him in the jaw with the butt.

More Rebel soldiers had piled over the barricade, but our groups to the sides charged in, firing as they went. A few fell on both sides, and they crashed into a melee.

I aimed the rifle at another soldier on the bulwarks and jerked the trigger, but it didn't fire, so I thrust the bayonet into the man's chest.

He screamed and grabbed the rifle. I thought he'd give me another fight, but Van Benthuysen shot him in the head with the carbine.

Someone from the other side shouted, "Retreat boys, come on and fall back, now!"

Our marines kept firing as the enemy withdrew, until Greene called a cease fire. We heard a burgeoning conversation, somewhere in the enemy's ranks.

"Where the hell are your officers, boys?" the new voice asked.

"Suh, Captain's over in the square, he took a hornet in the shoulder," someone replied. "We had two lieutenants, but they're somebody's darlin' now."

"Suh, you gotta watch out, them Yanks are near about to shootcha!" another soldier shouted.

"Well tell me what in tarnation's goin' on over here?" the original voice shouted. I eased my head up and found a Confederate officer on horseback about a hundred feet out, with a group of Rebels clustered about him. "Did you say Yanks, boy? My, that's a fine one. What makes you say they're Yanks?"

"Well, suh, some other officer, a colonel, I think, came by a while back an' told us they was in there," someone replied.

"Look over at that river yonder. . . now if there ain't any boats sailing up, there ain't any Yanks," the officer asked. "See anything that makes them look like Yanks? They got Yank rifles? Blue uniforms?"

"They ain't got rifles, suh," the sergeant replied. "Just shotguns, and the coats are all dirtied up, like they been crawling' in the swamp or something, but the colonel said—"

"What colonel, Sergeant? Did you get a name?"

"No, suh, and we ain't seen him for a piece, but—"

"I don't know who told you what, Sergeant, but that's just some jailbirds, or deserters, or muggins or something," the officer said. "You set a watch out here and do what you can to keep 'em in there, but I ain't letting any more of you boys muster out just so we can dig out some hotheads who ain't got the sense not to get themselves all stuck in a *prison* of all places. Now, General Lovell's given the order we all gotta skedaddle before the *real* Yanks sail up that river and pour fire into this city from the levees. You hold 'em in there 'til it's time to go, then they'll be the Yanks problem."

"Yes, suh," the sergeant replied. "Hear that boys? Let's make a line here, we'll hold 'em inside."

"Well, that's something, at least," Greene said, and he collapsed against the barricade.

"Yeah, but that's sealed it, I think," I said. I walked over to the first soldier I'd killed so that I could retrieve my knife. "Unless we find another way out, we'll—"

My vision exploded into stars. A split second later, the pain registered in my jaw, and I stumbled sideways. The knife fumbled out of my fingers.

"Sergeant Wilkes, what the hell?" Greene shouted.

"I told you the witch had his mind, Lieutenant, and now he's led us into this!" Wilkes argued. I put an arm out in an ineffective attempt to hold him back as I fell. After I smacked into the ground, he kicked me twice in the ribs. Though I still couldn't see, I timed the next kick and caught his foot. He beat his fists on the top of my head and I shrugged and curled defensively.

"He did not!" Greene shouted in reply.

I heard footsteps and felt Wilkes get tugged away from me. Someone reached under my arms and helped me up.

"It was my decision to accept these lodgings from the Native Guard, and mine alone," Greene said.

My sight returned, and I found Wilkes restrained by Tomasini and Niculescu, with Van Benthuysen standing between us.

"*First* Sergeant Phillips issued his protest at our accommodations when we got here, and I ignored him," Greene said. "Moreover, I accepted this spot on the word of a *different* witch. That's right, you heard me. A priestess of the local religion said we'd be safe here and I trusted her. So, the blame falls on me.

"But beyond that, Lawrence," Greene continued, stalking up toward Wilkes. "We've had this talk, and I thought the matter resolved. We came across that woman again, just before we got chased in here. *First* Sergeant Phillips didn't start following her commands, no, I saw it with my own eyes that she has no control over him. He got Miss Beauregard to safety. I mean, think about it,

Sergeant, if he'd set this trap for us, would he come straight into it and join us in here? Would he have killed that Secesh soldier?" Greene pointed to the first man I'd killed. "Or that one?" He pointed to the other.

"Sir," Wilkes said, full of vitriol, "Maybe he's in here so he can let them in later."

"That's enough, Sergeant!" Greene said with a burst of rage. He stomped up to Wilkes, grabbed him by the collar, and held his close. "You've showed your teeth, and that'll be the end of it. You got a problem with him, then you've got a problem with me. I'm not going to fight this battle over and over, do you understand, you damned blowhard?"

I pushed myself up, snatched the knife from the ground, and stepped softly toward the two men.

"Lieutenant, his problem *is* with me," I said, though it hurt to talk. "It's my battle to fight, and I'll be the one to fight it."

I put a gentle hand on Greene's arm and directed him aside. I spread my hands out to make room for Wilkes and me. Then, I flipped the knife in my hand and presented him with the handle.

"Maybe she is in my head," I said. "Though I swear to our Holy Father that I would never raise a hand against any of you. No matter what, I *will* keep my faith in this company. But just to make sure, Lawrence, why don't you come on and take care of the problem. Come on, then, take my knife and gut me so she can't turn me against you."

"Alex, don't be stupid!" Greene said.

I raised my free hand and pointed a finger into Greene's face, a warning to keep him back. I held the knife steady, waiting for Wilkes to respond. Shaking, he seized the knife. I spread both my arms wide, inviting him to do as he pleased.

Trembling, he stretched out his arm and pointed the blade into my face. After a good while, he snapped the knife down into the dirt at my feet.

"Well, goddammit," Wilkes said. "All I mean to say is, what the hell are we going to do now?"

Keeping my eyes on him and my body ready, I crouched and picked up my knife once again. I stood and slid the knife into its sheath.

"Addison, you go check on your woman, make sure the sawbones' is taking good care of her," I said.

"She isn't my—"

"Tomasini, Nick," I continued. "You two, Doyle and I are gonna get every barrel of gunpowder we can spare and see if that Prussian taught you enough to blow our way out of here."

I had deduced the night prior that escape from the upper level was impractical. We could have rigged a "rope" of sorts by connecting the men's shoulder belts. However, getting through the iron bars would take just as much work as blasting through the walls, possibly more. Once we'd gotten through the windows, we'd be left in the precarious position of sending men down one at a time. There would be far greater time to detect us, and any patrol could easily capture or kill the first few. If we blew our way out at the base level, we could, hopefully, rush out all at once. The former *might* have been quieter, but the latter kept us all together.

"Yes, Sergeant," Tomasini said. Niculescu nodded. Greene still stood there, dumbfounded. I waved him in the direction they'd taken Miss Beauregard. He released a deep breath and walked off.

"Charlie," I locked eyes with Daniels, "you keep whatever plan you had going. They could change their mind at any time, so make sure you keep us ready for another charge, but also make sure the men are getting sleep as well."

"As you say, Sergeant," Daniels replied.

I looked back to Wilkes. "Lawrence, you and Emile make sure Lieutenant Daniels doesn't muck this up, all right? You both also need to keep an eye on the men and make sure none of them are getting wallpapered. We can't have drunk marines when we try to break out."

Wilkes nodded, but kept his gaze on the ground.

"And Lawrence. . ." Surprised, he looked up at me. "You see that witch, you plug her between the eyes before she causes any more mischief, do you understand me?"

"Yes, Sergeant."

I'd intended, mostly for the theatrics of it, for my explosives experts and I to set off immediately to find a spot in the wall to blast our way out. However, I asked when they'd eaten and discovered none had done so since mid-morning. The Native Guard cook had left the night before and had not returned. The jambalaya and fresh bread had all been consumed before he left.

I directed them to a cell where they could rest up and eat however much hardtack they could stomach.

I stopped in on Miss Beauregard and found Greene dutifully by her side. I learned that Mr. Shilling had removed a bullet from her hip. The surgeon felt confident there was no serious damage, but feared it could turn gangrenous if not well attended. I gave Greene an encouraging pat on the back and said I'd pray for her.

"Alex," Greene said, as I moved to leave.

I stopped.

"I've meant every word I've said about you, and you just proved me right again," he said. "You are the man who leads this Company. Not me, and not Daniels or Meeker, though they're coming along. It was you who objected to my foolish acceptance of this spot and here we are, doomed to fail."

"We'll find our way."

"Maybe, but that's not the point," Greene said. "If we're going to see our way through this, it'll be you who gets us there. I truly believe that."

"I appreciate your faith, sir," I said. "And I am doing my darnedest to live up to it. But let me settle something. *You* are our commander. I might be the top Marine, but we'd all be dead in a swamp if we weren't led by a man who knew what we were facing. If it hadn't been me, Major Reynolds would have found some other sergeant. On the other hand, he couldn't have found a better man than you. Now, you make sure she gets better."

I moved to the next couple cells, where Shilling and Sonnier worked, and checked on our wounded. By some miracle, we'd lost only two men in the previous attacks. They were laid out as well, away from the dead Rebels. Six of the men had been injured, two of which couldn't walk. That would be a problem if we broke out. Five more had picked up the quick step in the swamp. I could count on them to run when needed, but they'd be miserable in a fight.

The sun had set as I stepped back out in the courtyard. I retrieved one of our small barrels of powder and circled our compound, making sure every Marine's powder flask was full. Then, I did the same with a box of shot.

When I returned to the barricade, I discovered Daniels had moved the Rebels we'd killed to a respectful row off to one wall of the courtyard. Their rifles and accoutrements had been collected as well, and I found a few of our marines now wielded Enfield rifles, each with about twenty cartridges.

Daniels presented me with a revolver they'd found on a dead Rebel lieutenant, secure in its leather holster. It looked like any other revolver I'd seen, except that it had a second barrel underneath the main barrel. To go with it, he handed me a pouch that was full of a mix of cartridges and twenty gauge shot.

"It's a LeMat," Daniels said. "Rebel officers favor them, so they can't be all bad. I thought you should have it."

"If you insist," I replied. I pulled the Navy pistol from its holster and handed it to him. "Then you make sure this finds its way to someone who doesn't have one."

He nodded and took it.

"She's out there," he said, and he pointed through the gate.

I eased my head up over the barricade and looked out. A line of Rebel troops still waited for us, though now they milled about restlessly. Fires burned on either side of them, presumably to give them light as much as warmth. I scanned about, but couldn't see what he was talking about.

Then, I saw her. She stood well off to the left of the Rebel line, closer to the center of the great square. She was as bone white as ever, still as a statue, and unmistakable, even in the dark at great distance. Though it was impossible to make out from where we were, I was certain she stared at us. At me.

I asked if Meier was around, but learned he'd gone to get some shut eye.

With a shudder, I nodded agreement to Daniels and continued on. Wilkes didn't look at me as I departed.

Content that all the men had the powder they needed, I collected the other barrels, one by one, and brought them to the room where I'd left my explosives men. All three lay flat on the earth, sleeping soundly.

I decided they had a good idea and lay down as well. I spent a few minutes examining and fiddling with my new pistol. Then, I drifted off to sleep.

Chapter 25: The Breakout

When dawn came, Tomasini, Niculescu, Doyle, and I started a methodical search around the compound, looking for the best spot to try and blow the wall. We decided that the side that faced the cathedral would be bad as it was the most likely to have foot traffic. I'd also worked out that the rear of the building was Chartres Street. If we could exit that way, we could follow it all the way to Poydras House. Then, we would just have to hope Greene was right about it.

I feared there might be patrols at the intersections, but there was nothing for it. My best hope was to blow through as close to the back corner of the building, opposite the cathedral, and rush any troops who might be set up outside. We picked the second cell in from the corner.

Doyle informed me, and the other two agreed, that we shouldn't just set the barrels against the wall and blow them. Our best chance at getting through the wall, they explained, would come from getting the barrels into or under the wall. Seeing as it was stone throughout, I set them to work digging out whatever stones they could along the base of the wall. That effort alone would be time consuming as we had only axes, knives, bayonets, and rusty bars with which to work. Even more, I told them to prefer the bars, since I didn't want them breaking all of our good weapons trying to escape. We would need them.

Mid-morning, I returned to Greene to check on Miss Beauregard.

"Any improvement?" I asked.

"She's still got a strong fever and hasn't woken at all, but she's still with us," he said. "Sawbones doesn't think it's gangrene. Yet."

"I'll keep praying," I said. "But we need to have a plan to move her if we can get through that wall."

"Fire!" Miss Beauregard said. She sat straight up and tilted her head back. Her eyes were glazed over, milky white as if she'd gone blind.

"Ellie, it's okay, you're okay," Greene said. He grasped her arm and tried to hold her still.

"Soleil stands high and the innocent burn, and they call to him!" she screamed.

"When?" Greene asked. "Where?"

"Whole city is on fire!" she continued. "River, houses, shops, docks, ships, they be consumed in a murderous blaze. Kur Oto arrives!"

"She's seeing what's going to happen!" Greene said.

"Are you sure it's not just the fever?" I asked. "She's delirious, and that's what we've been afraid of. . ."

"Are we willing to take that chance?" he asked. I had no answer.

"The ships! The ships will burn!"

"The ships?" I asked. "If what she's seeing is right, it means they plan to burn the fleet, once it's in the city!"

"Ellie!" Greene shouted, his face close to hers. "When? When is this happening?"

"Soleil stands high! Soleil stands high!"

"Noon, then," Greene said.

"Yes," I agreed, "but *which* noon?"

She bucked and arched her back against the ground. Then, she collapsed. Greene put his hand on her stomach and leaned in. Shilling and Sonnier rushed in and pushed us aside.

"What happened, how is she?" Shilling asked. He put one hand on her stomach and leaned in close to her face.

"She's breathing," Greene said. He gave me a look which I took to mean we would keep her words quiet. We let the surgeon and the nurse tend to her, and we left the cell.

One we'd found a secluded place to talk, we discussed the revelation.

"I've never seen anything like that," I said. "Though, I realize I'm saying that more often these days."

"It was Laveau speaking through her," Greene said.

"How can you know that?" I asked.

"I know Laveau and that's how she speaks, using *soleil* for *sun* and whatnot," Greene said. "And Laveau has visions like that, though I can only guess she knows how to project them through people. Maybe she used Ellie's fever to send us a message, I don't know."

"I thought you didn't trust anyone who uses that kind of magic," I said.

He shrugged.

"Moreover, us being here in the first place was part of *her* plan, was it not?" I asked. "That hasn't gone too well, *sir*."

"Dammit, Alex, what other ideas do we have? Besides, this only supports the idea that we gotta get out here, now don't it? I thought that's what you wanted. Do I have to make it an order or something?"

"No, sir," I sighed. I had to admit, even if they were crazed rantings, they did support our need for escape. "Wouldn't want you to have to go and do that. Either way, we still don't know *which* noon she was referring to."

"We can only assume it's noon today," Greene said.

"I don't think we can get out by noon, that's only a couple hours," I replied.

"We've gotta think of something before it's too late," he said. I could tell his frustration was rising, which was understandable.

"If we try to blow the wall early, it might not work, and they tell me they need most of the day," I explained. "We could try to break through the bars upstairs and lower ourselves down, but in the daylight, we'd be spotted for sure, and they could just pick us off one by one. If we try to break out through the front gate, well, that's about the stupidest thing we could try. Even if we can blow through the wall, the noise will announce everyone. I think the only good time to blow it will be in the dark, so we have a chance at escaping through the streets. I still don't know what we can do about the wounded."

"We'll have to carry them as best we can," Greene said. He sighed. "And I see what you're saying about all the rest, but if she means noon today, and we *have* to assume she does, then we *must* get out today."

"Let's go take a look at the windows on the second floor," I suggested.

I could see the hope drain from him as we looked up at the narrow little openings. I boosted him up at every single one and he tried all the bars, hoping to find a weak one. On the fourth window, a bullet zipped into the stone while he pulled on the bars. He flung himself backward and toppled over me.

"I suppose that confirms they're keeping an eye on us," he said. He pounded his fist into the stone floor. "Damn! So close, yet here we are, failure all but assured."

We sat in silence for a moment. I strained the corners of my brain for another option, but found none.

"We're going to have to try to blow the wall early, and take our chances on getting out in the daylight," he said. "And we'd better hurry, we're even shorter on time now than we were."

"Addison, you just saw that they're watching the streets and watching the windows," I said. "We blow our way out in the daylight, they'll stack us up, same as if we charged out the front gate."

Nonetheless, we went down to where Tomasini, Niculescu, and Doyle worked. I found they'd recruited a few others to work the stone out, but their progress was slow. They confirmed that, based on what Kroehl had taught them, they didn't think we'd get through the wall if they didn't dig into it, place the gunpowder, and pack dirt around it.

I had another thought and took Greene to the barricade at the front gate.

Daniels had turned the gate over to Meeker in order to get some sleep. We crept up and lifted our heads to see over the barricade. The same line of Rebels stood there, and tents had sprung up in the square. There was no sign of the witch.

"See that?" I asked.

"I see they're still there, so what?" Greene said.

"Well, as you said, it's getting close to noon," I replied. "Ellie saw the ships on fire and the city burning at noon, right?"

"Yes, exactly."

"If the ships were sailing up the Mississippi, in order to be here at noon, they'd only be a few miles away right now," I said. "The Rebels would know they're only a few miles away, and they'd be breaking camp and heading out, assuming what that Rebel officer said is true. But instead, they're just hanging about, having a picnic, watching the grass grow."

He released another low rumbling sigh and continued to search the square for another minute.

"I sure hope you're right," he said. "If today is not the day, then we break out tonight."

Doyle struck the match and lit the line of gunpowder that led to the barrels they'd buried into the wall. I watched it burn for a moment, mesmerized by how slow it went. I'd never witnessed a line of gunpowder burn, and it went much slower than I had imagined.

"Out!" Doyle shouted. He grabbed my arm and tugged. I regained my senses and ducked out of the room. We stopped another ten feet away from the cell entrance.

Doyle stood with a finger pointed and his gaze upward as he counted. The men of Special Unit Thirteen and I waited.

The longer we waited, the more I noticed the men glancing about nervously, questions on their faces.

Doyle's ministrations ceased and he screwed up his face.

"Prussian said it always takes longer than you think," Tomasini said.

"I know that, ya' know, but it should've—"

A great boom erupted throughout the prison and the floor rumbled. Rocks and dust blasted out from the cell in which we'd laid the powder. Everyone tensed and moved forward, but the explosives team and I held them back for a brief moment.

"Okay, out wit' ya's!" Doyle shouted. I sprung forward, having given clear instruction I'd exit first. Greene insisted on joining me. He'd waited on the other side, and we met up at the entrance to see the damage.

A large, magnificent hole existed where the wall had been. The powder had done its work. We could see only darkness on the other side. That was a good sign, any light would have indicated the torches and lanterns of a patrol.

"Move quick, everyone!" I shouted.

Leading with my shotgun, I sprang through the crevasse. Before I could even look around, someone grabbed the shotgun with one hand and my collar with the other. I tensed up, ready to fight. My carefully crafted plan to escape had immediately failed.

"No sign of them!" Captain Golis shouted in his thick, guttural accent. He shouted for someone else's benefit. "Sergeant, get the men ready and we'll storm inside!"

As I relaxed, partially from confusion, I found a cluster of the Native Guard gathered on both sides of the hole, facing away from us. I couldn't help but release an exasperated chuckle.

"Sergeant," he said to me, "leave your wounded inside for us to find and capture. We will take good care of them. The rest of you get out, quick. Follow Orleans up to Bourbon Street and follow that to Julia."

He released his grip on my collar and shotgun. Greene emerged, looked at me, and ducked his head back inside.

"Leave the wounded!" he ordered. "The rest of you get out here, double quick!"

Angry protests erupted from inside, but Greene calmed them and explained in further detail.

Golis stepped back and shouted more directions to his men, though none of them moved.

Greene reemerged and moved toward Golis with a stern look.

"Miss Elizabeth Beauregard, cousin to General Beauregard, is inside," Greene said. "She was shot getting inside, and now she's in there, sick with a fever. I request you get her to a doctor immediately."

"She will be well taken care of," Golis replied. "You have my word."

"You know the city better than I do," I said to Greene. "You get moving that way and we'll trickle after you. I'll wait until the last man's out and catch up. Go on, sir, lead the company!"

He nodded agreement and gathered the first few men.

I wanted to ask Captain Golis how he'd known we would come out when we did, but I did not.

As each man came out, I directed him to follow the trail of marines that lead up the street and away. We still had around three dozen good men. Daniels came out last, having been in charge of the gate detachment until the last moment.

"Some of those colored men were storming in as we left," Daniels said. Then he saw Golis and instinctively raised his pistol. I grabbed hold of it and pushed it back down.

"They're here to help us out," I said.

"Captain Rey of Economy Company leads them," Golis said. "The other soldiers are more than happy to let us die taking the prison. Except," he shrugged and frowned, "It seems there were much less men in here than we thought there were. Very strange, no? Now, go! Bon chance, *mes amis*."

Chapter 26: Campbell House

I urged the trailing men to move faster so we could catch up to Greene. Shilling insisted on staying with the injured and I allowed it. Sonnier, our nurse, remained with us. Twenty-seven Marines, to include Greene and I, had departed the prison. Behind us, we heard shouts and sporadic gunfire. Though I trusted Golis and his men, I prayed to God that I wasn't wrong to do so.

Two city blocks up Orleans Street, the road that led straight from the rear of the St. Louis Cathedral, the trail of men turned left onto Bourbon Street.

Once we were clear of the sights and sounds of the troops around the prison, we slowed our pace, formed into a respectable looking group, and acted as a militia would. We needn't have bothered for most of the march as it was after midnight, and we saw very few people. Those we did see were too focused on their purpose to give us a second look. As I'd guessed, the people of the city were in a panic to either fortify their homes and shops or abandon them.

When we'd crossed Canal Street, the road made a slight left turn and became Carondelet Street. We moved another eight or nine blocks without issue, at last arriving at Julia Street. Watching behind us, there were no signs that we were being pursued. I took that to mean the

Native Guard had done their part, which gave me greater hope for our wounded.

We gave Daniels the formation and we posted a rough approximation of pickets to watch the surrounding streets. Then, Greene, Meier, and I eased forward to take a look at the mansion. It was a two-storied white Italian-style mansion, though I guessed there might also be a basement. It had windows evenly spaced all around and a white stone trellis across the front on both levels. The whole property was surrounded by a wrought iron fence as tall as my shoulder, with a well-tended garden as well. As we'd been told, it looked as if it had just been built. From the angle we were at, we could see a carriage house attached to the rear of the building.

Remaining one street away at all times, doing our best to hug the other buildings so as not to be seen, we circumnavigated the entire mansion. The front of the building, which faced Chartres Street, had a grand double staircase that curved up from the sides to an enormous front door. There was a patio with a low stone fence in front of the house, with a balcony to match on the second level. A group of six armed men, in no sort of Confederate uniforms, milled about in the front of the house. Two more sat above them on the balcony at the second level. As we peeked around corners, we found two guards on a slow patrol in the large garden west of the building. Two more stood at the door to a smaller house, servant's quarters we guessed, in the northwest corner of the property. Two more stood outside at the carriage house on the northeast corner. Those men conducted a slow walk back and forth on their respective side.

Fourteen men were visible, which would be easy for the company to take down. The concern was what lay inside, but we'd have to deal with that as it came up.

"Are we sure this is the place?" I asked. Though Greene had his suspicions, there was still no hard proof it was the right place.

"Well, we narrowed down all the other candidates, and we don't exactly have time to go check them again," Greene said. "It's central to the city, just a few blocks from the river."

"It sure is the oddest house in the area," Meier said.

"Explain," I replied.

"Every other house around here is either boarded and abandoned, turned their lights out for the evening, or full of frantic Secesh folks packin' up everything they got," Meier said. "Whereas this one's lit up and heavily guarded, and yet it's quiet as a grave.'"

"Like the calm before a storm," Greene added.

"Well, similes aside, how do we know it's not just—"

Though it was faint and quickly muffled, a high-pitched scream sprang from the innards of the mansion.

"Not so quiet, it seems," Greene said.

"There," Meier said, excited but keeping a low tone.

"What?" I asked.

"I just saw her, the witch," he said. "She just went by that window."

Greene and I stared for a few minutes, but neither of us saw anything. I did hear the flapping of wings, which made my skin crawl, but I could find nothing flying in the darkness overhead. Though I didn't want to rely on my instincts, they told me we had the right place.

"I swear I saw her in there," he repeated.

"What do you say, Alex?" Greene asked. "That's two or three of us certain this is the place. What do you think?"

I took a deep breath and thought about it.

"It's like you said, Addison," I replied, "It's too late for us to search back through the whole city. If this isn't it, we're too late anyway."

Doing our best to remain discreet, we separated the men into four groups. Five each would assault the carriage house, servant's quarters, and through the garden on the west side. Those groups were led by Daniels, Meeker, and Benthuysen, respectively. The carriage house lay against a wide street, which would make a simpler approach. The servant's quarters and the fence around the garden were both only accessible through narrow alleyways. Those two groups would have to time their attacks carefully.

Ultimately, we planned to rush the house from every direction at once. Greene instructed the other three leaders that they were expected to be ready as soon as they heard gunfire at the front. Meier would start the assault with his Whitworth Rifle, and the rest of us would charge in.

Some time later, we'd set ourselves up and were ready to go in. From the corner of a building on St Mary Street, I stood next to Meier as he lined up his shot.

"There they are, right where she said they'd be, come on, boys!" someone shouted in a strong, southern accent. I turned and found a group of Rebel militia marching toward us from Lafayette Square. Without thinking, I fired my shotgun in their direction.

"Paul, shoot that officer!" I directed. Meier swung the Whitworth around, let out a breath, and fired.

The one who'd shouted jerked backward. The other men in our group fired as well, and the militia scattered to the sides of the street. We moved out along Julia Street for cover.

"Reload!" Greene shouted. "Then forget them, let's go take the house!"

Shotgun, carbine, and pistol reports echoed from all around the mansion. I figured the other squads, having heard gunfire, assumed it was time to attack. I popped out my expended cartridge, turned about, and fumbled for another one as I walked smartly toward the mansion. While we finished reloading, our group piled up against the north corner of a row of houses across the street from the Campbell House. Impatient, Greene leaned out and fired his pistol.

"Form a line, aim at the men atop those stairs!" Greene demanded. He still hadn't learned drill orders worth anything, but the direction was clear enough. Our detachment spread from the corner at the quick and aimed.

"Fire!" I commanded when all were ready.

"Come on, then!" he shouted, and ran across the street. I double checked the alignment of the pin on my cartridge and ran after him, shouting for the other men to follow. As I did, I saw the carriage house group, under Wilkes, had already killed their two guards and were kicking the carriage house door open.

One of the men up on the balcony twitched and tumbled over the trellis, dead. He landed, with a heavy thump, in the grass to the left.

The guards at the front of the house had taken cover under the stone trellis and fired erratically through the gaps.

Greene and I took refuge on the columns to either side of the double staircase, not ten feet from the guards. With a nod, we turned and fired at the group of men on the front patio. The guards fired at the same time we did. Greene and I were unscathed and returned behind our respective columns, but I don't think we hit anyone either. The other men in our group caught up, splitting themselves between the two columns.

I recognized the report of the Whitworth, followed by a yelp and gurgle from the other man on the balcony. In response, more fire came at us, nicking fragments of stone from the columns. I holstered my LeMat revolver and retrieved the shotgun, which hung from its strap.

"Men, open up on them when I say, then charge up the stairs," I shouted. "Ready? Now!"

Shotgun blasts and pistols barked while I ran up the right stairs as fast as I could. Greene came up the left. As we reached the top, I turned without thinking and fired to the right along the patio. The first man stood as I approached, but bucked as I blasted him. His face splattered into a bloody pulp, and he slammed against the guard behind him. A third guard lay dead beyond them, presumably killed by Meier's shot.

While the second man wrestled the corpse off, I released the shotgun, drew my sword, and chopped at his neck. He raised his right arm in defense and my blade cracked against the bone. He fumbled to bring a shotgun to bear with his left arm. I let go of the sword and stepped off to the left. I drew my revolver, cocked it, and fired into the man's stomach.

I glanced in the window and saw no one inside, then I looked toward the other end of the patio. Greene had collapsed on one knee next to a dead guard who had a knife in his throat. Two other dead guards were slumped, unmoving, against the trellis.

"Damn, Lieutenant, Sergeant, you could've saved some for us," Samuel Cash said as he stepped up the last step.

"Well, we're not done yet," I replied. I knelt to collect my sword, sheathed it, and plucked a cartridge from my pouch to reload the shotgun. "There's sure to be more inside, though I thought they'd be storming out by now. Lieutenant, are you all right?"

"Bastard cracked me in the ribs pretty good," Greene said with a gasp. With a grimace, he drew the blood-covered Bowie knife from his foe's neck and wiped it off on the dead man's coat. He struggled to stand, sheathed the knife, and reloaded his Dragoon pistol.

I heard shouts from the militia men who pursued us from St. Mary Street, so I moved to the door and pushed inside. I swung the shotgun up as I entered and panned it around, looking for anyone to shoot. The foyer had an elegant chandelier overhead and led to a grand, spiraling rosewood staircase. The mansion was spacious, with gorgeous, intricate marble columns, rosewood panels, and fine, expensive furnishings. The walls were adorned with artwork, and almost everything else was made of gold or silver.

"Everyone inside, quick!" I shouted. Our assault was to immediately become another siege. I touched the cross against my chest and prayed we had the correct house.

The twelve of us crowded into the house and shut the door behind us.

"Well, that wasn't so hard now, was it?" Greene asked with a pained smile. I shot him an angry look.

"Don't you ever say anything like that, again, *sir*," I said.

I tasked Meier with shooting whichever militiaman appeared to have taken charge and left Private Wiatt to stand with him. Hopefully, that would slow the militia and further erode their resolve to follow us into the mansion. I directed Cash to take two men through the house to the back, to make contact with Meeker's group. With all proper deference, I politely asked Greene to take three Marines in a quick sweep of the floor and then to take up a defense of the entryway. I led Privates Young and Chase through the kitchen to exit the house to the west. I planned to meet up with Benthuysen and McDaniel's groups.

The well-tended garden muffled the sounds of gunfire, which became infrequent. In the dark, it felt eerily calm as we stepped along paths between flower beds. Not a dozen feet out, the thick vegetation blocked the light from the house. The moon was a waning sliver and was, in any case, blocked by tall trees. My eyes fought to adjust to the heavy darkness, and we crept forward as a result. Apprehension turned into dread as I discovered a powerful stench, reminiscent of blood and viscera.

"Emile," I said, louder than a whisper but quieter than a shout. "Benthuysen?"

My boot bumped again something heavy and made a squishing sound. As I bent to feel what it was, Private Young bumped into me, and I tumbled forward onto it. My knee came down on mushy cloth. My hand flew forward on its own to catch me. It landed in a pool of warm, viscous liquid. Blood, and a lot of it.

Light emerged from my right and blinded me.

"Sergeant Phillips?" Daniels inquired. "Oh God, what happened here?"

Squinting, I discovered I'd fallen into a mass of crimson-soaked corpses. My knee sat atop the remains of Sergeant Emile Van Benthuysen.

Chapter 27: Into the Depths

Corporal Clark's body lay a few yards further back. His head rested in some bushes beside it. Privates Edson, Rich, Simms, and McCawley, all newly recruited after the action at Saint Augustine, were scattered about as well. It was difficult to determine which pieces belonged to who. Up against the iron fence lay the two crumpled bodies of the guards that Van Benthuysen's group had been tasked to deal with.

Private Chase retched into a collection of flowers. Young followed suit. I fought down my own nausea and leaned back off the corpses. I wiped the blood on my hand off on the grass.

"Lieutenant Daniels, sir, how is your squad?" I asked.

"Better than this one, Sergeant," he replied. In the lantern light, I could see he'd gone pale, and he carried a grim expression. Two other marines stood behind him. "We took down the guards at the servant's quarters easy enough. We found a bad sight, though not as bad as this, on the upper story. A group of three men and two boys, servants by the look, all dead. None of them were torn up like this, though."

"Just men and boys, Lieutenant?" I asked. "No girls or women?"

"No, Sergeant," he replied.

I recovered Van Benthuysen's sticky red carbine, collected myself, and stood. The carbine had a full load, he hadn't even had time to fire.

"Well, this can't be helped," I said. "You leave the other two in the building?"

"Yes, I—"

As he spoke, two shotgun blasts barked from the servant's house, followed by a shriek. Daniels spun about with the lantern, and we saw Sergeant Wilkes crash through the door from the servant's house. I sprung past Daniels and ran toward Wilkes. He staggered out of the house with a hand on his neck. He carried no weapon, and his left arm hung limp at his side. As I closed, he fell forward into my arms.

"Sh-she got Martin," he muttered. He was shivering, and it took most of my strength to hold him up. "Damned. . . witch. Shot her in the face." He gulped hard and his eyes rolled back. "She didn't like that, no sir."

I dragged him backward toward the others.

"Get back to the mansion!" I shouted. I kept my eyes on the servant's house. A soft white glow grew at the doorway. The white witch stepped into the opening. The white shift dress she wore was darkened all over. Her eyes burned red, and she ran a finger around her lips. If Wilkes had shot her, I saw no sign of it.

Daniels appeared at my side to help with Wilkes, and we struggled to carry him away faster.

"If it isn't my paladin," she said. She smiled and licked the finger. "That's right, rabbit, run! Run away! Go hide in that tomb, there!"

She broke into hysterical laughter as we lurched through the garden, and she disappeared from sight. My boot crushed some shrubs, and we stumbled back into the lit area beside the mansion.

The four other marines pushed through the door to the kitchen ahead of us. I took one last glance back as we carried Wilkes into the house. I saw only the trees and the flower beds, stretching back into the shadows. She had not followed us. Her laughing had ceased.

Inside, we laid Wilkes out on a table in the kitchen.

"You four," I said, looking at the four privates who'd escaped inside with us, "Watch that door. You shoot the hell out of anything that comes through it."

"Won't do any good, First Sergeant," Wilkes groaned.

"You just relax, Lawrence," I said.

Gently, I pulled his hand away from his neck. The leather stock around his neck was ripped, as if it had been scratched or cut by a sharp knife. His neck had two deep scratches as well.

"She tore Martin apart like he was a doll made of straw," Wilkes mumbled, and then coughed. I realized he had a blood trail on his left arm, from a wound between his shoulder and his elbow. When I touched, the arm bent inward with no resistance. He screamed in agony.

"Arm's broken right there," I said. "Sonnier, get in here!"

"What the hell happened outside?" Greene asked as he ran in.

Dan Sonnier rushed in, pushed us aside, and went to work.

"What the hell happened to him?" the nurse asked. He ripped some bandages from his bag. "Water or whiskey or anything? Someone get me something to wash this off."

"He says the white witch did, and I believe him," I replied, turning to look at Greene. "Benthuysen's whole squad was torn apart by something. If what Wilkes says is true, and I saw her myself, the white witch did all that."

"That's absurd!" Greene said. "Witches can't do that sort of thing. Where was this? Out there?"

Before I could stop him, he'd grabbed the lantern from Daniels and stormed out of the house. I ran after him, unable to let him face the witch, or whatever she was, alone. I muttered for everyone to stay where they were and keep an eye on the militia. Nonetheless, Daniels and two other Privates followed us out. I focused my attention on the servant's quarters, searching for any sign of the woman.

Greene found the grisly scene and stopped for several moments while he looked about.

"I've been a fool," he said. "Let's get back inside."

We returned to the house much faster than we'd left it. Inside, we checked on Wilkes and learned he'd survive. Sonnier explained he'd been bitten "by something" but the stock had protected him. At that news, I noticed all the men tugged about at their own stocks, each man ensuring theirs was well secured. I guessed we'd have less complaints about the horribly uncomfortable accoutrements going forward.

Greene tugged my arm toward the foyer, and we left the kitchen. Daniels followed us. The men had moved a couch to block the front doors, and Meier knelt on it. He'd cracked a small piece of the window out to put a rifle through.

"She's not a witch, Alex, I've been wrong all along," Greene said. "I always thought it didn't quite fit, but you see a woman who seems possessed of some sort of magic, well, you just think *witch*, don't you? I'm the one who should know better."

"Then what is she?" Daniels asked.

"Could be a number of things," he replied. "Demon, most likely, succubus, maybe, that would be a devil woman. *Loup-garou*, which is the local term for a sort of wolf-man, though I've never heard of a woman being one. Of course, no one's ever really seen—"

"Addison," I said in a stern tone.

"Yeah, sorry, but wolf-man, or wolf-*woman*, doesn't really fit either," he continued. "Which is good, because despite my requests, we have yet to receive any silver ammunition."

His gaze floated around us.

"Though now I mention it, there does seem to be quite a bit of silver in this house," he said. "Let's make sure to do something about that, we might really need it later."

"Addison," I repeated, my tone even deeper.

"Yes, sorry," he said. "But Wilkes' neck. . . I'd guess she's a vampire. A vampire is a—"

"I know what a vampire is," I said. "My mom told us all the stories when I was a boy."

"So. . . what?" Daniels asked. "Wooden stakes? Garlic? Can she come in here uninvited?"

"I don't really know, truth be told," he replied. "I've never come across one. And she might be a succubus or something else, besides. Safest bet, I'd think, would just be to sever the head if we can. Cutting the heart out could work, but it'd probably be a good deal harder to do. Either way, even if she's one kind of demon, beheading would do it."

"Behead her, then," I said with a hint of cynicism. "Bully. I'll make sure to pass that around. Now, on our other score. . . any sign of, well, anything, in here?"

"Not so much," Greene answered. "House is empty. Meeker took the carriage house, didn't find anything in there, so I brought them all in here and now I've got all the men who aren't watching doors and windows searching the place. I got Meier making the militia think twice about coming in here, though he's using the southern rifles we got from the prison to save his Whitworth cartridges."

"Well, that's something," I said. "But anyway, this house was well-guarded, which might just be because of all the riches in here, but she's here, and McDaniel's found the servants in their house, well, men and boys, at least, all slaughtered. Something's going on here, we just gotta find it."

"I agree, and I was about to get working on that, but then you came in with Wilkes and news of Benthuysen," Greene said, and then he shouted, "Tom!"

"Yes, sir!" Archibald replied from upstairs.

"Report!"

Sergeant Archibald appeared at the banister of the spiral staircase.

"Sir, I found the family huddled up in a room upstairs," Archibald said. "Woman of the house, four children, and a baby. Looks like they haven't left the room much in a while. Boys tried to fight us off, and the whole group's a bit hard-nosed."

"I see," he said. "Bring the woman down."

"Yes, sir!"

There were shouts and screams from both girls and boys. It all ended with the sound of a door slamming, after which we could only hear the protests of an upset lady. Archibald and one other Marine dragged her down the steps. The diminutive dark-haired woman fought the whole way down and, when presented to us, raised her nose in the air and spat. Greene, who'd seen the gesture coming, ducked his head to the side.

"I've nothing to tell you!" she shouted. Her accent was somewhat plainer than that of the southern women I'd encountered.

"Madame, there is no time," Greene said. "Now, we're not here trying to—"

She screamed.

"Help me!" she shrieked. "If there are any good gentlemen left in this city, please! Help me!"

I struck her, backhanded, across the face.

What would Cassie Paul think to see me strike a woman?

I brushed the thought aside.

The screaming stopped. I grabbed her by the shoulders.

"Dammit, woman, listen to us, we're trying to save you just as much as us," I shouted at her. "We're not here for the Union, we're here to save the whole damned city, and your house and family, too! From what we know, some damned fools mean to burn the whole city down or some nonsense, and we're just trying to stop them!"

Doubt flashed across her face. Her gaze flickered off to her left, toward the stairs. Then, her eyes narrowed, and her frown re-emerged.

"Help!"

I smacked her again and thrust her toward Archibald. Greene had already moved to the staircase.

"Get her back upstairs!" Greene demanded, and Archibald pulled her along.

"You saw that?" I asked.

"Yeah," Greene replied. We stomped about at the base of the staircase, which was covered by an ornate rug. It was hard to hear anything over the screaming, but it felt soft, as if the floorboards might give way.

We threw back the rug and crouched along the floorboards. A few inches from the baseboard at the bottom of the stairs, I found two small holes, no larger than a quarter dollar coin.

"Get me a poker from the fireplace," I ordered.

Someone handed me one, and I wedged it into the hole near the center. It gave way a little, but I found no leverage, so I tried the other one. As I heaved on it, a curved panel lifted from the floor. I pushed enough so that Greene and a few others could get their fingers into it. They lifted the panel up, which revealed stone steps that spiraled down below the house. I checked my shotgun, checked the load on my revolver, and edged my way down the steps.

I was only a few steps down when I heard a smattering of gunfire erupt up above. I climbed back out.

"Reb's are trying to make their way in!" Meier shouted. The rest of the window he sat behind shattered at that moment and he dropped down.

"Forget them! Everyone down into the hole!" I shouted. I looked to Greene to confirm the plan, and he nodded at me. "You just hold that door until we get everyone else in, then we'll all head down and hold them there."

"I'll lead us down," Greene said. "You make sure everyone makes it in, Alex."

"Yes, sir," I replied. "Dan! Can Wilkes walk?"

I ran into the kitchen, pushing men the other way as I went.

"I'd rather he not, Sergeant," Sonnier replied.

"It's that or be captured, or worse," I replied.

"I'm fine," Wilkes said weakly.

"Then help me help him up," Sonnier replied.

"First Sergeant," Wilkes said, droopy-eyed, as we swung his legs off the table and lifted him under the shoulders. He spoke in a low, slow drawl. "I'm sorry. She's a devil, and I can't be mad at you just 'cause she's a devil. And I don't mean your average woman devil, she's a real, Bible devil. You're a good man, Sergeant."

"What did you give him?" I asked Sonnier.

"Laudanum, last bit I had," he replied. "Doc Shilling had all the good stuff."

"You're fine, Lawrence," I said. "Come on, let's get you down the stairs. Can someone take him?"

Private Young took my place. I checked the door from the kitchen to the garden, deduced no one was going in that way, and ordered the men there down the stairs. I went back by the foyer, found the Rebel's hadn't broken in yet, and I went to the back door, toward the carriage house. Meeker and two privates guarded that entrance but hadn't seen any activity, so I sent them to the stairs.

When I returned to the front, I witnessed Meier shoot a man directly outside the window. I heard glass break in the sitting room to our left. I ran to the double doors from that room and closed them before anyone climbed inside. I shoved a table over to brace the doors.

"That's the last of you, down the stairs, men!" I shouted. Private Chase fired his shotgun through a window, and then turned and barreled down the stairs. Corporal Meier and the other three remaining privates went as well. I stood at the top of the stone steps until they'd gone down. Bullets clipped the walls around me as I followed. Both sets of doors groaned from getting battered from the other side.

"Good luck down there."

I almost jumped at the woman's voice. I'd never thought about it before, but her diction was focused and succinct. The devil woman leaned, casual as ever, against the doorframe to the kitchen. Her otherwise white dress was painted over in a crusty reddish-brown. She carried a bemused smirk on her luscious scarlet lips, where I discovered long, fang-like teeth on the sides of her mouth. I'd never seen anything like it. The pupils of her eyes burned like a crimson fire. She took two short steps to the couch at the door, put a hand under it, and flipped it away as if it were light as a feather.

I darted down the stairs as the doors flew open.

"Well get down there, already! After them!" she commanded, as I tore down into the depth below.

Chapter 28: The Devil Woman

I dashed down the first dozen steps until I lost the light. Then, I slowed enough to feel my way on every step. The stone was slick with humidity and slime; I had to be careful not to slip. A soft glow of light from further ahead became apparent. I found the shadow of another Marine just before I bumped into him. He brought his shotgun around, and I pushed it aside as he fired.

"It's Sergeant Phillips, dammit!" I said.

"Sorry, First Sergeant!" I recognized Private Matthew Baker's voice. "I heard the commotion upstairs, and you didn't follow, so I thought they'd got you."

"If I'd been them, you'd have been a mite too slow, Private."

The sound of boots behind stole my attention, and I swung my own shotgun back up the steps. I caught a shadow a few steps up and fired. A large Rebel militiaman took the shot in the belly and tumbled down toward me, his bayoneted rifle clattering down first.

"They got the sergeant!" someone cried, just a little further back up.

I pulled my revolver as I descended a few more steps. The marines below me moved slower than I would've liked, but at least we hadn't been stymied by some other force lower in the earth. I fired into the darkness at any shadows and was rewarded with a curse more often than not. When I'd emptied my revolver, I arranged to alternate with Private Baker and Private Forrest Marston, the next Marine down, to watch the steps above. The light grew and we found torches had been set periodically as we wound our way down.

There's no good way to measure how deep into the ground we went. The staircase ended abruptly in a tall, arched tunnel which was also lit by torches. Two more dead guards, along with the corpse of Private James Edson, lay slumped on the stone floor where the stairs ended. Further into the tunnel, Sonnier tended to Private Charles Wiatt, who had a blood stain on his shoulder.

Tomasini and Niculescu stood closest, and I learned they were directed to help watch the stairs until everyone was down. Tomasini informed me they were held up by a sealed door at the other end of the tunnel. Greene was working out how to proceed. Before I could move to rejoin Greene, Tomasini shouted and fired his shotgun. In the narrow confines of the tunnel.

Deafened, I spun about and found a dead Rebel militiaman face down on the stone. The next yelled as he charged down into the chamber. Meeker shot that one in the gut with his pistol. Another came down behind him and soaked up a few shots.

More than a dozen militiamen stormed down the stairs. Each one carried a look of pure wrath on their faces.

Their shouts became more desperate as the bodies stacked up at the base of the stairs. A few were able to fire off a shot from their muskets before we cut them down, but we only suffered a few new injuries.

I had to admire their courage, but I was confounded by their reckless, last-ditch effort to stop us.

Another floated down behind him, his feet barely dragging along the steps. I saw a trickle of blood from the man's neck, and knew he was already dead. Private's Baker and Marston both shot that one before I could stop them. His clothes and flesh fluttered apart as the two blasts of shot cut into the rebel soldier before he fell forward onto the pile of corpses.

"Worthless militia," a familiar voice cackled. "Paladin, where are you?"

By the time it dawned on me she'd carried the last two militiamen, the devil woman had sprung over the corpses. She flew towards Baker and jammed a clawed hand into his throat. Faster than I could follow, she flew at another private. Both of her hands shot into his belly and ripped his guts out in one quick motion.

Marston, having an empty weapon, swung the shotgun at her like a club. She grabbed it out of the air with ease and flung it away. She spun to attack Marston next, but Niculescu, who hadn't fired yet, blasted her midsection. The shot dug into her, yet she seemed unfazed, only angered.

I aimed my shotgun, but she was on Niculescu before I could shoot, and then I feared I'd hit him as well. One of her clawed hands flew deep into his stomach, the other shot behind his head and pulled him toward her mouth. She bit and ripped away his stock in one fluid motion. Then, she tore into his neck. Tomasini stabbed her in the side with his Bowie knife, and she slashed across his chest in response. I could see he was shouting, but I could not hear it over the ringing in my ears.

Knowing Niculescu was already dead, I took a step forward, aimed the shotgun at her head, and fired. The blast shattered the side of her face, but I watched in horror as she remained latched onto Niculescu's neck and sucked at it. In the blink of a bloody eye, the tattered flesh on the side of her face pushed the shot back out and smoothed over. I drew the revolver with intent to hit her with the LeMat's single-shot, twenty-gauge barrel, but she released Niculescu into a heap on the ground and spun to face me. As Niculescu dropped, I saw that he'd buried his knife into her sternum.

Marston rushed in with his knife, but she caught him by the neck and squeezed. A great crack echoed, and she tossed him aside like a puppet. The distraction gave me time to shoot her in the head again, which stopped her for half a second. For a slight moment, seeing blood trickle from a neat hole in her temple, I believed I might have killed her.

I had not.

Enraged, she threw her arms up to her sides, opened her jaws in a furious snarl, and came for me. In that moment, I was certain I would die.

Accepting my fate, I charged toward her, wrapped my arms around her, and hugged her tight. I tucked my chin, closed my eyes, and prayed that my death would give the others an opportunity to kill her. I expected to feel her claws dig into my rib cage, to feel her fangs dig into my face, or neck, or shoulder, but none of that happened. I felt pressure on my neck, and she dug into my stock. Her teeth wriggled about, caught on the hard leather strip.

Why doesn't she rip my stock off the way she did Niculescu's?

Opening my eyes, I found Tomasini grappling with her right arm, screaming in anger. Samuel Cash had joined the fight and driven his knife through her left arm. He quietly held the arm with one hand and maintained his grip on the knife with the other. Two more Marines, one on each side, came up and aided them in restraining her.

Addison Greene slid up behind her, as smooth as a snake. He sliced his Mameluke sword across her neck and proceeded to saw it back and forth. His left hand held the end of the blade, and a trickle of blood dripped from it.

She crouched, pulling us all down with her, and then leapt up, cracking my head against the stone ceiling. My vision blurred and I fell limp against her.

As she landed, she flung herself backward against a wall. I hung on for dear life as I heard a crunch. Greene cursed. Unable to see, I put my hands up and felt around for the sword. My hands wrapped around the metal, and I pushed it further into her neck. The vampire woman twisted and jerked. A clawed hand slammed against me and shoved me backward onto the ground.

As my vision settled, I saw her flail about while Greene hung tight, working the blade back and forth against her. She threw herself violently backward, slamming Greene against the wall once again. He collapsed and let go of the sword, though it remained lodged in her neck.

Tomasini was on her in a flash. With a deep, primal scream, he grabbed her hair in one hand, and chopped a hatchet through her neck with the other, finally severing it. Greene's Mameluke sword clattered to the ground. I spent half a moment confused, as Tomasini hadn't carried a hatchet. With a glance at Niculescu's dead body, I realized Tomasini had taken it from his dead friend.

I laid back against the ground, closed my eyes, and caught my breath.

The ringing in my ears faded and, when I opened my eyes, my vision had cleared.

Tomasini stood with a hand against the wall as Sonnier accepted strips from other men's shirts to use as bandages on Tomasini's chest. The Italian gazed at Niculescu's dead body, fury burning on his face. Greene had a bandage wrapped around his hand and stood above me.

"Back with us, Alex?" he asked. "Or, should I say, *Paladin?*"

"You should not," I replied with a hoarse throat. "I wasn't napping on you, was I?"

"No, we understood you just needed to rest your eyes," he said. He put his right hand out to help me to my feet. "I always seem to lose your attention when she's around. But that'll be the last time that happens. Damnedest thing I've ever—, well, it's the damnedest thing I've seen this week, at least. I was pretty darned sure she was set to rip you to pieces."

"Me too," I replied.

"Then why the hell did you go and do that?" Greene asked.

"I figured it might give all of you a chance to take her down," I said.

"It certainly did that, my friend," Greene said. "I can't explain it, but it was almost like you caught her off guard. She hesitated for half a second, and it was all we needed. Damnedest thing."

I stared at the headless corpse of our so-called white witch while I collected my faculties. My gaze drifted to where the head lay, a few feet away. The great fangs had receded. The skin had shriveled and pulled taut against her skull.

"Do we have to burn her?" I asked. "This may be the dumbest thing I've ever asked, but is there any chance of her coming back?"

"Excellent question, Alex," Greene replied. "I think she's down, but yes, just to be sure we'll turn her to ash when we get the opportunity."

Two Marines watched the stairs we'd come down, but I didn't think anyone would be coming down. At the other end of the tunnel, four Marines cracked away at the stone around the heavy metal door, trying to chip their way through the sides. Greene pointed.

"If you're quiet, you can hear some damn fools chanting some nonsense on the other side," he said. "But I'm not too sure we're going to get through it in time."

"Do Doyle or Tomasini have any ideas?" I asked.

"What do you mean?" he asked in reply. "The only powder we got is what the men got on themselves, and we'll need that."

"We got a few pistols, and a few carbines that don't need powder," I said. "The rest of us got those knives, hatchets, and swords. I say we collect all the powder up, see if they think it'll be enough. It's worth a try at least, seeing as we don't rightly know how much time we've got left. I mean, hell, I would've thought it was too late already."

His gaze wandered around while he considered my words.

"Hell," he said after a few seconds. "Tomasini, Doyle! Collect all the powder from all the men. Pile it up in something. . . Actually, Mister Sonnier, we're going to have to borrow your satchel. It's empty, isn't it?"

"Well, yes, sir, it is, but—"

"I'll see to getting you a new one," Greene said. "That's it, collect all the powder in his satchel, there."

A quarter hour later, every ounce of powder had been collected in our nurse's satchel, placed at the base of the door, and tamped down with all the dirt and rock chips we could collect. For good measure, we'd placed the vampire's body against the mound. A thin, short line of powder trailed out from it. Tomasini, face still hard with anger, lit the line with a torch and sprinted back toward the rest of us. The remaining Marines lay as flat as we could behind the piled corpses of the two dead guards and the dead militiamen.

I plugged fingers into my ears, squinted my eyes, and waited.

There was a great boom, and the whole tunnel rumbled. A few rocks fell from the ceiling and the dust exploded in a haze throughout.

The metal door stood firm in its portal.

"Damn!" Greene said as we walked up to it. "Well, let's get back at it."

I walked up and inspected the hinges. Curious, I pushed my knife into a gap near the top, between the metal and the stone. I levered between the two and, with little warning, the metal door fell toward me. I barely dodged aside as it slammed down hard onto the ground.

The way was clear. Steps continued straight downward into darkness.

"Looks like it did better than we thought," I said. "Dan, you stay here with the wounded. You two, keep an eye on that stairwell, shoot anything that comes down. The rest of you, come with me."

I un-holstered my revolver, cocked it, and stepped into the abyss.

Chapter 29: The Ceremony

As I walked down the steps, I could hear the faint sound of chanting, though I could not yet make out the words. There were no torches lining the way, so I half-stumbled as the steps leveled out at the bottom and smacked into a wall a few feet further along.

While I recovered and turned, I thought of requesting a torch. However, I changed my mind as I discovered a dim glow of light emanating from a second set of steps, which descended opposite the direction of the first set.

"Are you all right?" Greene whispered.

"Yeah, they're back down that way," I said. "Let's stay close, move slow and careful, but be ready to rush them when we get close. Pass that along."

"Yes, sir," Greene said with a soft chuckle.

We felt out each step on the way down, cautious and mind-numbingly slow. After several minutes of this, my eyes had adjusted.

The voices below were a steady, moaning chant, more unnerving than anything I'd ever seen or heard in a church or the like. I could not identify the language, it sounded nothing like Latin or any other European language with which I had any experience. There was one thing I recognized, the name "Kur Oto".

"Lord protect us," Greene whispered.

Over the drone of the deep-voiced intonations, I discerned soft, high-pitched sobbing noises. Recognizing the lamentations of young girls, I picked up my pace. The glow from the base of the steps resolved to a dimly lit room, with shadows dancing about.

One of the girls shrieked, followed by a chorus of terrified screams. I broke into a run down the steps, unable to control myself any longer.

When I leapt into the opening at the bottom, I found a large, domed room. In the center sat a marble-encased pool of smooth, reflective water, raised a foot from the floor. Evenly spread around the base, with their feet chained to the edge of the pool, were a dozen young, long-haired girls in simple, white shifts. I guessed none were older than twelve.

The shifts all carried a crimson blossom at the breast. Rage flared within me as I came to realize that none of the girls moved or made any sound. Standing at the head of each girl were tall, black-robed figures, who each held a bloodied knife in the air as they chanted louder and louder. If I'd arrived one minute sooner, the girls might have lived.

"Kur Oto!" the cloaked figures howled. "Give us your blessing! Bestow your power on us! Kur Oto! Grant us the power to destroy our enemies!"

Movement on my left stole my attention. A plain-dressed guardsman lifted a rifle toward me.

I lurched to the side as he fired, caught my footing, and fired my revolver at him in response. As he crumpled, I received a powerful, burning blow to my hip on the left side. Another guardsmen had shot me and charged toward me with a bayoneted rifle. Anger overpowering the pain, I retained my footing, cocked the revolver, and shot him as well.

Marines poured into the chamber and engaged the dozen or so guards. A deafening cacophony of gunfire burst across the domed room. After the initial blasts, the fight devolved into a desperate melee.

I cocked the revolver again and charged at the circle of robed figures, who in no way regarded our invasion.

The water in the pool had, in a mere few seconds, turned to a great boil.

I ran to the closet figure, raised the revolver at his back, and squeezed. He spasmed and dropped the knife. Dumbfounded, he twisted back to look at me. His crazed, wide-eyed face carried a wicked smile.

"You're too late!" he said. Then, he coughed and crumpled to the ground.

I slid my hand across the LeMat to cock it again, but it caught and would not do so. Rather than fumble with it, I dropped it and drew my sword. I took two steps toward the next robed figure. My periphery caught something rising from the pool. Looking upon it, I froze in horror.

A large, slime-covered skeleton emerged from the boiling water. Antlers grew in a tangle all around the skull and an intricately carved golden disc was perched on its shoulders. Fiery red orbs blazed in the eye sockets and its jaw hung open in a macabre smile. It carried an ornate collection of feathers and smaller gold discs all over its torso. The skeleton unnaturally stretched a long, boney arm toward the cloaked figure next to me.

One of our marines, I could not tell who, screamed and ran from the room.

Another pair nervously glanced around and stepped backward. Archibald grabbed both by the collar and said something I could not hear. They steeled with resolve, tightened their grip on their weapons, and moved forward.

"For the love of God, Alex, kill them!" Greene shouted.

I came to my senses and grabbed my sword with both hands. The skeleton's boney index finger tapped on the cloaked man's chest as I reared my sword back to swing.

The cloaked figure burst into flames and screamed. I swung.

My blade caught on his neck bones. His burning hood fell back. Though he should have been dead, his eyes rolled over to look at me. I wrenched the sword out and swung again. The head fell and the fiery body dropped.

More skeletal arms had cast out from the bony demon and ignited all the other cloaked men. They turned about and launched themselves at the Marines. I watched one grab hold of Private Thompson, who shrieked as they burned together.

It occurred to me that we should focus our attention on the boney demon who'd emerged from the pool, but we became mired in melee with its fiery minions.

The marines hacked into them with knives, swords, and hatchets. A few pistols and carbines barked here and there. I saw one burning figure take three shots and continue forward.

After the initial screams as they lit up, the burning men became enraged, yet acted unaffected by the pain of the fire or any Marine-inflicted injuries.

One of the figures clapped their hands together and a column of fire shot out in a line toward a hapless private. The Marine burst into flames, let out a piercing wail of agony, and fell to his knees.

Tomasini stabbed that one in the chest and chopped with a hatchet at the neck like a man possessed, acting impervious to the blaze. His coat burned away as he hacked the head off. The fiery ball rolled to the ground, and the flaming body collapsed. Tomasini stepped back and beat at the flames on his chest. He coughed and lolled his head around dizzily.

The burning men swept around the pool and charged for the stairwell, directing their ire on anyone who got in their way.

"Stop them, Marines, stop them!" I shouted. "If they get to the city, it's over!"

Samuel Cash swiped his knife across the throat of one, but it didn't kill the man. Stumbling away from the burning man, he flipped the knife and drove it into the stomach. A moment later, he snatched his hand away in agony. I thought the fiery man would get Cash, but another Marine drove a bayonet into his face and pushed him back.

Daniels, calm and collected, followed one burning man. He fired his carbine into their back, at which point the burning man spun and clapped his hands toward Daniels. The lieutenant dodged aside the column of fire, reloaded, and fired again until the man went down.

A burning figure ran toward me. Flame and smoke trailed him. I barely got my blade up in time and jabbed it into his thigh. His arms spread apart and swung toward each other. I released my sword and fell to the side to escape a line of fire. The heat washed over me and singed my face. The explosion of Greene's Dragoon pistol burst my eardrum. The fiery man's head snapped back, and he collapsed.

Greene stood next to me with an outthrust hand and helped me to my feet.

Eyes burning from the smoke, I squinted and looked about. The Brotherhood by all reason, lay lumped, scattered around, in flaming mounds. The surviving marines, less than twenty, stood about, vicious hatred on their blackened faces and blood trickling from various wounds. They scanned for any remaining enemies, but found none.

I locked eyes with Greene and gave him a nod of thanks. Simultaneously, we turned to look at the pool.

The skeletal demon had disappeared. The water lay still and placid, reflecting the light of the dozen fires scattered about.

"Where did it go?" I asked.

"Kur Oto, you mean?" Greene asked with a sly smile. "I told you it was real."

"Yes, but where is it?"

"I imagine it gave them what they wanted," he said with a shrug. "It granted its blessing and decided to immediately depart from a potentially dangerous situation."

"Do you really think it considered *us* a dangerous situation?" I asked. "It could have just lit us on fire."

"In my experience, the more powerful a creature, the more cowardly they are."

My gaze returned to the dead girls, laying in a somber circle around the pool. My heart dropped as I was reminded of my failure.

"Don't ask me how the devil thinks, Alex," Greene replied. For the next statement he raised his voice to a shout. "And yes, Sergeant, I do believe that demon had something to fear from Special Unit Thirteen. We killed his vampire, we killed his Brotherhood, and we defeated his plans for the third time in a row. We saved the city, men, and we saved the Union Fleet!"

I retrieved my sword from the dead, roasting corpse at my feet and thrust the blade into the air.

"Unit Thirteen!"

The voices of the other marines joined me as we shouted to our victory at the tops of our lungs.

Chapter 30: The Capture of New Orleans

Dawn had arrived by the time we re-emerged from the bowels of the mansion. There were no signs of any militia in the mansion or its surroundings. We queried Mrs. Campbell, who'd sealed herself and her children back in the master bedroom upstairs. She claimed ignorance of everything.

Greene's first order of business, on returning above, was to set the Special Unit Thirteen flag, with its glorious golden dragon on a field of red, out on the second story balcony.

Horses and wagons raced by the mansion in a frenzy to abandon the town. Oblivious to our nature, passersby shouted to us to leave the city. We learned the Union fleet was coming up the river and would arrive within the hour. I set pickets around the house and ventured back inside.

With great care, we moved the bodies of the murdered girls out of the catacombs and arranged them in the carriage house. We had great concern that we might be accused of their murder, so we planned to deliver them discreetly to a coroner as opportunity allowed.

One by one, we retrieved the bodies of our fallen from below and set them with care in a row in the garden. I led the detail to collect the remains of Emile Van Benthuysen's squad, as well as Private Martin, who we discovered ripped apart in the servant's quarters. We respectfully wrapped them into blankets, so they'd be easier to move and bury later on.

We collected the wounded in the main sitting room, and Dan Sonnier worked feverishly to tend to the burns, stabs, and bullet wounds. As few men did not carry an injury of some kind, Sonnier did his best to address the most serious and released the most capable as quickly as possible. Most of the marines claimed perfect health, despite clear signs of contradiction, and volunteered for the various duties.

When the streets cleared, I sent two men as runners to check on our injured back at the prison.

On Greene's direction, Meeker led a detail to collect every bit of silver we could find from the mansion. Mrs. Campbell would have a very unpleasant surprise when she re-emerged.

"Alex, come see this!" Greene called. I followed his motion to join him in a small library. It had a mahogany desk with ledgers and letters piled all about in a haphazard fashion. Samuel Cash was in there with him, his right arm wrapped up in cloth and hanging in a sling. His left hand held a letter, which he studied with great attention.

"What's all this?" I asked.

"Reports, diaries, ledgers, of all kinds about this 'Brotherhood'," Greene said. "There's references to generals, ship captains, spies, and all sorts throughout the Confederacy."

"Are you saying this *Brotherhood*, under the command of this demon of yours, Kur Oto, is running the whole damn Confederacy?"

"I don't know yet, but I don't think so," he said. "There's a lot going on here, and a lot to sort through, but from what I've seen there's definitely a great deal of influence spread all over."

"This letter here is from a man who's an aide to some cavalry general, and the man reports that he's helped the Rebel cavalry run rings around our boys between Virginia and Washington," Cash said, keeping his gaze on the letter.

"I just read one who says he works for a ship captain, who insinuates 'their master' has blessed him with some kind of fortune telling, such that they've wreaked quite a bit of havoc on our blockade fleet," Greene said. "We're gonna keep at this, I've a strong feeling it'll be a hell of a guide as to where we go next. Biggest problem might be deciding which of these to follow up on and in which order. You do what you do and keep running the company."

"Yes, sir," I said.

Greene snickered at my formality.

"I imagine this city will be filled with our Union brethren by nightfall," I said. "I'll make sure we're ready to receive them."

An hour later, we received reports that the Union fleet had indeed arrived in the city. There was a great deal of protestation from the remaining citizens, especially the women, but there was no armed resistance left and the city fell without a fight.

Captain Golis and a contingent of the Native Guard arrived at the mansion, escorting Doctor Shilling and our wounded men from the prison. I gathered my two runners had filled them in on the events below the mansion, as they all seemed forlorn and ashamed to have missed the big fight. I did my best to reassure them that they'd done their job, and that there would be plenty of fights to come.

I inquired about Miss Beauregard. Captain Golis told me she was well enough and that she'd been safely delivered to the Slidell House. I quietly discussed the fate of the poor young girls we'd found and asked if he might be able to get them delivered to a cemetery for burial. He agreed to do so.

"Thank you for that, sir," I said to Captain Golis. "Now, sir, don't you and yours gotta be getting out of this city?"

"I tell you, mon sergeant," he replied, "Our allegiance is to New Orleans. We will remain, and we will do just fine. Our colonel and his friends, yes, they have left, but we will not miss them. For the rest of us," he shrugged, "if the United States retakes ownership of this city, then maybe we fight for them. We will see."

"I see, sir," I replied. "Well, best of luck to you, whatever lies ahead for you. Either way, sir, you have my greatest thanks for your help back at the prison. That might otherwise have been the end of us."

"It is I who should thank you, mon Sergeant," Golis said. "The city stands because of you. I would offer you my hand if you would take it."

He put his hand out, and I took it. After a solid handshake and an approving nod, he ordered his company to march around the corner to the carriage house. The First Louisiana Native Guard took up positions all around Campbell House, and for the next few days, none of the fleeing soldiers or citizens gave them a second glance.

For the next several days, we tended our wounded and searched through the stacks of documents. A few at a time, the wounded we'd left at the prison hobbled in to rejoin us. When Greene felt the streets were safe enough, he dressed in plain clothes and went to visit Miss Beauregard. He returned to report she was recovering better than expected.

We were tempted to blast the lower tunnels and the ceremonial room with whatever we could find and bury them for all time, but we feared how much of the city might sink when it collapsed. We settled on carrying as much stone and dirt into the tunnel as we could manage and sealed it up as best as we could.

Although most of the militias had left and the Union Navy commanded the entire river, the mayor stubbornly refused to surrender. At the end of April, some of our fellow Marines entered the city to claim City Hall and raise the US flag.

In the afternoon on the first of May, a squad of Union soldiers marched by Campbell House, and we greeted them. It took a good deal of work to convince them we were Union Marines and not Confederates, but the accents and my knowledge of Philadelphia won them over. On my recommendation, Greene came out and gave a simple, much reduced report to the blonde lieutenant who led the squad.

As the sun set, a larger contingent of Union Soldiers approached, including a horse which carried a rotund balding man with droopy eyes and a mustache. When he got closer, I saw he carried stars on his shoulders.

"It's as splendid as I was told," he said as rode up to the front of the Campbell House. "That settles it, men. Captain Greaves?"

A thinner soldier with a full head of hair, but similar mustache, ran up to his side.

"Yes, General?"

"Set my headquarters in this building, if you would," the bald general ordered.

"Yes, General Butler," Captain Greaves replied. The blonde lieutenant from earlier strode up. Within earshot of the general, Greene reported to the captain that our company had already taken residence in the mansion. He explained we had a great number of killed and wounded, and that it would take some work to relocate us.

"Well then, by tarnation, you best get them to work on moving out, by God," General Butler growled. "And get that damned strange flag taken down at once."

"And Captain, one more issue for the general," the lieutenant continued, careful to ensure he addressed the captain and *not* the general, "The family is still living here as well, the Marine lieutenant here reported to me that the madame of the house is upstairs with her children and one baby."

"Captain, kindly go find this woman and explain to her she is now in a city occupied by the Union Army, and that, as a secessionist, she has forfeited all her rights to any property while so occupied," General Butler said. "Get this woman and her family, and this curious company of marines as well, to vacate *as soon as possible*, Captain. Do I make myself perfectly clear?"

"Yes, General."

Upon receiving the news that we were to find alternate lodging, Greene set every man to collecting the last of the silver. He packed it up with the great collection of correspondence we'd found and had us sneak both collections out through the carriage house. We requested wagons from the captain for our dead and wounded, which he provided.

As we loaded things up, a courier arrived with letters for the company. Greene accepted all of them and sent the man off.

Once everyone and everything was loaded, we departed the mansion. Our first order of business was to find a place on the outskirts of the city where we could bury our men.

"Probably for the best, Alex," Greene said, as we walked along next to the wagons. "Now that general can take the blame for everything we absconded with."

"Couldn't happen to a nicer general," I replied.

"If you would, while we head out of the city, please distribute our mail," Greene said. I nodded and took the sack full of letters that he offered me. Twelve of the letters were addressed to Greene from various offices, and I passed them to him. A substantial stack of the letters was addressed to men who had not survived the mission. I tucked those back into the sack and made plans to respond to them myself. I passed out the rest of the letters as we traveled.

Three of the letters were for me. One was from my mother, two were from Cassie Paul. I stuck them with a stack of similar letters I'd collected but could not bring myself to read. I resolved that I was ready to read through them and would do so that evening after we'd buried our dead.

Job complete, I returned to Greene's side. I could see he'd broken open a few of the letters he'd received.

"Would you like the good news or the bad news?" he asked. Taken aback, it took me a moment to respond. My mind flew through all the possibilities of either, but nothing I could think of made any real sense.

"The bad news, I suppose, just to get it out of the way," I answered.

"I thought you might say that," Greene responded. "Well, our great benefactor may be no more altogether. Major Reynolds has been brought up on a set of charges and faces his court martial as we speak, or near enough. Though Major Zeilin promises to do what he can for us, we might be on our own for the time being."

"Could be worse," I said. "We can do the job well enough with what we've got and what we can find. Now, what's the good news?"

Instead of answering, he handed me one of the letters. I was not as well versed as he at walking and reading at the same time, so I carefully read a few words at a time and frequently checked my path ahead to avoid tripping. Of immediate note, I read that the letter had been addressed from the Department of the Navy. As I read, little by little, down the message, my breath caught in my throat.

"Congratulations, Lieutenant Phillips," he said. "It seems Reynolds made the recommendation, and they signed the orders before the charges were brought against him."

My heart swelled. I can only imagine the stupid sort of grin that overtook my face, but I could not control it.

"Lieutenant *Paladin*, maybe?"

My smile faded.

"*Phillips* will do just fine, Addison."

"Before you get too excited, they've made me a captain," he said. "It seems you're doomed to continue teaching me how to be a Marine for the rest of your days. Beyond that, they're expanding the Unit. It will take a while before the assignments and requisitions find their way along, but Special Unit Thirteen will soon muster two full companies. Just imagine the damage we could do with that!"

"What *are* we going to do with it?" I asked.

"That's the easy part, Alex," he replied. "With what Sam Cash and I found, it looks like we got our work cut out for us. By the time we've rested, refit, and rebuilt, we'll have a pretty good idea of what the Brotherhood's doing, and where. Opportunity abounds, Alex. Our war's just getting started."

The End

Casey Moores was a USAF rescue/special ops C-130 pilot for over 17 years- airdropping, air refueling, and flying into tiny blacked-out dirt airstrips in bad places using night vision goggles. He's been to *those* places and done *those* things with *those* people. Now he lives a quieter life, translating those experiences to fiction.

He has written in the Four Horsemen universe with stories in numerous anthologies, several novels about Bull and his black ops rescue company, and much more to come. In the near future he will be expanding in the Salvage System and Fallen World universes as well. He has several stories out in his Deathmage War fantasy series, one of which—"A Quaint Pastime"—was a finalist in the FantaSci fantasy story contest.

This novel is his first foray into the chronicles of Lieutenant Greene, Sergeant Phillips, and M Company, the first of many.

A Colorado native and Air Force Academy graduate, he is now a naturalized Burqueño, having retired in New Mexico.

Casey Moores

Historical Commentary

As much as this is a work of fiction, I did my best to tie it into actual historical events and to include actual historical figures as much as possible. My primary references for this was David Sullivan's The United States Marine Corps in the Civil War series. Beyond that, I used some wikipedia pages and an assortment of civil war history pages. I must note that I am not a historian, although I did my best to find multiple sources to confirm just about everything. When different sources conflicted, I tried to determine which were more reliable or which details were more preponderant among the different accounts. When all is said and done, I will repeat that this is a work of fiction, meant only for your enjoyment.

Chapter 1

Major Reynolds was the officer who'd led the Marine contingent in the Battle of Bull Run. He was assigned as the commander of the Marine contingent sent south to take Port Royal as part of the South Atlantic Blockading Squadron. Led by Captain Samuel DuPont, they departed to capture Port Royal on 1 November, 1861.

The sinking of the Governor was a real event, which played out mostly as described with the exclusion, of course, of mini-krakens in the water devouring the men.

The original plan was to distribute the Marines among the ships of the fleet, but at the last moment it was decided to consolidate them onto a single large steamboat, the Governor, which was poorly suited to the sea. It quickly succumbed to a storm during the trip. The Marines held it together for more than two full days while seeking assistance. There was a sailor who was crushed between the boats and there were six men who attempted to leap across as the ships pulled apart, and none survived.

Chapter 2

In the end, the bulk of the Marines were moved to the Sabine in the manner described- by tying a rope to themselves, tossing it to the boat crew, and jumping into the water.

Chapter 3

Arriving late due to the sinking of the Governor, Port Royal hd been taken before the bulk of the Marines, led by Major John Reynolds, arrived.

There are records that indicate the idle Marines became bored and unruly in the days afterward, and Major Reynolds did indeed order them to drill until they were too tired to fight. The Marines even wrote some disparaging songs about him as a result.

Colonel Harris was the commandant of the US Marines at the time, who were based out of Hampton Roads, Virginia. The term Hampton Roads is sometimes used to refer to the entire area, which at the time included the Confederate held Portsmouth and Norfolk. However, in Union correspondence, they used the name Hampton Roads to refer to the Union held area on the north side of the James River.

Chapter 4

My apologies to Lieutenant Cartter, who was a real person and whose letters provided an abundant source of information for David Sullivan's research.

Chapter 5

Aside from being a great way to provide a diverse group of folks for M Company, it was a fact that the US Marines were far less geographically homogenous than other Civil War units. Army regiments, particularly Volunteers, were mustered in ways that most of the soldiers already knew each other, or at the very least came from the same general area.

Marines mustered from all over and were more likely to come from a wider range of cultural and geographic backgrounds.

Major Jacob Zeilin was in Hampton Roads at that time recovering from wounds received at Bull Run. He would later become the Commandant of the US Marines.

Chapter 6

The Ketchum grenade was developed in the years prior to the Civil War and used by Union soldiers.

The Whitworth rifle was one of the premier long range rifles of the time, but was both expensive and difficult to re-supply as it fired an unusual hexagonal bullet.

Chapter 7

Molino Del Rey was a key battle in the lead up to the taking of Mexico City and the Battle of Chapultepec. However, there is no evidence that anyone was attacked by Quinametzin, a race of giants in Aztec legends.

Major General Ambrose Burnside, for whom sideburns were named, led the army units for the expedition along the North Carolina Coast from

February to June of 1862— it was known as the Burnside Expedition.

Chapter 8

The approach to Roanoke Island, the site of one of early Americas greatest mysteries, is as described. The term "Mosquito Fleet" shows up regularly in accounts of the Union blockade- it refers to the small, poorly armed groups of ships the Confederacy threw together in vain attempts to oppose Union Naval operations. The Mosquito fleets usually scattered after being fired upon by Union gunboats.

There were also small shore batteries around Roanoke Island, but the only one that threatened the Union approach, the four guns of Fort Bartow, was silenced by Union ships, as described.

Two hundred Confederates of the 31st North Carolina under Colonel John V. Jordan attempted to oppose the landing, but were also driven off by Union gunboats.

Acting Master Charles Daniels and Flag Officer's Clerk Edward Meeker were two sailors who were put ashore under the command of a young Midshipman Benjamin Porter to provide artillery support to the Army on Roanoke Island. Both Daniels and Meeker did, in fact, subsequently transfer to the US Marines.

Midshipman Benjamin H. Porter was seventeen at the time that he lead the Navy's howitzer detachment. He is recorded as having been a remarkable officer and great leader even at such a young age. He was killed leading as assault on Fort Fisher in 1864. The six howitzers he commanded were the only Union artillery pieces to participate in the battle.

Lieutenant Cartter was present in the Battle of Roanoke Island as he was the overall commander of the Marine contingent for the entire expedition.

Chapter 11

Brigadier General John Gray Foster led the First Brigade through the initial landing and maneuvering on Roanoke Island.

Opposing them was Brigadier General Henry A. Wise, who had collected approximately 3,000 troops on the island. 1400 of them, with 800 more in reserve, three guns, and a hastily erected barricade, stopped the Union advance in a swampy clearing roughly halfway up the central road of the island.

Union troops were held up by this force throughout the morning of 8 February, 1862.

Brigadier General Jesse L. Reno arrived midday with the Second Brigade. He ordered his troops to attempt to navigate the impenetrable swamp on the left. Foster ordered two of his reserve regiments to do the same on the right.

The Aztec Club was an actual organization of officers formed after the capture of Mexico City.

Chapter 12

The Confederates had assumed the thick, swampy brush on either side was impassable as well. By sheer coincidence, the two flanking forces emerged at the same time on the Confederate positions.

Chapter 13

Minty was Harriet Tubman's nickname. I have not found a direct connection between her and the founding of the Freedmen's Colony, but that doesn't mean there wasn't one.

After the battle, slaves who'd been used to build fortifications were collected, labeled "contraband of war", and emancipated. A lot assisted the Union troops in rebuilding forts on the island and in surrounding areas.

The Freedmen's Colony was soon joined by runaways from across the state. Its population peaked around 4000 by the end of the war, when government support ended. The population dwindled until the colony was decommissioned. However, many descendants live and work on Roanoke Island to this day.

Casey Moores

Chapter 16

On 1 March, 1862, Captain DuPont, still leading the South Atlantic Blockading Squadron, ordered an attack on Fernandina. Gunboats and the Marine Battalion, led by Major Reynolds, captured Cumberland Island on 2 March and occupied Fernandina on March, both being abandoned just prior to the attack. St. Mary's, Georgia was occupied on 4 March as well, followed by Simon's Island on 9 March, then Brunswick and Jekyll Island on 10 March. There were only a few, limited exchanges of fire as these were taken.

During this time, Major Reynolds sent numerous complaints concerning supply and paymaster issues to the Marine Commandant.

Commander Christopher R. P. Rodgers accepted the surrender of St. Augustine on 11 March. As some 800 Confederate troops were rumored to have just left the town, "he put Captain Doughty and the Marine Guard of the USS Wabash ashore at St. Augustine, along with the 7th New Hampshire Volunteers."

Chapter 19

Julius Kroehl is the most curious historical figure I came across in the course of my research.

Born in 1830 in Memel, East Prussia.

Emigrated to US in 1844, worked as a civilian in the US Navy with mention of a history in artillery and profession of submarine engineer.

He was an assistant engineer in the construction of New York's Crystal Palace, held a patent for a flange forming machine, won a contract to build the Mount Morris Fire Watchtower (which still stands in Marcus Garvey Memorial Park). Then, he and a partner won several contracts to clear underwater obstructions all around New York.

At the outset of the Civil War, Kroehl was proposed as a captain of pontoniers in a New York volunteer regiment, but the regiment was not formed.

He then served as a civilian contractor for the Union Navy, in some accounts as an underwater demolitions expert.

He was first hired to perform minesweeping in the lower Mississippi River. He attempted to break the chain barrier that held up the Union fleet at Forts Jackson and St. Philip, but was unsuccessful (Farragut reportedly called him a "failure").

He served with Admiral Dixon Porter up and down the east coast, demonstrating electric torpedoes (mines) and eventually serving aboard the USS Blackhawk. He helped develop navigation charts and continued to develop strategies to employ the torpedoes.

Back in Mississippi, he sank a coal barge on his own initiative to allow Union ships to withdraw from a tenuous position. He worked during the siege of Vicksburg until he contracted malaria and returned to New York.

In 1864, Kroehl then became the chief engineer of the Pacific Pearl Company. He designed and constructed the Sub Marine Explorer in 1865, considered to be a highly advanced submarine for its era. It was tested in the Brooklyn Navy Yard in May 1866, then shipped it down to Panama in March 1867. He died 9 September 1867, though it's unclear if it was due to lingering malaria or decompression sickness.

He designed and built one of the most advanced submarines of the time period and was one of our Navy's early underwater demolitions pioneers.

As described, Farragut and Butler massed their ships and troops at Ship's Island before the attack on New Orleans.

Chapter 20

As expected, the major barrier to approaching New Orleans up the Mississippi were Forts Jackson and St. Philip, located across the river from each other at a significant bend. A massive barrier chain was strewn across the river north of Fort Jackson.

On 18 April, mortars opened the Battle of Forts Jackson and St. Philip. David D. Porter led a semiautonomous fleet of 21 mortar schooners in an attempt to damage or destroy Forts Jackson and St. Philip. However, over the course of five days, little damage was done.

Deciding the mortars would not do the job, Farragut ordered the gunboats Kineo, Itasca, and Pineola to attempt to break the chain. As described, an attempt by Julius Kroehl was defeated when the current carried the Pinola away too quickly and tore the wires from the explosives he'd set.

The crew of the Itasca, as described, disembarked onto the hulk the chain was connected through. They worked for half an hour with chisels and sledges and broke the chain. The Itasca was then caught by the hulk and the chain as it swept towards the shore. The Pinola arrived and was able to attach grapples with hawsers and a cable to tug the Itasca back to safety.

Throughout the battle, the Confederates sent numerous fire ships at the Union fleet, but to little effect.

Chapter 21

During the Battle of Forts Jackson and St. Philip, the Pinola was struck by a shell and set aflame.

Gunner's Mate John B. Frisbee shut himself inside the gunpowder magazine to keep the flames from spreading into it. One year later, he was awarded the Medal of Honor for the action.

Casey Moores

Jean and Pierre Lafitte are said to have used the area between Barrataria Bay and New Orleans for smuggling, leading a group known as the Barratarians. They helped US forces in the Battle of New Orleans of the War of 1812, for which they received pardons. The are is now the Jean Lafitte National Historical Park and Preserve.

The First Louisiana Native Guards were a militia unit of New Orleans freemen who mustered for the Confederacy. In a curious footnote of history, they claim the first African American officers in North America.

Chapter 22

Captain Louis Golis is recorded as the commander of the Beauregard Native Guards company of the 1st Louisiana Native Guard.

General Mansfield Lovell, a Mexican War veteran, was in charge of the defense of New Orleans when the Union Navy launched the attack on it. Generals PGT Beauregard and Braxton Bragg had both been favored for the role, and Bragg in particular felt personally snubbed for not having gotten that assignment.

In a map of 1854 New Orleans, the corner of Chartres and St Peter streets, next to the St. Louis Cathedral, is listed as an "Old Prison". It is also the site of the Cabildo, which was used as a courthouse, and the Arsenal, which was used as a supply depot by the Confederacy. For the purposes of simplification, I used it as an old prison in this novel.

When New Orleans was attacked, Caroline Beauregard, the wife of General PGT Beauregard, and Mathilde Slidell, wife of politician John Slidell, were indeed cousins in law and were in New Orleans at the Slidell House at the time of the attack on New Orleans.

Madame Laveau, the famed Voodoo Queen of New Orleans, was alive and prominent in the city throughout the Civil War.

Chapter 23

The Poydras Asylum was where I described it, and was similarly moved further out of the city prior to the war, at which point it was bought by the Campbell's. Mr. Campbell was indeed a surgeon and he was away during the attack on New Orleans.

Chapter 24

The LeMat pistol was carried by a number of Confederate officers. It had a 9-round cylinder of either .42 or .36 caliber ball and a single 20 gauge shot barrel.

Chapter 30

The Confederate First Louisiana Native Guard disbanded on 25 April, 1862, and re-formed under the Union Army and later became the 73rd Regiment Infantry of the United Stated Colored Troops.

In my favorite happy coincidence of this entire novel, I accidentally set my climax in the very residence that General Butler took as his headquarters after taking the city. I honestly did not realize I had done so until I was almost done writing this. It only made sense to have a monster hunting unit collect silver. General Butler was criticized for many things in his administration of New Orleans, one of which was his confiscation of silver.

If you enjoyed Witch Hunt by Casey Moores, then check out these other JTF-13 titles.

JTF-13 Origins Anthology

Original cover art ISBN <u>1951768167</u>
Legacy Cover art ISBN <u>1951768337</u>

Made in the USA
Coppell, TX
14 January 2024